HERSELF SURPRISED

HERSELF SURPRISED

A Novel by J O Y C E C A R Y

H A R P E R & B R O T H E R S *New York*

Queens House

Larchmont, New York

Republished 1977 by Special Arrangement
with Harper & Row, Publishers.

Library of Congress Cataloging in Publication Data

Cary, Joyce, 1888-1957.
  Herself surprised.

  Reprint of the ed. published by Harper, New
York.
  I. Title.
[PZ3.C25884H3   1977]   [PR6005.A77]   823'.9'12
ISBN 0-89244-070-8   77-21373

QUEENS HOUSE
Larchmont, New York 10538

Manufactured in the United States of America

To MARY OGILVIE

HERSELF SURPRISED

Chapter One

THE JUDGE, when he sent me to prison, said that I had behaved like a woman without any moral sense. "I noticed," he said, and the paper printed it all, "that several times during the gravest revelations of her own frauds and ingratitude, Mrs. Monday smiled. She may be ill educated, as the defense has urged, but she is certainly intelligent. I am forced to conclude that she is another unhappy example of that laxity and contempt for all religious principle and social obligation which threatens to undermine the whole fabric of our civilization."

When he spoke in this way I was upset and wanted to tell him that I had never been against religion; far from it; but the policeman stopped me and afterward I saw that I had no right to be angry with the judge. Perhaps I had smiled when some of the lawyers brought up old stories about me from years back. It is strange to stand in that box and hear yourself taken to pieces by strangers.

At first I could not believe that I was anything like the woman they made me out to be. But the chaplain tells me that nearly all the women who come here to prison have the same story, that the lawyers were wrong and made

1

them seem worse than they were; and I couldn't deny that each little bit they brought against me was true; or nearly true; and that some things they did not know were worse.

I was shocked by the prison clothes, and the way I was treated, as if I were a criminal. Now I see that I am a criminal just like the others, and that perhaps some of the others became so in the same foolish way, without knowing what they were doing. So perhaps some who read this book may take warning and ask themselves before it is too late what they really are and why they behave as they do.

"Know thyself," the chaplain says, and it is true that I never knew myself till now. Yet I thought I knew myself very well, and that I was humble enough, and I remember the first time I saw myself in my true body. It was on my honeymoon, in Paris, in a grand shop, the grandest I had ever seen. It had big mirrors in the showroom, between the pillars, like glass doors, and I was walking to the stairs in my new hat as big as an Easter cake, and feeling the swish of my new silk petticoats and the squeeze of my new French stays. I seemed to be looking into the next saloon, and I thought: Look at that fat, common trollop of a girl with a snub nose and the shiny cheeks, jumping out of her skin to be in a Paris hat. Wouldn't you bet she was out from Dartmouth fair last week? You can almost smell the cider on her lips. What a shame to expose herself like that —and her nation—to these foreigners.

But in the same flash I saw that it was me. It stopped me dead with the blow. I knew I was not a beauty, but till that hour I had not seen myself with the world's eye. I had made a love of my nose, snub and broad though it was, and my eyes which were nothing but brown. Are not any eyes wonderful if you will look at them alone and forget the rest? I had praised the shining of my hair and even the shape

2

of my big hands and every bit of me at one time or another. So I had made a belle of myself when I was nothing, as they used to say at home, but maiden meat. My husband Matthew saw me stop and said: "What is it, love, is it the hat? I thought perhaps it was a bit bright for your complexion."

I was going to say, "Yes, indeed," but instead the words popped out: "No, it's not the hat—it's the glass. I never saw one so big." So I kept the hat, and if people looked at me I thought: If I am a body then it can't be helped, for I can't help myself.

So I would think in those days; whenever I wanted to please myself; even against my husband. Yet I meant to be as good as my vows and better. For I could not but wonder that he, a gentleman and rich, had taken me, an ordinary country girl, neither plain nor pretty, with none of the advantages he might have expected. I would think that perhaps it was only a fancy in him; for I knew that Nature made men mad now and then, when they would catch at the nearest woman, but when they were tired of their play, they waked up and wondered how they had been taken in.

So I was in terror that Matt would wake up, especially when I mistook in conversation. For though I could speak very well, like any farmer's daughter in those days, I knew very little of geography, or music, or languages. I remember in my first month I asked a lady who had been on the Rhine about the Russian food, thinking she had been in Russia. But the worst thing was when I saw Matt turning red, I went on to mistake things which I knew quite well, and said: "Oh, I didn't know Russia was in Germany," and so on, trembling at my poor Matt's feelings and yet going on with my nonsense, only to make the woman think me more ignorant than I really was.

3

I knew, of course, that all the ladies of Bradnell Green, which was where we lived, were studying me and telling the news—"a month ago she was a servant."

Chapter Two

FOR THAT was how I began with poor Matt. I had been cook to his mother, Mrs. Monday, who was a widow. It was true that I had come from a good home, for my father was a freeholder and working foreman, and my mother had been a teacher. I myself had prizes from school for recitation and Scripture, and a certificate for sewing; and afterward I had a very good training as kitchen-maid under a man cook in a good religious house with a very rich brewing family, who never allowed as much as an ounce of margarine or custard powder or any made-up stuffs in their kitchen, even for the servants. My mother wanted me to be a first-class cook fit for the best service; and so did I.

Indeed, even as long ago as the Diamond Jubilee I had a pick for my first place, as cook. I could have gone to a general. But I chose Mrs. Monday's because the house was not so big, or the family; and it was not too far in the wilds. I liked to stay south, too, and Bradnall, though it is fifty miles from the sea, is still south feeling. It stands in a valley among orchards, which I liked, from the cider orchards out at home; and yet the Downs were not too far.

It is true Bradnall town was nothing much except for the cathedral and the close; just shops and streets as dirty as you please; but Woodview, which was the Mondays'

4

house, stood two miles out at the Green. It was not too quiet either, but right on a main road, with carts and carriers passing all the morning, and in the afternoons always some good carriages. I could see the coachmen's hats from my kitchen window, coming up the hill; then I would often go down to the back gate to see them trotting past on the level. I always loved a good carriage and pair, with its shining horses going up and down like rockers; and silver on the harness; and spokes twirling like an egg beater; and the coachwork so bright that you could see the hedges and the sky in it.

Then the village was close, and it was a good village with five or six real shops and a real draper, I mean one that sold only drapery and could find you a draw ribbon or match your wool at the last minute.

The house was very pretty too, all covered with trellis in front, for roses, and creeper behind. It reminded me of a picture out of *Mrs. Ewing*, with its high chimneys and trellis roses, except that it was not really old. But then again, if it had been old, it would not have had such good sinks and hot water laid on, and a porcelain bath that cleaned with bath brick; and looked clean when it was done.

Woodview had a good garden, too, and especially a good kitchen garden. I always like to see a kitchen garden in a house, to know that my vegetables are fresh, and to walk in. For servants can use a kitchen garden, and what I feared to miss most, in service, was a garden. All my friends in service said the same, that they had no garden. You might say that country girls do not set much store by a garden when they have one, but then, country girls at home have the lanes and the fields. But a girl in service can't run about the lanes in her kitchen print or her uniform. Every-

5

one can recognize her a mile away and say: "There's Min-
nie or Millie again, running after young So-and-So," and
it will soon come to the mistress. The very names of hay-
cock and housemaid, put together, will terrify any mistress.
But in a kitchen garden a maid can walk and look at the
world, I mean the growing world, and sometimes even
bring out a kitchen chair and shell her peas or shred up her
runners, and feel the open air, a feeling which you don't
have walking in a road.

I'll own I soon found a corner in the kitchen garden at
Woodview where no one could see me from the house, and
where I was well away from the rubbish heap, with a sweet-
brier hedge at my back and the cabbages in front; and
beside the cabbages, a great bed of larkspur, which they
grew there for cutting; and then I would often bring out
my chair and read all afternoon between luncheon and tea.
It was at Woodview I first took to reading. For though I
had been a prize winner at school, I never knew how to
read for myself and get the sweet pleasures of a good book
until I came to Woodview. They had books there, put in
the servants' rooms; religious books. So I began with them,
with missionaries to the Kaffirs. Their name was Moffat,
and I have never forgotten their goodness and bravery; for
truly they offered their lives to God.

Then, too, it was in that happy, quiet time at Woodview,
before I was married and while I was still a sober maiden,
that I first read Charlotte M. Yonge. Of course, I had heard
of her fame before, because my mother had the *Young Step-
mother*, and my teacher at school taught us that she was as
great as Shakespeare, and truer to life. But it was only
now, when Miss Maul asked me if I would like a good
book, that I remembered the name and asked her for a
Yonge. And Mrs. Monday had the *Pillars of the House*,

6

which Miss Maul lent me, and it gave me such pleasure I was quite mad for reading and could not eat or sleep for thinking of it. I was glad that being cook I had my own room, for I read often half the night, and, I'll admit it, was so excited that even in my work I would be thinking of that poor family, thirteen children left without a father, and the noble Felix who gave up his education to support his mother.

My own daughters laughed at Miss Yonge's books and at me for upholding them, but I told them often and I believe it still that great books should tell of good, noble characters and show them in the real trials and sorrows of life, for God knows there are enough in every life, and every one of us wants help to face them. I know that Miss Yonge did me much good and gave me strength in adversity, and I have often thought, in my bad times: How would Violet Moss have borne this?—she would have made nothing of it; or What would Mr. Underwood have said, though he was dying of consumption and leaving a sick wife and all those children behind him in poverty?—and then I got courage again and cheerfulness.

But even when I was still in the Woodview kitchen, the Moffats and Miss Yonge did me good. They made me ashamed of my comfort and my spoilings. For now when I look back on that time it was not only good religious thoughts that came into my head. I say I was a sobersides, and I was certainly shy in strange company, but I know I had begun to spoil myself. I always had my fingers in some sweet thing, and often, even from that same quiet corner in the garden, with the *Pillars* in my hand and tears in my eyes, I would jump up and rush to the back door, only at the sound of the milkman's voice. Because he was a good-looking boy, and a charmer. Indeed, I let him flirt with me,

7

though I knew he was a philanderer and had misused several poor girls, and, what was more, I used to forgive myself afterward, saying: "I'm only young once," or "That's the way I'm made." Indeed, I think if I had not been sober brought up by a good mother, I might have gone to the bad in my teens. But my mother was a good woman, one with a conscience. She never minded giving me a hard smack now and then where it did me no harm (for she never boxed my ears and would rage against any parent that did, saying it was dangerous to the drum), and when she saw me lolling and lazing and skimping my work about the house she would tell me so in plain words and say: "You can do your work properly, my girl, or you'll get nothing from me but bread and water and sackcloth." So indeed she has given me bread and water only for my breakfast and, when I sulked, told me that I was a fool to spoil my temper as well as my welcome. "For if you want to get a husband," she would say, "you'll have to do it on your temper and your character. Your face and your shape will take you no farther than the workhouse."

Chapter Three

I KNEW my luck at Woodview, and, indeed, I did not know how there could be such delight in the world, and especially in service, even good service. So when Mr. Matt began to wait about the back stairs and to come upon me in the attic landing, I was angry with him for bringing me into the fear of losing such a good place.

I could not blame the poor man himself; he was so

8

held down and cramped by his good mamma and his older sister, Maggie, or Maul as they used to call her. It was Matt, Matt, all day; and where have you been and what do you want in your best suit. It was a shame to see a man already up in his forties so hampered and hagged, like a child, and kept from his rights as a man. All we girls pitied him.

But I had been well brought up, as I say, and I asked him to leave me alone.

The truth was that though I pitied him then for his poor creeping life, I did not greatly like him. I thought him a poor thing, with his long neck and long nose, his bulgy eyes and his bald head. He would look as startled as a hare when I told him that it was not honest of him to lie in wait for me; and then when he looked at me through the kitchen window, from the garden, his eyes were as sad as a wounded hare. And that, God forgive me, made me want to laugh. He was a joke to all of us girls, for we were a young, careless lot, always ready to laugh.

He kept away from me for a time, and then he began to be more than ever in love. I could not stop him. He came breaking into the kitchen whenever he thought I was alone and then he would take me by the hand or arm and falter out: "How are you, Sara?" or "What a nice girl you are." Never a word of love. But his face would grow red all the way up to his baldness.

I could not be too angry, for I saw it was Nature working in him. Yet I was frightened and so sharp enough. "Mr. Matt," I said, "have you no shame behaving so in your own mother's house? If you want a girl, go and take one in your own class and don't pester servants who have their own way to make."

When at last he wrote me a note, proposing that we

should go off and get married, I could not believe him. As I say, I didn't like him then; he seemed too old and serious; besides I was afraid to marry a gentleman, with all their rules and manners. But he would not take no. He kept on asking me every day; and one day, when he asked me if I could not like him enough, though I meant to say no, yet the words came out of my mouth that I would try.

I don't know what was in my mind, for though in our parts girls did sometimes try a marriage with a man and marry him after, I can't have thought that. I wouldn't have thought it with my religion, and I know, too, that Mr. Matt wanted a marriage at once.

All that evening I was surprised at myself. Yet it seemed to me that I could still draw back, and that it was all a kind of play.

But not a bit. For now I was caught up and couldn't get out. He brought me the ring that night and how could I say no then, with it around my neck? It was the ring on Monday and the registry office on Thursday and London that night and Paris on the next Tuesday. In one week from that idle word my whole state was changed as much as if I had been made over into another woman. I could not believe it myself and still it seemed to me that I was play-acting, or that the world was more like a play than I had thought.

You will say that was just what a flighty girl would do, marrying for a whim. But I was not flighty then. I was a sobersides. If I had been flighty, I would not have been so surprised at myself, as I was for many a day, until I had no time to think of anything.

10

Chapter Four

MATT HAD left behind a letter for his family, but you can guess how I was in terror of them. I hoped, indeed, that they would never forgive him, only that I might not have to face them again.

But Mrs. Monday, though stiff and proud, was a noble soul and a true Christian. She called me daughter in her first letter and summoned me home. Miss Maul, indeed, was another mold, for though she was polite enough when I came, she soon found how to quarrel. She was a cross kind of woman and I think she suffered from losing her power over Matt, who had been like husband and son to her from his babyhood.

I could not blame her for being cross and she had one reason to find fault. For as it happened, no sooner had I reached home than my friend, Rosina Balmforth, came to visit me.

Rosina was two years older than me and my mother had never liked her. She had always been a bold girl, talking broad and dressing in a way that gave a wrong notion of her. For though she had little enough religion, she never allowed any freedoms with her nature.

Rozzie and I had lived at the two ends of one double cottage in Rackmill where we were both born, and though we were different, she was my best friend. She had such spirits and she never let anything put her down. Yet she had no luck and no prospects. She came from a bad poor home. Her father used to knock her about and she was always in

11

rags. She had no proper education. Her looks, too, which might have been her hope, were spoiled by a bad skin, and in those days a girl could not powder and paint to give herself justice.

Yet Rozzie had made her own way. She had got herself, at only fifteen, a good place at The Case Is Altered, which was then a rough enough house, though free, and doing the best business in the village. And once she was there she made herself respected by the worst. She would fight off the men with her fists and her tongue. So, before she was eighteen, she was the real manager and married the landlord, Willie Balmforth.

This was a good match, for, as I say, Rozzie had nothing but her health and go, and a good bust. And Willie owned the house and fifty acres of good land besides. He was a striving man, too, who meant to make his fortune. The village all wondered at his taking Rozzie. But I thought it was Rozzie who had taken him and I admired her for the way she had fought herself up out of dirt and rags and ignorance.

But it did well. Rozzie stayed behind the bar and managed that side of the house better than any man. She would throw out a drunk with her own knee. She made the Case so respectable that the vicar would come there, yet consumption went up by barrels a week. She would fix a man with her eye in such a way that he dared not hang over a pint for more than twenty minutes, or a quart for half an hour.

Meanwhile Willie built out a wing in iron, bought secondhand, and took cycle clubs and Sunday schools and Buffaloes. He had summer visitors and sent them out by charabanc to the beaches.

The only trouble at the Case was that Bill could not hold

12

his drink, nor Rozzie her tongue. They were cat and dog and Rozzie would write and tell me never, whatever I did, to marry a man, for they were all hateful.

Chapter Five

BUT THOUGH I admired Rozzie for her character, I could have wished she had not come to see me quite so soon after my marriage and I had great harm from it. Yet it was not Rozzie's fault, but my fault. You might say, I had reason to be flighty; a young girl, I wasn't yet nineteen, just married to a gentleman with his strange nervous ways, and never knowing whether they were Matt's own ways or proper rules of the class I had come into. But it was not that I was flighty, but that there was a bad spirit in me ready for mischief and for any temptation, and I would not fight it.

Yet now I was growing in love with my Matt. No girl could have helped loving a man so kind in himself and so loving to her. So it was the last thing I wanted to upset my poor Matt, and when Rozzie came I went to meet her at the station to warn her that the Mondays were a strict family and that Matt was a shy man and a true gentleman, easily put out of countenance among women.

But Rozzie was full of confidence. "Don't tell me," she said. "A word to the wise. I'll butter them all up like a sore tail. What about the costume? It's the one I use for customer's funerals, old ale color." It was true she was in a dark brown cloth dress, very quiet and respectable, but her first words to Matt were: "So you're another of them."

13

"I beg your pardon," Matt said, all eagerness to make my friend welcome, especially because his mother and sister were looking at her already as if she was dirt on the carpet.

Rozzie knew as well as I did that she was going wrong. She turned purple and stuck out her big chest. But do what she would, she looked bolder and fiercer than ever and fairly shouted at Matt: "I meant husbands, not pigs. I respect pigs." So then she turned to old Mrs. Monday without being introduced and gave her a nod and said: "We know men, don't we, ma'am—hogs by night and monkeys by day."

Matt tried to laugh but could only move his lips and I was in despair for him and the Mondays. But I couldn't blame Rozzie, for as soon as I had got her out of her room she stopped and said to me: "You can kill me, Sara; go on, give me a good smack in the mouth"; and she asked me: "Whatever did I do that for?—a nice beginning, I must say. But curse me if I let out another fly word. From this lamppost to around the corner, I'm a lady in both legs."

But though Rozzie tried to hold herself in, she couldn't do it. She told Matt at dinner not to kick her under the table. "If you have enough for Sara, it's as much as your life's worth"; and she said to me: "Don't be jealous, Sara—I wouldn't have him for a back-scratcher, in spite of his nose."

Poor Rozzie was in as much agony as I was, and when I went to her bedroom I had to console her and tell her that nobody minded. But she was no fool and she would say: "Of course they mind, Sara. And I'm doing you a lot of harm. I wish you could just give me a good kick in the stomach—it would make me feel better. But I'll go away tomorrow and never come back."

14

Of course, I could not bear that. For the truth was I was glad to have Rozzie. I had been feeling lonely with no woman to talk to.

So Rozzie did not go, and on the third day she came out in a pink silk with a green sash and she had a green hat with ostrich feathers almost to her waist.

She was a little ashamed of it and yet I could not tell her it was on the loud side. For even Rozzie could be touchy when she knew herself in the wrong.

When I went out with her people turned to look at us in the streets. Then Rozzie would stare at them and say in a loud voice, to be overheard: "What's wrong with the mumpheads—or aren't they used to seeing a lady in these parts?"

But I think Rozzie liked to be stared at, and I couldn't blame her, for it was all in her bravery and her go, which were what I admired.

But the worst was this: that I went shopping with Rozzie and bought the same kind of clothes. Then not to waste them I had to wear them and we gave Bradnall a fine spectacle. This in my first six weeks when I was on my trial, and I thought myself so dutiful.

Poor Matt did once try to make me wear something more ladylike, but I pretended that I did not know what he meant. "I like a little color," I said. But I knew quite well that I was making an exhibition of myself and that everyone was saying: "There goes the girl poor Monday married—she was a cook and doesn't she look like it!"

Chapter Six

ROZZIE WASN'T gone a day before Miss Maul was at me about the clothes. "I think," she said, "that you'd better not wear that new pink to Lady So-and-So's."

"It was my own choice," I said, for fear she should abuse Rozzie, and then I should be cross.

"Oh," she said, "I only noticed that it was like that terrible dress Mrs. Balmforth was so fond of."

So then, of course, I had to say that Rozzie was considered to have very good taste, and Miss Maul answered that it was not a suitable taste for young married women, at least in Bradnall.

Of course, she was quite right but I could not allow it, and so I had to go out in the pink dress and shock another party and make Matt wretched. For though he never noticed for himself what I wore, Miss Maul soon showed him that it was vulgar and such as only a common woman would wear, and so he was in agony for me.

I tortured him so and suffered for him, but so it was. It seemed I was two women; and one of them a loving wife and the other mad and wicked. I did not know how to manage myself, any more than a filly foal running about the field with her tail in the air and pretending to bite the trees, and to kick at her own mother. And as I say, I was frightened too, for I thought: This luck can't last. Think of all the girls prettier than me, and ladies, too, that never get husbands at all.

16

So I was reckless, too, and it's a true word that the reckless are meat for any devil.

Chapter Seven

THE WORST battle with Miss Maul was when she told me, in anger, because I would not change my style of dressing, that I had set my cap at Matt and caught him. This made me angry, too, and I was going to tell her how I had fought against him, when it came upon me that perhaps it was true. For though I had run away from him and told him to let me be, and kept out of his way too, all these could be for leading on as much as putting off. Hadn't I played that very trick on the village boys, when a girl?—running off from them, when, God pity me, my aim was only to drive them mad and take them away from their own belles; and to be caught at last and kissed. But what before all confounded me with Miss Maul was that at that very moment, I was playing upon my poor dear man. For the more I loved him, and I had never loved him as much as then when he had to stand up for me before the world, the more I held away from him, and pretended to be nice and ticklish. Day and night I held him away, making him dancing mad for me and to fall down before me in worshipful gratitude for what was his by right and justice and all the time I wondering at my own luck and the sweetness and goodness of that dear soul, which I tried so much.

So, indeed, like the young fool I was, thinking all men hot knives to a woman's butter, and never to be hurt or blunted by them, I did him great harm for which we both

17

suffered and which still comes upon my conscience when I least expect it. For men are far more delicate in their ways and feelings than many girls, and so girls should be taught to be helping and not hindering with foolish tricks. I do not mean that the girls are bad by nature, for I would not blacken my sex; but only that they are simpletons as I was and ready for bad as good, just upon the way of the wind. But men are not so innocent and so they are more particular and more delicate in their nerves.

So though I told Miss Maul it was a shame of her to say such things to me, especially to my face, and to hurt me, I felt a terrible sinking in my courage. Indeed, I never again was easy on that point; to think that perhaps I had played so meanly upon my poor Matt. For make no mistake, he suffered by marrying me. No man can marry a servant and live on in the same place without a stab, even unmeant. Poor Matt would change color if anyone in the room should say the words cook or saucepan. Stove or kitchen would prick him like a gad. Only kettle and trivet were safe, because kettles can belong to a drawing room; so I would always say, if I wanted to run out to the kitchen, I think the kettle must be boiling, though it was the soup or the milk that I had on my mind.

Miss Maul gave him a hundred stabs a day. She could make him scarlet only by looking at my dress or my big hands. But to me she was as good as a sister. For if she blamed me and abused me for catching her brother (as she thought) with wiles, she was not the woman to bear resentment or keep up a quarrel. She was a Christian, too, like her mother, and she had a mannish manner of mind and face, able to feel hot and think cold. She gave me good advice about cards and visiting and conversation among ladies, which, except about the clothes, I took; and it saved

18

me from making a fool of my poor good Matt when all Bradnall was watching for my slips.

Yet with all my faults and Rozzie's visit, there were only two ladies that closed their houses to us. Our only trouble was that the better people, such as Matt ought to have known, always had engagements when we asked them to the house. But as I say, Matt had lived quietly and given no parties for himself, so we had no right to wonder that Bradnall did not flock into us.

Chapter Eight

IT WAS a great trouble to me to find how Matt had been put upon and lost his rights as a man. It was waste of both our pleasure, for he was always saying that we could not do this or that, only because his mother and Maul would not like it. But worse, he felt his own injury. He told me once, in our first weeks, when disappointed in the way you know by a failure of his nature, that he was too shy. "It's my great fault," he said, "and a very bad one, for it makes me unsociable. I ought to have asserted myself more," he said, "and had my friends to the house."

"How could you," I said, "when your mother and sister would allow no drink and no late hours? You can't have men in without offering them something."

"No, no," he said, "it wasn't their fault, but mine. I was afraid of it. I was always shy and I've given way to it."

So I said that at least he would get his rights with me and he could bring in his friends. I would be very glad to see them. For we had our private sitting room and I meant to have whisky there for men, and port for the ladies.

"You have only to ask your friends," I said, for I did not know then that he had none. I had thought, like other foolish young people, that everyone had friends, and it was only when I grew into the world that I found out how many people had none—to call friends—but only daily acquaintances. Matt truly had no friends, and when I said: "But what about so-and-so?" giving names, like Mr. Boler, his partner in the foundry, and Mr. Hickson, who did business with him, he cried out: "Good heavens, not Boler— and Mr. Hickson is a millionaire."

"But why should you not know millionaires?" I said.

"You don't understand, my darling," he said. "Mr. Hickson looks upon all Bradnall people as provincial people, and bumpkins. His real home is in London and his country place is a hundred miles away, almost in Devonshire. He uses his house here like a hotel and only keeps one because he likes to be on the council and to have his finger in every pie."

But I thought that a cat may look at a king and so I plumped for a stall in the church bazaar, in June, when I was a six-months bride. The Mondays had always had a stall. And when the committee, whose chairman was my chief enemy, said all the stalls were given out, though I knew they were not, I went to sell at Miss Maul's, for she couldn't refuse me. And when Mr. Hickson came over to the stall, for he went to everyone, I looked at him with a friendly eye.

Of course, all the ladies did as much; it was their duty to give kind looks for the men's money; but I'll own I put that in my eye which, among us village girls, had meant: "I have a soft place for you."

20

As well, I liked Mr. Hickson at first sight for his sad eyes; and perhaps for knowing he was a sad man. Although he was not yet at the middle thirties and married for the last four years, his wife was a gadabout, neither to cherish nor love, nor even to give him a home to make his friends welcome and hold up his position in the world. She was only a shame to him. I was told that all their houses, in London and the west and at Bradnall, where she was never seen, she had her own rooms and her own bed and never came to his and gave him no comfort even in duty. It seemed very wrong that so rich a man, who had worked hard for riches, should get so little for it, not even as much as any plowman with a simple woman to his bed and his table.

Yet he was not so bad looking a man; neither crooked nor bald. He was on the short side and his head was on the big side, with a very big face, and big nose. But he had very good eyes, brown and clear, and a handsome chin with a cleft. His teeth, too, were beautiful; too good for a man and nearly as good as my own. As for his complexion, true, it was rough and brown, like coffee, and full of holes from smallpox because he had been born and brought up in Africa, but that did him no harm in my eyes. I never liked pretty boys. A man's face should be for use in battering at the world, and show the scars of it.

Now whether it was because I was a bride, or so much talked about as the cook who married upward, Mr. Hickson stayed chatting for ten minutes and showed by many signs that he was ready to know me better. He said, too, that he had known my husband for many years; and was delighted to know me.

All this, I admit, was a triumph to a silly young girl, for Mr. Hickson was the greatest man in Bradnall; and

21

as Matt said, he used to go among us, especially at bazaars, with a face of duty. He was affable as any prince, but you saw that you were of his daily work and not of his pleasure. And there he was talking to me with his hands in his pockets and his eyes jumping about, and standing on his heels and laughing with all his teeth, like any boy that has just picked up a belle at I Spy corner. All the other ladies, and especially poor Maul, were smiling one way at their customers, and looking the other, with their eyes, at poor me and my conquest. And so it was. For to my great surprise, while I was still planning how to bring great Jack to the jug, as they say, and trying to get Matt up to a garden party, which would not fix Mr. Hickson to an hour and which would bring in all the doubting ones to see him, he walked in to tea, all by himself, as cool as you please. Imagine Matt's surprise when he came home at half-past six and found me talking art with Mr. Hickson, and Mr. Hickson hanging upon my words as I had been his doting piece these four days.

Now I know nothing of art, as I told Mr. Hickson, who was a great collector and had his houses full of pictures; but he made me talk, all the same, of what I liked, such as Marcus Stone and Raphael; and also of my young life in the country and that sweet land where I was reared.

Matt, as I say, was amazed. Yet I was glad to see how, shy as he was, he came out when Mr. Hickson used his fascinations upon him, and talked and laughed. I had been afraid of Matt's fumbling and stumbling with him. But no, and this was the advantage of his good education, for though he was shy, he knew himself Mr. Hickson's equal, and could say, "when I was at the varsity," to which Mr. Hickson would answer that he had been there too.

He asked Matt to luncheon, on some business which he

said he had for him; but I believe he invented it. And after he had gone, Matt was in such a state of wonderment and joy, and pride in himself, and pride in me, that he seemed quite comical. He talked about it all evening and half the night and said a dozen times: "The truth is, my dear Sara, you've bowled him over. What a joke and what a slap in the eye for the Upper Road," which was that part of Bradnall where the best people lived, like the colonels and the knights.

And so it was. For when I got Matt at last to give my garden party, though he would give me no band and no strawberries, only in the plates four at a time till they ran out, yet because Mr. Hickson brought the county member, who was a lord and a famous cricket player, I could have had all Bradnall, and those that were not asked were ready to hang themselves.

And afterward Mr. Hickson stayed to a little supper, just the three of us, in our own sitting room, not to trouble the Monday ladies, and was so sweet to Matt that he was touched to the soul; and said afterward that Mr. Hickson was worthy to be rich because he was a noble-minded man, and set the things of the spirit above the body.

Chapter Nine

SO IT came about that Mr. Hickson called in almost every day and had tea with us; or if Matt could not come home to tea, with me alone in our own sitting room. And he talked to me about everything and listened to my words, as no one had ever done before. I thought that this was in compliment and only to flatter me. Mr. Hickson was a clever man, I knew, and though still in his thirties, a man old in the world; he would know how to fiddle all tunes which women dance to. But I found now that he truly pondered my words, and gave them back to me, many times, with improvement. As when I was disappointed of a party by the children being ill and said, after my good mother's words, that "life is a gift that Solomons miss; and none so plain but the sun will kiss," and he came back the next day and answered that life was not only a gift, but to him, a very real gift; for he was blessed with riches and some very dear friends. "No," he said, "I ought to be a very happy man, and you have made me ashamed of my grousing."

For Mr. Hickson did often complain to me of his sad life, without home or wife or children; and indeed I thought he might well be envious of Matt and me. For though, as I say, I had made things hard for Matt, in his nature, and my own ignorance, yet it was not fourteen months before we had our first child, a girl Belle. She was a lovely girl from the cradle and never gave me any reason for those fears which every mother has.

And in only eleven months after, I had another daughter, Edith, who though small and frail seeming, was always the healthiest and most independent of my children. Even as a tot, she kept herself close and made up her own mind, as sweet tempered as she was sure of herself.

Yet though I was so much in the nursery, Woodview was already another place. For Hickson brought friends to tea and we went out to dinners. And Matt joined a golf club.

Chapter Ten

IT WAS Mr. Hickson who got Matt to play golf; and just as I had hoped, that led to a golfing suit and at last, after another year, to brown shoes. He would not buy them for me, but when Mr. Hickson told him of his own bootmaker who made the best brown shoes in the world, then he got a pair.

I could not say thank you to Hickson for anything so private and so small, but I told him how I was grateful by my handshake and by a joke about my going to the new shoemaker. I was indeed grateful; who but Mr. Hickson would have guessed that I wanted anything so little and ridiculous as for my Matt to wear brown shoes on Sunday afternoons, and to have a knickerbocker suit like other gentlemen. I was ashamed to say it to anybody, knowing that women are named for just such littleness. Yet that clever little man knew my wish mind only by the way I had admired his own breeches and said that they were good for the long grass; and by the way I had only looked at his brown shoes and then at Matt's city boots. I believe he knew the map of my whole soul better than myself.

On that first day when Matt went out in his new suit and brown shoes, Mr. Hickson came back early from golf, having got a twinge in the wrist, and when we went into the garden before tea, he held me by the top arm the whole way around the rose garden. I noticed too, how he mentioned Matt, saying: "He's coming out a bit, isn't he? We'll make a prime minister of him yet."

I did not know how I liked his pressing my arm, especially where Maul might see, and saying that we would do so-and-so for Matt, who was worth ten of Hickson, in spite of his riches and cleverness. And then he began admiring my frock, which was a Russian blouse all ruffled down the front, lifting the ruffles and pretending to see how they were sewn to the bodice, but really to touch me. I did not think I liked it, and yet I thought, what harm if he enjoys it, poor little man. I owe a great deal to him, I thought, for he has got for me much I could never have got for myself. How could I have gone to golf clubs and county clubs and shoemakers and tailors or made Matt do it? In all my life Matt would never take my advice about anything except a menu or the kitchen crockery. A woman can do as little for a man in a man's world as a man for a woman in hers.

But since Mr. Hickson had flirted so with me once, touching me, he had to do it again. And this is the great difficulty for a woman. How to put an uppish kind of man into his place, without hurting him more than he deserves. For after all, it was no great crime in Mr. Hickson, to be a man and like me as a woman. Or if it was so, then Providence must answer for our shapes.

Yet, as I say, since I did not know how to stop the man, he ended by going too far and bringing upon Matt and myself a great misfortune.

Chapter Eleven

THE FIRST time this friendship with Mr. Hickson brought our happiness to danger was just after Edith was weaned; and I was coming down to a reasonable size, and going back also to some outdoor gaieties. For I nursed all my babies nine months and could have nursed them for a year, I was so strong and healthy.

Now Mr. Hickson had bought a car, the first in Bradnall, and the dearest of all to my memory; for in it he gave me my first airings after all my first four babies. It was an Argyll, green with brass lamps like trumpets; and what I liked, very high in the back seat, so that you could see over the hedges. Not like your modern motors, with windows like cracks in a door; and so near to the road, you see only half men and half women, trousers, and skirts, much less the fields. But what a delight to go bowling along in the old Argyll and look once more on the fields, especially about harvest time when Edith was born; and the corn as ripe brown as a duck's egg and the barley as white as a new-washed hairbrush. And three larks at a time trilling and tweeching as if the sun had got into their brains and made them glorious.

Oh, that joy, to feel the open again and to see the lovely world and know that your nine months are over, when you felt like a parcel coming out of its string; and to have a new baby at home. Matt and Mr. Hickson would laugh at my spirits and my calling out "There's the Green Man," or "the Blue Posts," as if I had never seen them before; or driven along that road.

So, as I say, I loved the Argyll, and I was delighted— when Edith was weaned at last, the most difficult to wean for the obstinate thing meant to have my milk even with six teeth, biting holes in me—that Mr. Hickson proposed a long trip, to his great house at Addingley. It was shut up, as nearly always, since Mrs. Hickson did not like country; but we would see the pictures and gardens and have tea and supper there, and stay the night and so home the next

27

day. A good holiday without taking me too long from the children.

So we drove through plenty of dust, I'll admit, but what was dust then to a motorist? and got to Addingley for tea. All the furniture in covers; and no footman or grandeur, only a caretaker and Mr. Hickson's own man, to see about our meals.

But such rooms and pictures that made you say: "Oh, to be rich!" Here I saw for the first time pictures of women quite naked and Mr. Hickson was amused when I was shocked. I had seen that one before, of a girl with a water pot, but she was sideways, and besides, not in colors. But it seemed to me, and does still, a queer thing that for a girl to go naked would be shocking; but not her picture done from life, on the wall.

The house outside was not so much, though big and old; a great square block like a box, with stone railing around the top and statues all along; as if someone had opened the box and left the nails sticking up. But the gardens were a wonder; and to beat Babylon, falling down by terraces, and fountains in every one, to a lake, and on the other side of the lake, rising grounds with woods and single trees and Jersey cows as fine as deer, and pale as lemon, grazing and drinking. It was about sunset with a sky like a kitchen fire, all sparkles below and blue ash on top; meaning perhaps a storm tomorrow. But the air as warm as new milk and still as water in a goldfish bowl. The water was as soft and bright as sweet oil; it seemed that you could have put it on your tongue and tasted its luxury.

There were many islands on the lake, one with a bridge to it, like a willow pattern; but the bridge in white stone and the temple on the island like a little Royal Exchange,

28

with pillars; but all white and clean, as if from a wedding cake.

There was a boat waiting as if by chance, and Mr. Hickson said, "Shall we go for a row?" But of course the boat was prepared, with cushions ready.

We said we should be delighted and Matt said that he had rowed at his college, though in the second boat. But just then Mr. Hickson's man came down with a message, on the telephone. Matt and Mr. Hickson went to the house and Mr. Hickson came back alone. It was urgent business, for them both, at the Hickson works, thirty miles away, but Matt had said he would see to it alone; and the car would take him.

How like Matt, I thought, not to want to spoil my day. For Matt was the most thoughtful man I ever knew, to give another pleasure. So that was how Mr. Hickson took me out alone in the boat.

I always loved to be rowed on water, for the feel of that wonder; all that weight of boat and people floating upon the air as you might say, for it seems but thicker air; and so smoothly as an angel might slide in the air; and I liked to watch the splash of the oars coming upon the trees turned upside down in the water as still as sleeping princesses; and making them shiver and wriggle and stretch themselves as if the prince had touched them with his finger.

Even the knock of the oars I liked, because, on the water, all sounds are like music and make you feel that joyfulness in the body which would be like dreaming if it was not so lively, and sometimes bad. For every knock was closing the eyes of my soul and opening the thirsty mouths of my flesh.

So when we came to the little temple and found there all kinds of lemonade and wines and sandwiches and sweet

29

cakes laid out upon a clean cloth—and garden chairs with silk cushions—I was very ready to drink some sweet wine, and eat and compliment Mr. Hickson on his water party. "You spoil me," I said, but he answered no, he could never do enough for me in return for what I had done for him, and so on. He had often spoken so and I did not greatly attend to it. And at the same time, I admit, he would take and press my hands and even kiss them, and once or twice he had even kissed my cheek and squeezed me a little.

Why had I not stopped him? I can't tell except that he was my friend and Matt's and I did not want to hurt his feelings.

So now in the temple, what with the water and the stillness of everything, even the aspen leaves seemed to be asleep, I did not notice Mr. Hickson or what he was doing, but only felt the joy of the evening, until I came to myself and saw that he was going too far. Then I was so angry that I hardly knew what I said. I told him, of course, that I would never see him again, and he apologized a hundred times, and blamed my beauty and his own love and so on, as they always do.

Yet I insisted on going back to the house at once and I wanted to telephone for Matt. But Mr. Hickson asked me if I wanted to upset my poor Matt and I saw how wrong that would be.

So I shut myself in my room till after suppertime. Then Matt or no Matt, I had to come out and I could not snub Mr. Hickson with his own man behind my chair. So we chattered and not to spoil so good a supper, I let myself be a little gay.

The upshot was that Matt did not get back that night. The car had broken down. But I took care to lock my door, and Mr. Hickson was wise enough to let me alone.

30

But it came out in Bradnall, I daresay by Matt's own innocent talk, and made a scandal, which Miss Maul brought, all hot and peppered, to me first and then to Matt. She was too honest to go behind my back, but she took care to see Matt before I could catch him. She told me that I was imprudent and I would come to disaster unless I was careful. For Matt was a jealous man, and if he was once made jealous he would tear down the world for his revenge.

What she told Matt I don't know, but he was in such a fury that I heard him from three rooms shouting. And I quaked to my bones. For though I was not truly guilty in my soul, yet in the world's eye, which does not look at the mind, but only the flesh, I had gone far to break my vows.

Yet all Matt's raging was at Maul. For he said that Bradnall had a mean mind and so had she to repeat it; and he came into me straight and told me that I was not to let myself be hurt by any of their vile gossip which attacked me and Mr. Hickson, only because we were above such meanness ourselves, and provincial prejudice.

And when I said that all the same, I would like to be more careful in future, Matt said no, he would have no truckling to meanness. For friendship was innocent and a noble thing, and should not bow down before idle spite. And as for jealousy, he said: "I know my faults, I hope, and they are plenty, but I hope jealousy is not one of them. For it is the most contemptible of vices." A very good true speech, and what was better, all meant. For Matt was good all through, without a bad bone anywhere.

The end of it was that Maul left the house and took another small one of her own. I was sorry for her, and we were always good friends; yet I was glad too, because she could not help thinking that she knew best for Matt. Even though she saw him so happy that he was a different

31

kind of man, yet she would make herself believe that happiness and gaiety were bad for him. If it wasn't his liver, then it was his character and religion. And I was rattling him into his grave.

Chapter Twelve

SO ALL was as before, and I forgave Hickson; not, I mean, by words, for words would have brought it all up for talk, and talk is dangerous in such a case. But it was understood that he was not disgraced, and in a week, he was holding my hand as before and telling about his sad life and his need of me.

But now Maul was gone and Mrs. Monday had died the year before, we began to give more parties. There were luncheons and dinners every week. For Matt, with his clubs and his knickerbockers, and his Homburg hats, like Mr. Hickson's and the new king's, was fast coming out of his creeping ways that the Monday women had put on him. He had begun to be bold on all sides; not only in clothes, though they are always the beginning. He had even turned against the church and criticized the sermons and the prayers and even Heaven and Hell. I was sorry for this change around in Matt, but I could not be sorry to see him acting the man and the master of the house; and sending the port around his own table, as a gentleman should; and calling the men out from the drawing room after tea, to have a whisky with him in the library. The first time he did that, I could have hugged him; not Mr. Hickson could have done it better. For he looked as if he enjoyed the very idea of it; and poor Mr. Hickson for all his polite easy ways, never looked as if he enjoyed anything except what he should not, philandering with me.

And I'll admit that I was too careless and too easy with him. A woman grows easily coarse, as she is made for the rough work of childbearing, and so things that would have shocked me as a bride were so little to me now that I did not even notice them at all.

But then, my boy Matthew was born and died of croup in the first month.

I had had no fears for him, as for the others; nor for myself. I was so well and gay in my carrying, and he so fat and strong and greedy. But he died in ten minutes when I was only gone to choose a chicken for Matt's dinner, and even before he was dead, and I saw the maid running for me, I knew that he must die. So, I thought, God strikes when you least expect and His wrath is terrible.

I could barely cry and Matt wondered at me. He was afraid for my health and my looks too. For though my breasts were sore and running with milk, I grew so thin in the face that my friends would have me take tonic and oil and my enemies rejoiced and said: "At last that fool Matt Monday will have his eyes opened and see that he was caught only by the girl's country colors, and that she is really a plain common lump."

It has come, I thought, and it is just what I might have expected, for as my marriage was far beyond my due, so out of my marriage comes my punishment and my destruction.

I remembered then all my provocations, and Hickson, and that I had put off my blacks for my poor mother after four months, only to go to a garden party. For poor little Matthew I wore them like a widow, and the coarsest linen

33

and wool stockings that made my legs itch. I would not let Matt near me and mortified my life. I trembled for the next stroke, for Belle and Edith and for Matt himself.

But at last poor Matt was fretted into such a state that I could not hold him off. Only I took care to take no pleasure myself and to think meanwhile of my grief and danger. However it was, within another two months I was carrying again and full of terrors.

But my girl Nancy was a kind baby from birth, and never a day's illness. Not as pretty as Belle, or as clever as Edith, but the sweetest affectionate nature to make up for it. So God struck the balance for the child.

Here was I then, not yet twenty-four, with a house of sixteen rooms, and five servants in and three out; and my landau and my victoria and my governess cart; and my at home days; and three children; and another started; Mrs. Matthew Monday of Woodview on the county nursing committee.

You may say that it was no wonder I forgot those warnings and gave myself up to the sweet world; but the truth was that at my very worst, and when I least expected it, the fear would strike me like a cold shiver, and I would say God is not mocked. Then, indeed, I would wonder at my lightness and folly.

Chapter Thirteen

BUT NOW I was in the fury of my life when a woman has no time to know herself or anything else, unless she is strong in remembrance of her religious duty and can fend off the world. I had never less than two thoughts jumping in my head, if not a dozen, and the telephone as well. Our telephone was not a year old, but it was already as much as two more children.

I gave myself no time to think, except of trifles and vanities, arranging the dinner guests or paying a call, or altering the girls' frocks, or giving them their medicine. I don't think I ever read a book in those years; not really to read it and feel it; for even when I opened one of my old favorites, I would find my mind wandering off upon some rubbish. Though my eyes would be reading of Violet Martindale with her husband going to the bad and not knowing how to stop it, my mind would be noticing the children's voices in the garden and saying: "So they're back already. I wonder has Belle changed her stockings."

And this, though I knew my books as well as my kitchen and could open *Heartsease* at the very page where Miss Yonge says of Theodora Martindale: "Many thoughts floated through Theodora's mind; but whether the better or worse would gain the advantage seemed rather to depend on chance than on herself."

It might have been written for me.

Yet even in that page, though I saw the words, I did not feel the truth and the meaning of them. What was worse, I would be deceiving myself. I would think I had been spending my time seriously when I had only been fritting it away, just as before.

But what took up more time even than the children was the parties and the calls. For Matt had come right out from his timid ways and we were as gay as the rest. Indeed, looking back at that time before the war, in the 1910's, it seems to me that the world was all gaiety; delights crowding together till there was no room between. For it was parties, parties all the time, in summer, croquet and tennis and luncheons and teas and pageants and plays and regattas; and in winter it was dinners and balls, and such balls. Even at our Bradnall balls we had the cotillions and prizes for everybody; good prizes. Matron as I was, I won so many favors that I didn't know where to keep them. It was a heaven for girls in those sweet days, for the men had not lost their manners and at all dances there were chaperones to see that they danced with even the plainest. So they did too, for they knew their duty as gentlemen.

Then there was Henley too, and Wimbledon and the Eights at Oxford. Matt had been to Oxford and he had a cousin there, a professor. So we always went to the Eights and then again to commemoration. I would dance all night, three nights running, for though Matt could not dance, his cousin would find me partners and come himself. But what was sweeter than dancing and the lovely waltzes of those days were the gardens gay with paper lanterns, and the trees as green as lettuces over the fairy lamps; and the smell of the limes and the nightstocks hanging on the dark, and the lovely girls in their trailing skirts walking under the old walls, like the ghosts of queens. Then we would go out in the early morning, all as we were, but wrapped up in furs, and take breakfast on the river; so sleepy and lazy that the noise of the water sent us to sleep.

And not only at home in England did it seem that life was nothing but joys and new dresses; for when you looked in the illustrated papers there was nothing but gaiety abroad. There you saw that the emperor of Austria had given a great ball and that Paris was mad about the new dances from Russia, and in Germany the kaiser and the czar had had a great review and a yacht race and more luncheons and dinners and balls. Of course, all this gaiety meant plenty of work, too. As I say, I spent half my days

36

making up parties and some of the ladies at Bradnall village were busier still. For we were not the gayest, as we were not among the rich, as riches went then. Yet we lived in glory and luxury. I don't know how it was but everybody seemed to have money then; and money seemed to go further.

You may say that such a life was bad and trifling. Yet I think people were no worse then than now, and perhaps better. For in all our happiness there was more religion, and no one in Bradnall, however gay, would have thought of tennis on Sunday, or of not going to church. If I went to the bad at last, it was not the fault of the times, but of myself. It was not because I loved the parties and the gaiety and even as a mother and a matron up in the thirties, danced through twenty pairs of shoes in a year; but because I did not remember my weakness and study my faults, and because I forgave myself too easily for those evil deeds which always took me by surprise. For many were as gay, who were also good, and happiness was a grace to them, as it is God's most precious grace; they lived with God and never forgot their gratitude. So I have thought, even at a ball; this sweet pleasure is provided for me, and felt the wonder of God's providence and my own especial luck.

This was a happy time for Matt, the happiest in his life, before his troubles began. He would groan indeed that he had never peace in his own house and make a terrible outcry about the bills. He would say that it was me only who liked the parties and that he bore all the noise and expense only for my sake; but I, who heard him talk afterward of what he had said to this man, and how he had set that other right, knew well his gaiety on party nights and the good to his natural spirits, which indeed made

37

him so lively and boisterous that he often left the proof upon my skin; I say I knew differently. So I did not argue with him but was content. I was a foolish woman enough but I knew that what a wife may lose in justice comes back ten times in kindness.

Chapter Fourteen

BUT OUR chiefest joy was Matt's new glory when they made him a councilor. After that, no one could say I had dragged him down. And this was through Mr. Hickson, and through a mere hint of mine that Matt, though he laughed at the council, would not be against it, if he could be sure of getting in.

Mr. Hickson said only that it was an easy thing, and sure enough, he had Matt in within six weeks; and nothing said to him of our private chat. Yes, I may reproach myself for being too free with Mr. Hickson, over so many years; allowing him so much that I can't believe the eyes of my memory, or its feelings; yet he did me great services, and was a good close friend.

For you may say that a married woman cannot be close friends with a man without wrong. But wrong is not a steady thing; and if I did wrong with Mr. Hickson so often, I can't believe I did but right.

He would come sometimes to supper, just with us two; when he was most cast down. Then Matt, seeing his grief or his need, would say; "Take Sara out for a walk—she's had nothing but children all day and she needs some peace and fresh air. But please excuse me—I'm too busy."

So I would put on a shawl and we would walk out through the lane and the fields, which were being built over so fast that every day there was a new tree down and a new stream turned into a drain. Indeed, by daylight, Bradnall, with a new motor works and a new cement works, had come out to us, so that we were built in on three sides. If I had seen Woodview now, when looking for a place, I would not have called it a country house, but a villa in a suburb. Out of my own bedroom window I saw not fields and willows and the stream winding away to join the Thames, but rows of little houses like kitchen fenders, with blue roofs, and, beyond them, a gas works. It had become an ugly place where no one cared to live, and already some of the big houses were sold and their grounds built over. I don't know how it was that in so gay and sweet a time, such ugliness came into the town and the country; but wherever we went we heard the same tale, of villages spoiled and parks built over, and rivers turned into sewers, and the country paths stopped up. It puzzled my daughter Belle, who was a clever girl, and when she asked me how it was, I asked Mr. Hickson and Matt and several more councilors and public men. But none of them could tell me. It seemed that it was something you could not stop like mold in a bread bin, without cleaning everything up and starting again. Which, of course, is nonsense in a nation.

But on the one side there were still some meadows and some poor old willows, bald and broken, and a clear stream; and here Mr. Hickson and I would walk and he would think himself as well off as in that beautiful land around Addingley.

So we walked about the lanes until dark fell thick and the fields were as black-green as well moss and the trees quite black except at the top; and the sky like the water when you wash an ink bottle; as black as blue can be in the middle and paling away to skim-green at the edges; and the owls calling like ship horns as I used to hear them from Rackmill, on their way to America. And the cows breathing in the dark so quietly that you thought it was the field itself, until they heaved up and trundled away. Then Mr. Hickson was at his truest and best; his soul came out of him and I could no more have set him down than if he had been a child. And to be fair to him, he never thought of me then as flesh, but as a friend and a woman's ear; to listen and understand what men could not: his loneliness, and his wonder. For he too would wonder how he had missed his happiness after working for it so hard. He knew it was not all his wife's fault, for he had asked me often should he be divorced, and then he said: "No, what good? Another scandal among the rich, all for nothing." But I thought he thought too much about himself, and what was due to him in joy, to get any. So I have hinted, but he never heard me, to understand.

I do not say this, that there was true friendship between Mr. Hickson and me, to excuse myself for what was more than only friendship allowed, but to show that it is hard to judge people as all of a piece.

For Mr. Hickson could not only be a true friend to me, but to Matt, and he gave us both happiness when he brought on Matt, in business, to be richer, and in the council, to be more known. Matt was the best of men but had no push, and so he owed all his success to Hickson.

And a successful man is a comfort in the home even when you are not thinking about him. Indeed, I always thought the house itself looked brighter and the fire drew better on a day when Matt had made a good stroke in his business or asked a question in the council and had come out in the paper. Success was good for Matt if it was bad for me. It took away the fret of his nervousness. Even after quarter days when the bills came to light, he would no longer cry out that he would be ruined and really fear it. He would only shout a little, as indeed he had a right to do, and then remember himself as a man acknowledged in the world, and say only: "But goodness knows, Sara, I hate all this fuss as much as you do. It's so undignified. If only you would keep some check," and so on, and then saying: "Well, my dear, I suppose I'll have to pay it," and paying it and giving me a kiss and telling me not to look so upset. Which more than anything made me swear I would reform. For God knows I would catch myself looking upset when my mind, knowing that the worst was over, had flown onto the children, or the larder, or even another new frock.

Chapter Fifteen

NOW I come to the time of my meeting with Gulley Jimson, who was the turning point in my downfall, and, I dare say it, the instrument of Providence, to punish my prosperity and forgetfulness.

I say that Bradnall village was now joined onto the town, so that people even wondered why we lived there any more; and many poorer families had moved out. But we would say, since Matt was a councilor, he must live in the town. And the new building made it the more interesting. Always new schemes and new committees. We had already a new union workhouse, two new hospitals and an asylum, and now there was to be a new town hall.

So we told people, and it was quite true, that Matt took great pleasure in the council work. He had always been interested in architecture, especially Tudor architecture, which the new town hall was to have; and both he and Mr. Hickson were on the building committee.

They had planned a fine lobby for the entrance and Mr. Hickson proposed that it should be painted with a decoration or scene by an artist called Gulley Jimson, who, he said, was going to be famous, but who was still cheap.

No one had heard of Jimson except Hickson and Matt, who only knew the name through Hickson, and the committee asked to see his work. Mr. Hickson showed some photographs, but no one liked them. So in the end, not to offend Mr. Hickson, they proposed to put up the wall for competition.

Every artist was to send in a colored drawing, eighth size of what he would do on the wall.

Then he asked Matt if he would give Jimson a room while he came to measure the wall and to make his first sketch. He said the man was very poor and besides needed care and comfort.

"Only starting, is he?" Matt said.

But Mr. Hickson said that Mr. Jimson was not very young and had been at work for many years. He was a true genius in his way but poor because no one would buy his pictures and the critics despised them. "I wonder he has gone on," Mr. Hickson said, "he has had no encouragement to do so."

"He's had a bad time," Matt said and I could see he was coming around to Mr. Jimson. For being himself so open to be put upon, he hated all oppression and tyranny. I saw how he felt and willing to bring him out in this new way,

42

I said that we had the pink room with a good window and a lovely view, which any artist would like.

"We have several rooms free," Matt said, "and I should be delighted to put the best at Mr. Jimson's disposal. Delighted," he said, "it's a privilege," and then he said that it was a duty to support artists and especially original artists. It was the fault of our democracy that it neglected art and culture. Mr. Hickson said that he was quite right and then he asked if he might bring Mr. Jimson at once to introduce him. So he did, for it turned out that he had him waiting in the road.

Chapter Sixteen

MR. JIMSON was a little bald man with a flat nose and a big chin. His head was big and hung over so that his face was hollow in the middle. He was much older than we expected, getting on for forty; very shabby too, and had a front tooth missing. He said that he would bring his painting things next week and all he wanted besides was a room with a good light from the north.

We had never seen an artist before and though Mr. Jimson was not my idea of an artist, he was better because he was so simple and gay, never minding his own shabbiness or his lost tooth. He smiled away as if he had no thought of it. I thought: You're not one to care what the world thinks, and so I warmed to him at first.

When he had gone again to fetch his luggage, Mr. Hickson told us of his struggles and his poverty and how hard it is for a genius to make his way against the ignorance and jealousy; and how he had been a gentleman before he took up art.

This, I thought, made it still worse for him to be a failure in life, and homeless, especially by the spite of others. But then, as Mr. Hickson said, he had no push and a man who takes up art needs push before all things, or money, or he will be trampled over. Both Matt and I were sorry for Mr. Jimson and thought that he should get a chance at last. "It's a scandal," Matt said that evening, to a party we had, "that such a man is still almost unknown and can't even make a living. I don't agree with those who say that our industrial civilization is bound to be selfish and materialist, but we have to admit that it has very grave faults and the chief of these is its neglect of original art. That indeed is a blot upon our recent history." This was from a speech Matt was going to make next week, at the prize-giving in the girls' school. He had it on his mind for he was always very nervous before a speech, so he brought it out now.

I loved to hear him speak so, and it seemed to me that our own lives, running so sweetly, were a temptation. "God knows," I said, "we might be ruined tomorrow and homeless and not so ready for it as Mr. Jimson. The rich grow soft to sorrow. That is God's own plan for their punishment."

"We have much to be thankful for," Matt said, "but we mustn't forget our luck. No, I shall give every word of that speech even if it does get me into trouble with the agent, and I'll send it to the papers tomorrow in case I can't be heard properly or forget some of it."

So he did, though luckily the papers did not print the strong parts on account of the big election that year; it

44

must have been about 1910 because I remember a mourning dress I bought for King Edward.

I was glad in myself that the speech was not printed because I was always afraid that Matt would make enemies who would play some mean trick on him. Indeed, for a long time I thought my downfall would come from that side, since that was my glory.

But Matt himself grew more fearless every day, and more happy and more easy in his mind, so it seemed that what little we had done for Mr. Jimson was coming back to us.

Chapter Seventeen

WE WERE so excited on the day that Mr. Jimson came that Matt stayed away from business to receive him. But Mr. Jimson made little of that. He did not even say how do you do, but only: "I'll just look over the rooms and see what you've got." Then he darted over the whole house, even in the servants' rooms and the schoolroom, where the girls were doing their homework, and said that the only room he could take was the morning room where we sat when we were by ourselves and where I did all my accounts and sewing.

I was afraid that Matt would say no, but not a bit; he answered certainly, he was very glad there was a suitable room; would Mr. Jimson like any changes in it? Mr. Jimson said only to take all the pictures out of it. So we went at once and stripped the walls. It was like a holiday and it made me laugh to see us pulling down our own things

45

which we had picked so carefully, just at a word from a stranger. Indeed, Mr. Hickson, finding out how Matt was giving Jimson all he asked, warned us not to let the man be a nuisance. "Don't spoil him," he said. But Matt said it was a privilege to assist Mr. Jimson and spoke of a great poet, Coleridge, who had been taken in to live by a doctor.

Chapter Eighteen

THE NEXT thing was that a party got up in Bradnall which said that they would have none of Mr. Jimson. His pictures were indecent, because he painted men and women naked. I knew now that this was nonsense and both Matt and I told everybody we knew it would get Bradnall a bad name because artists had always been allowed to paint naked. Yet when I saw Mr. Jimson's first colored drawing I was startled and so was Matt, though he did not confess it. It was not the nakedness of the people, but their shapes and colors. They had very short legs and big heads and especially very big eyes. The women, too, were all in red and the men in green.

This began our first trouble with Mr. Jimson, not because either of us thought at any time of criticizing his way of painting, for, as Matt said, we were learners only. But that when we tried to understand the pictures, he laughed at us or put us off. I did not mind this for myself, but I minded for Matt who was very sensitive to snubs. I never admired poor Matt more than in the way he would face up to Mr. Jimson and try to get something out of him, in spite of terrible snubs.

46

He would look at the canvas a long time and say at last: "I think I see what you mean."

"It's more than I do," Jimson would answer, turning and grinning at me. When he grinned like that, the gap made him look wicked.

Matt would grow pink, especially his nose, by which I could tell that he was hurt. But he did not give way. He said that it gave him the feeling of poetry and the secret influence of Nature. The green men were like trees and the red women like flowers.

"More like mud," Mr. Jimson said, laughing.

"Our human clay," Matt said.

"I'm not a poet," Mr. Jimson said, "I'm a painter."

"But you must have a reason for painting your figures in that way."

"I paint 'em as I see 'em, Mr. Monday."

When I saw Matt turning scarlet, I thought I would change the subject and I said that everyone saw it differently.

But he only laughed in my face and said: "That's right, Mrs. Monday—they do. Different is the word. But excuse me—" and he put down his palette and walked out.

After the first week, every time we looked at his picture he said: "Excuse me," and walked out, so we gave up looking at it. But we both felt we were right in encouraging Jimson. And when I puzzled over our troubles with him, as I did many nights, and wondered if, after all, we had been tricked by Mr. Hickson who was using us to push Mr. Jimson and to take the risk of looking great fools before the world, I thought that no, for at least Mr. Jimson is not in the plot. For what does he get out of it? Nothing but poverty and misery. It must be that he is chosen for it and so we must be right to keep him.

Chapter Nineteen

THOUGH JIMSON was so hard on Matt, he was very friendly to me and even on the very first day he began drawing he opened his door when I was going through the hall and called through the hall to me. "Give me your hand a moment, Mrs. Em—"

I was surprised. But it turned out he wanted only to draw my hand. And the next day it was my arm, which he pretended to admire. I had been ashamed of my great thick arms, but one night at a party, given for him, he took hold of my arm, all mottled as it was in the cold weather, and lifted it up before all and asked them to admire it. I did not know whether to be angry or not. But there was Matt looking very serious and saying: "Yes, yes, I see—I always thought so myself"; and as for those who were laughing and saying to themselves: "A regular cook's arm, got from pounding steaks and whisking soufflés," I could laugh at them too.

But Jimson was always calling for an arm or a hand or a neck or even a leg; though he did not get it; and while I sat, he would make talk and so we were howdedo friends, and had some private jokes. As I say, what I always liked in Jimson was his gay spirits, little enough as he had to keep them up.

So one day I dared to ask him why he was so scornful of Matt. I told him that Matt admired artists and wanted to help them.

48

"Oh," he said. "I suppose Hickson has been talking to him. Hickson tells everyone about my genius."

"So he does," I said, "and isn't that a good thing for you?"

"And for him," he said. "He's invested in me, you know. I painted about twenty-five square yards of his hall wall at about forty shillings a yard. He wants to push up the stock."

"So much the better for you," I said.

Mr. Jimson said nothing to that but kept on laughing at me. He never paid any attention to my words, like Mr. Hickson, and he thought me a fool about art, as indeed I was.

Yet I did not dislike him for that, but for something much worse. After he had been with us about three weeks, he went away suddenly and stayed away two months, so that we gave him up and put back the pictures in the morning room and hung a curtain over his picture. For Matt would not have it touched and yet he did not want the children or visitors to see it.

But no sooner had we got back the use of the room than Jimson walked in, one afternoon when we were all out, and brought a wife with him. When we came back late for tea, there they were having a high tea in the dining room. At first we were both glad to see them because though Jimson was a nuisance, he livened us all up; but afterward we could not bear the way he treated his wife. He made her a slave; and as we found out afterward, would even beat her.

Chapter Twenty

THE WIFE was called Nina. She was a little thin thing with a long neck and a very big forehead. Her nose and chin were small so that the forehead seemed out of proportion, especially with the style of hairdressing at that time, all on top, with rats underneath to puff it out, and a bun behind. Nina had blue eyes, not big, but a very pretty color, like forget-me-not. She was dressed very badly; a kitchenmaid in a good house would have scorned to go in such dowdy clothes; a flannel blouse, a black skirt all down at the back, and long cracked boots.

But she was so gentle and sweet that we both liked her at once, and Matt asked her to stay as long as she liked and complimented her on her husband's genius. He made her blush with pleasure and I must say I was delighted with him.

Nina was no trouble to anyone, always neat and clean and punctual, very quiet and serious. Indeed, she saved us trouble, for she waited on Jimson hand and foot, as he demanded; and kept their room beautifully clean and tidy and tidied him up too.

Now I don't know what it was but I fell in love with Nina almost from the first day. You would say we were very different and when Rozzie once came for a week end, while the Jimsons were with us, Nina could not bear her and Rozzie despised Nina and said she ought to be in the Salvation Army.

It was true that Nina seemed very religious. Yet she was

not a Christian. On Sunday she behaved as on other days, waited on Jimson, and sat with him while he drew or painted. Her sewing was beautifully fine and she took commissions for work on trousseaux and she would embroider initials and monograms. Then every afternoon, wet or fine, and this was January, she would go for a long walk alone. For Jimson never took any exercise. He would either work all day, or stay in bed till tea time and then go to a public house, where I heard he would cut jokes by the hour and drink beer.

When I knew Nina better I asked her how she could bear to walk alone and she said that she liked to go out alone every day, as a duty. "If I don't go out to see Nature every day, I forget what it is like, and how beautiful the world is."

I thought that Nature was not very beautiful in January, except in snow, but then I knew that I was country bred and that townspeople like Nina often thought more of trees and fields, even when bare and dirty, than I could in full summer. It is like a religion to them, and I'm sure it is a good harmless one, though, like Nina, they don't know an elm from an oak, and think that all corn is wheat and all green, grass.

Mr. Hickson used to laugh at Nina to me and call her a romantic soul, but I knew she was better than either of us. She accepted her hard lot with so sweet a mood, better than patience, for she set no value on herself as a patient sufferer. Then when she went out to walk so seriously, she was full of delight and thanks even for the dirty fields around the village. I never knew anyone who took such happiness from so little.

I don't think Nina ever cared much for me. That was natural; for I was now getting full blown in the rushing tide of my worldly delights. Matt had given up trying to

51

control my dress and Bradnall was used to it. But when a little while ago I looked at old photographs that Jimson had kept and saw the woman I was in my thirties and early forties, frilled and flounced and laced and thrusting myself in front and behind, I can't believe my eyes. There is no doubt that in those days I outdid Rozzie herself. I seemed a very bad kind of woman, worldly, common and worse.

The wonder was not that Nina drew away from me but that I had still the sense to like her and know my need of her.

Chapter Twenty-One

MR. HICKSON was always trying to get portrait commissions for Mr. Jimson and so did we. We gave two big parties for him and showed two of his portraits. But no one liked them. At last Matt ordered a portrait for fifty pounds.

I was against the portrait and yet I was for it. I knew that if Matt was not painted now he would never be painted at all, because he would think it too conceited to order a portrait of himself, except as a charity; but then I was afraid, too, of how Mr. Jimson would paint him.

I was quite right, for first he would not paint him, as we both wanted, in his golf suit, with grass and trees behind, to make a picture of it, but he would have him in a black coat and a stiff collar. The next thing was he made his nose so big and his forehead on a slope and his chin so little that he looked like a goose peeping out of a jug.

52

As soon as I saw how the portrait was coming out I knew we should have trouble with Jimson.

So the next time Mr. Jimson wanted my hand, I said to him that his portrait might be good but it wasn't my husband.

"Oh," he said, "but he's not my husband. He's Mr. Monday and that's the way I see him." And he would make no change.

I knew it was no good to ask Nina's help, for she would never interfere with her husband, and as for Hickson, he was away in London, and besides, we were not then good friends.

The truth was that Mr. Hickson had given me a great surprise, by warning me against Jimson in a way that I could not brook. For he seemed to say that I was too much with Jimson, and had shown him too much for his drawing. Which was false, and what was worse, unfriendly.

This quarrel with Mr. Hickson was another cause that brought up my reckoning. But I must not say it was a cause either; but rather all my indulgence that went before, to him and to myself, which spoiled my modesty, and his manhood. For to hear him in our quarrel you would have said he was a little spoiled boy with a pain that is told he mustn't have any more sugar.

Chapter Twenty-Two

NOW, ALL this time, I was complaining to Matt and trying to get him to suggest another position, with his head more up and a winged collar. But Matt only laughed and said that he did not mind how he looked. "What does it matter?" he said. "If he paints me like a baboon—those who know me won't mind, and those who don't know me, can think what they like. After all, Sarry, I never was a beauty!"

Yet I knew that this was only his bravery, because he would go in to look at himself often six times in half an hour, when Jimson was at his bar, and when you saw his face coming out, you could see he was troubled. And one day, when I caught him coming out from the room, God forgive me, like a fool, I burst out at him and said: "You're not going to let him hang that up in an exhibition."

So Matt was taken off his carelessness and let himself out, and said: "Well, Sarry, it's not for myself but the children. Perhaps there is a ridiculous side to me or at least my face, but it's not what I would like to be remembered by."

Then I was angry with him, for I knew this was a sore place with Matt, that people might laugh at him. Indeed, I had got a picture, bought from a curiosity shop, only because it was Matt's image, and hung it in the bedroom corridor, "General James Wolfe, Victor of Quebec," saying I had my sister in Canada, but really to show him that a delicate chin and a sharp forehead could go with a general, and who had once been a famous man.

So I told him that long faces are among the highest dukes in Europe, and considered to be the mark of the blood.

"If only my face were long," he said, "but the whole is squat—it's the shortness at the ends throws out the nose. You'll never make me into a donis with all your fussing about my clothes and my shirts and my shoes."

I told him the truth, that it's not the face that matters but the spirit, and a man that carries his features like a first prize will make them a model.

54

But Matt shook his head and I thought he looked smaller and older. "No," he said to me, "he's seen me as I am— and he's brought it out in the portrait. That's his genius— to put a man's character into his picture."

I argued with him and I got him around to saying that it was not really himself in the picture, not the one who got on the council and made the speech against civilization, not my Matt, but only a little bit of Maul's Matt. But I felt frightened, as well I might have been, and so I took the bull by the other horn and went to Mr. Jimson with a photograph of Matt. It was by a very good man in London who had brought out the distinction of his character by electric lights. So first I made myself as nice as I could to him, and, as it seemed, more than I need have, for he rose like a fish, and I was in terror that Nina would come in or Matt himself. He surprised me then, the nasty little man, but I dared not put him down too hard. So I took out the photograph as quickly as I could and said: "Mr. Jimson, you say we are friends and that I have helped you at your work, and you have done a lovely picture of my husband. But yet it is not quite the man I know. For how could you see him as we see him and know his fine character and his courage in standing up to corruption? This is the Matt we would like painted."

Mr. Jimson looked at me laughing and said: "You say we are friends, Mrs. Em, but you want me to destroy one of the best things I ever did."

"No," I said, "only improve it."

But he said only: "Tell your husband that if he doesn't want the portrait, he needn't pay for it. I'll keep it," and he opened the door to let me out.

"At least," I said, "you won't show it."

But the very next week it was in an exhibition in Bradnall town, labeled "Portrait of a Gentleman."

55

Of course the opposition paper put Matt's name to it and besides everyone recognized it. Though Jimson had taken an inch off the forehead and put it on the nose, clever as he was, he had made it the Devil's likeness of my poor Matt.

Indeed, everyone who knew Matt recognized it and all our friends came to sympathize with him and with me and to see how we took our misfortune. Now if the Devil had contrived such a trick, he could not have found a better to drive my poor Matt mad. For it hit him in his two sorest places at once, his great modesty left over from the creeper days, and his decent pride, new got in the clubs and by being master in his own house. It had him between two irons like a lemon squeezer and it squeezed the life out of him. For pride would not let him complain that he minded what face he was given, and modesty could not bear the exhibition of his weaker parts and the laughter of the very workmen in his own foundry. It gave him no peace. All night I would feel him wriggling there beside me, and when I asked him, had he a pain, he would answer in a despairing voice that there was nothing the matter with him and tell me to go to sleep.

I could not bear it so I went to Mr. Jimson and told him that it was a wicked thing to show the picture. "Not that my husband minds," I said, "it's a trifle to him. But I mind."

"You don't appreciate my masterpiece," Jimson said smiling.

But I was angry and lost my temper and said that even if he was a genius, he had no right to do a cruel thing.

Then he was furious too, and said that it was not cruel to paint a fool in his own colors; for how else could fools be painted? So I answered him that he was mistaken in

56

Matt, who was worth ten artists, and twenty Jimsons. I always hated meanness, for it frightens me. So I went out for fear I would take the man and shake him.

It happened we were out to tea, and I was glad to be out. But still I knew that I had been foolish to quarrel with a man like Jimson. You never know what an artist will do. I came home early to apologize to him and win him over again. But, I could not believe it, he had packed already and gone off, in two cabs, and nothing left but a letter from Nina, thanking us for our great kindness and saying that the insult to her husband could never change her gratitude to us.

I was shocked, but Matt suddenly changed over and said: "Good riddance." He said that Jimson was not even a true artist, for the true artist was never spiteful or cruel. It was impossible because, if he was inspired, it must be by God.

Then, too, I had to confess that I had quarreled with Jimson and might have been the cause of his going. So he raged against him and said that he would like to kick him. I had to smooth him down.

I was glad to see Matt take it in this style, with spirit, but I think now I was wrong and that he was giving way to himself more and more.

Chapter Twenty-Three

THE JIMSONS took a room in the village, over the stable in the Swan yard; not half a mile from us. Matt was afraid that he would meet the man and never went through the village. He was still in a fury against

Jimson, and I think he was afraid of what he might do next.

"Keep away from the Swan," he said, "he might get hold of you and worry you. I don't want him to upset you again."

But even then I had seen Jimson, in this way. The first market day I saw Nina at the fruit stalls and the moment I set eyes on her, I knew how I had missed her.

She was looking serious as ever with her head in the air. Her nose was red as usual in a wind, but no one ever minded poor Nina's nose; she did not mind it herself. She despised looks. Her hair was in a bun so neat that it might have been carved on a stair knob.

There was no one like her, so neat, and yet dowdy. You would have thought her a Christian except that she never preached and never thought evil. It was a pleasure even to think about her.

She had a big bruise on her cheek and I asked her how she had hurt herself. But when she said, "an accident," I asked no more. I saw she did not want to speak of it. I had no notion then that Jimson beat her.

I asked her about her room and the picture. She said that the room was a good light but Jimson had not gone on with the picture. It was still lying on the floor, rolled up, and he would not touch it.

"But there's only a fortnight before the sending-in day," I said.

"I know," Nina said, "and so does he. But it's no good trying to make him paint if he has lost his inspiration."

"Inspiration is all nonsense," I said. "He told me so himself. He only wants to be put at it."

But she looked grave and said that Jimson often talked

58

like that but it was not true. How could he paint without inspiration?

"This competition is the biggest chance of his life," I told her. "If he wins it, it will give him a real start. They are going to have a royal prince to open the hall and unveil the picture."

"I know," she said, "and he was painting so well even on Monday—but he has not touched a brush since." She said it in such a way that I knew what she meant and I said: "What, it's not me who's upset him."

"He was very upset," she said, "you know he looked upon you in a special way as his friend."

So I was astonished to think that I could have upset anyone so much—especially a gay, brave man like Mr. Jimson—with a few words. But I was put about too. For, I thought, if he loses the competition, it will be my fault.

"He *must* finish it," I said. "He simply must send his picture in. He *mustn't* miss this chance if he dies for it." So then I told her that if the picture was sent in it was sure to win, for Mr. Hickson had just got a grip on the third vote on the committee. I could not help telling her but I made her promise not to tell. "So whatever you do, see that the picture goes in."

When I met her the next day she told me that Jimson would not even look at the picture. But I could not sleep for thinking of how little would save them both and change their whole lives.

The end of it was that the next day, happening to go past the Swan yard, I had a sudden idea and went up to their room. There was Nina sweeping the floor and Jimson on the bed, smoking. He frowned at me but I paid no attention to him. I said I had come to help Nina. "The first thing," I said, "is to get the picture up—there's no time to waste with that."

"What picture?" Jimson said.

"Your cartoon, as you call it," I told him, very short. "You only have ten days to finish it."

"I'm not going to finish it."

I said nothing but I began to unroll the papers and look for drawing pins.

"Where are your pins?" I asked him.

He stared at me as if he would bite me, but I knew that he would not behave like a fool before me, after his philandering. So I said again: "Here or there? Which is the best light? Even if you don't finish it we want it out of the way."

"Where you like," he said, "the pins are in my big box."

I began to pin up the sheets and asked him which was the middle one. He stared again and then he laughed and came to help me. "Are you going to take me up?" he asked. "I suppose you're tired of bridge parties and want a new toy."

"Maybe so," I said. "I don't know. But you will look foolish enough if you throw away the chance of your life when you have it in your hand."

"A chance of making money," he said, "and being taken up by snobs."

He kept on laughing at me, which I thought a good thing. He said at last: "You're like a train—nothing will turn you when you get started. It's a good thing you're not my wife or I should have murdered you long ago."

"Maybe," I said, "but I am not your wife and if I were perhaps I should do the murdering."

This was the kind of thing he always made me say, pert and foolish.

When we had finished putting up the sheets of paper, I began to admire the work and say that it would be sure to win the competition. But he put on his hat and excused himself and went out. Nina was still cleaning the room. She said now: "Never do that again, Mrs. Monday—interference drives him mad."

But I thought only that her interference might drive him mad. Indeed, next day when I called, I found him hard at work on the picture and when he saw me he called out: "You see, Mrs. Monday, the result of your influence."

But I knew that he was trying to stab at Nina so I said: "Nothing of the kind. You would have started today in any case." She said only, in her serious way, that she had never liked to try at inspiration, in case she might do harm.

I said she was right, but I thought it might have been better for them both if she could have laughed more and enjoyed what little, poor thing, she had to enjoy. There's not so much happiness in the world that anyone can afford to waste it.

Yet she made me know my own wastefulness too. For one day when I stepped out of my carriage to ask if I could do some shopping for her, in Bradnall town, she said no, but she would like to drive the other way, into the country, to see the spring. "I'm missing it," she said, "I haven't seen any of it except in gardens."

"I would like that too," I said, "if I had only a moment. I lost last spring in the children's whooping cough and this year in parties. And now today I have to meet Nancy at the dentist's. He's a man from London and this is the only time he could give me."

But Nina asked me what I had to do after the dentist and proved that I could find time by going home late for tea.

61

I liked my tea in time but I did not like to admit it to Nina. I was especially anxious to do anything Nina asked, on that day, because I had just been told in the town that Jimson beat her. I thought I could see a mark under her left eye, like a bruise, and I was horrified to think of the brute hitting that saint in the face. So I could not say that I liked my tea better even than spring.

"It would be good for us both," Nina said, "to look at the trees and forget our stupid selves."

"You can't forget a child's teeth," I said, "when she's a girl and has no advantages. Nancy's are going already at thirteen, and she's growing plainer, too. Belle has everything, looks and brains, and Edith has brains; and Phyllis is the world's darling, but Nancy has nothing."

"You must forget them," Nina said, "it's a duty—you can't enjoy the spring while you're thinking about teeth."

For Nina, of course, trees and grass were holy. Indeed, I think everything was holy for her and I suppose, if God made the world, that she was right. But whether right or wrong, it was in her character and it made her different. And I looked forward now to my drive with her, for I thought: I've been getting too fond of my tea—I'm too fat too, which is just God's rightful punishment for indulgence. It will do me good to see Nature and enjoy it in spite of not having tea till five or even none at all. It's what I need, to clear all the rubbish off my soul. So I prayed that if I went without my tea and drove out to see the spring instead, the man would give me a better report of Nancy's teeth. My idea was that if I could save them till she was twenty-five or six, I would have six or seven years to get her married. I was determined to marry Nancy to make up to her for all her disadvantages, and I had begun already to tell Matt how I would like to travel some day and see

62

India where, Mr. Hickson told me, a girl with some money would always get something.

But the dentist gave me no comfort. I did not deserve it, perhaps, with the life I led; but it was a terrible blow to be told that the child had been neglected. She should have had a plate, he said—two of her teeth had been killed.

It was no good me telling him that we had gone to the best dentist in Bradnall. He looked into the air over me and pressed his lips together as if I were not fit to speak to. He would make me no promise even to save her front teeth.

I could see he was the kind of man who thought women were fools to think so much of looks, and I was in terror that he would pull our Nancy's front teeth only to triumph over me. I could not even be nice to him in case he thought that I was trying to charm him. He was the kind of man who would have turned spiteful to a charmer, and even as it was he kept looking down my figure and my dress as if to say: "a common cheap woman who might as well be on the streets."

Yet I had put on my best dress and powdered to please him, not knowing that a London dentist was almost the same thing as a doctor or a clergyman and that I ought to have dressed down for him, instead of up.

So I came out with Nina feeling like a murderess who had killed her own child by her follies. I felt such a weight on my breast that I wanted to cry out.

Nina did not even ask me about the child's teeth. She began at once to look about her, even at the trees in the gardens, and to breathe through her nostrils, trying to smell the blossom, so that I wanted to tell her that laburnum had no good smell and was a town tree.

I was angry with her for not asking about Nancy, and even when we came out into the real country, I would not

63

listen to her talk about the lovely day, or sniff at the air. But all at once she said to me that it was a day when God seemed so close that you could hear Him breathe. Then, I don't know why, my heart opened from its bitter clench and my anger against her changed to love. For Nina had great religious power so that though sometimes you hated her for her taking no notice of your troubles, the next moment she said something that went straight into your soul. She made you remember God and the shortness of your time on earth and your own littleness.

So I said: "Yes, indeed, you could," and took her hand in gratitude, and looked about me to make the most of spring. For the truth was since my difference with Mr. Hickson, I had not been out as much as usual in the country. It was Mr. Hickson more than anyone who used to take me away from the children and tea parties, to be quiet for a little and to admire beauties.

And this was indeed a lovely day, to make anyone religious. The apple trees were just budding with new leaves, and the sky so pale blue and clear as a baby's eye, and the air blowing fresh as if straight off a sea; and some little thin clouds floating high up like muslin sleeves on a washing day; and I could smell the new hawthorn leaves in the shiny hedges, like a warm iron when you try it on your cheek. What with this sweet beauty that was there for me to take and would be gone in no time, and my pain and guilt and wondering what would happen to Nancy with her plain face and Belle with her obstinate perverseness, I was in agony.

"Oh, dear," I said at last, "why don't I come out every day? Once in a way is making too much of it. I can hardly bear it."

"That's true," Nina said. "It's what my husband says—

we ought to live in God as familiarly as in a lodging, dining room, drawing room, bedroom, and kitchen. He did one of his best pictures about it for Mr. Hickson. But he would not take it."

"Where is it now?" for I was mad to see this picture and know Jimson's religion.

"I don't know—we had it when we were in London—it was in our lodgings, but we had to leave and the landlord kept all the canvases until we could pay the bill."

I asked her why Mr. Hickson would not take the picture. For I wanted still to know what it was like.

Nina hesitated a moment and then she explained that it was because the picture showed the plumbing—there was even a w.c. with a man in it. "But it wasn't Mr. Hickson, though I think he thought it was."

I said I didn't call that religion, and then the words jumped out of my mouth: "Does he really hit you?"

But Nina, good soul, answered me as simply as if I had asked the time, that Jimson never hit her unless she exasperated him. "I am not a very good housekeeper," she said, "and besides, think of all his discouragements; no one understands what he's doing."

"But why need he paint like that, Nina?"

"It's the only way he can paint. But I think sometimes he would like to stop."

I said that he seemed quite mad, but Nina answered me: "Oh, no, he's very sane—the other people are mad—to live as they do without happiness or God."

Then, again, I felt her goodness and I asked her how she could bear to live with a man who beat her. She said she had two good reasons. One was that she couldn't live without him and the other was that he needed her.

I said: "I suppose he is your religion."

But Nina was shocked. She said: "No, how could any man be your religion?"

Still I thought that if Jimson was not her religion, he was most of it, and perhaps the beatings were part of it too. For she hated to indulge herself and I know she always despised me.

Chapter Twenty-Four

I THOUGHT that I could not bear to see Jimson again after knowing that he had hit Nina, but I was wrong. When I went back with Nina to their room for tea, I stood off from him, but I saw he did not notice it. It was never any good to disapprove of Jimson because he did not care. So soon we were laughing again at some joke, and the next day I ran in again, between the shops and luncheon, to see how the work was going on.

I couldn't do without my visit, and if I had been a great churchwoman, like Maul, I would have thought I went there to be out of my tearing life in Bradnall, and out of worldly cares.

I was glad, too, when Jimson would call out, just as before, in my own house: "Give me your hand, Mrs. Em," or "your neck" and draw me for the picture.

Nina herself would ask me to sit and once she telephoned from the Swan for me to come and be drawn. She would have liked me to sit naked. It seemed nothing to her, I suppose, and when I refused to strip, she would look sad and say: "That's what he really wants, but he doesn't like to ask."

"I should think not," I said.

"Don't you think it's a pity when you could help him so much? He thinks you have the finest figure he ever saw."

"It's only a fancy," I told her. "He is a fanciful man and he likes fat women."

But I will confess that on the last day before sending-in day when we were all mad to get the picture done, she and Jimson so persuaded me that I sat for him down to the waist. I could not believe it was myself, sitting there, half naked, but there was my dear Nina in the room, as calm as you please, sewing a shift; and Jimson painting and humming and looking at me as coldly as if I had been a statue.

It seemed to me then that I had been a fool to be so prim before and yet I wondered at myself. I could not tell whether I had done a religious thing or a bad one. When I went home again, I was in wonder and dismay all the evening. I thought: What will I do next?—there seems to be nothing I wouldn't do.

Chapter Twenty-Five

AS IT happened, Matt had been very busy all that fortnight and with the children at school I had had plenty of free time, but on the sending-in day, Saturday, he came home early from the office, before lunch. I saw there was something wrong, but I could not tell what. I thought perhaps he had had a letter from some lawyer about some bill. That had happened before and made a terrible quarrel.

I was in a great difficulty, for I had ordered the landau at three to take the picture to the town hall. I dared not let Matt know that I was going to the Jimsons', but I could not disappoint Nina and risk the picture missing the competition. The man's whole life depended on it.

So I went around to the stables to get into the carriage there. But Matt threw up the library window and called out to me:

"Where are you going?"

"To make some calls."

"On the Jimsons, I suppose."

"No," I said, for I was not calling on them, only to fetch the picture.

I drove in the opposite direction to the village and left cards on some people. Then I went back to the Jimsons'. I had feared the picture would not be ready, but it was ready, only Jimson had not troubled to finish any of the faces.

He said: "Here you are—take it away quickly. But if I had not promised you, Mrs. Monday, I would much rather burn the thing."

I dared not ask him to touch the faces. We were glad to get the picture away from him. "It won't matter what it looks like," I told Nina, "for Mr. Hickson has the committee in his pocket. He has just given a big contract to Mr. Jones's son-in-law and Mr. Jones was the only doubtful one."

When we had left the picture safe, I was so happy that I almost cried. Nina, too, was pleased and when we came back to the Swan I suggested we should have a celebration tea. So I ran out to buy cakes and Jimson to get some port wine. Jimson was in his most outrageous spirits and I could see he wanted to flirt with me. He looked at me now with a different eye from the day before when he had drawn me. But, as I say, I was wild too, and I admit it, I didn't mind

68

for anything, not even for his squeezing and pushing me on the stairs, or his risky jokes. I felt as I did with Rozzie and if he had asked me to drink in some public house, I might have done it, in spite of all Bradnall.

Luckily he did not. He was satisfied with his jokes and his eyefuls. So we made tea and we were joking and using all our private jokes, like Jimson's with me: "Your hand, Mrs. Em," or mine with him: "Your ear, Mr. Jimson," meaning not that I wanted to talk into it, but box it—when a girl came up from the Swan to say there was someone on the telephone for me.

Down I went in wonder and fright. And it was my nurse, a nice little thing from my own village and my good friend, to tell me that Matt had just set off to find me, and seemed to be upset about something. "And I thought if you were at the Jimsons', ma'am, you might like to know in case the master could not find you."

The clever little thing meant to tell me that Matt was coming to catch me at the Jimsons' and that he was in a terrible rage with me.

I felt so bewildered I didn't know what to do, but while I was standing there, Nina came down and asked me what it was. So I told her, and she said I had better go home at once and she would swear I had never been there. She didn't want any scenes between Matt and Jimson, I could see that.

I had sent away the carriage, not to betray myself to all the town, and so I had to walk home. But I was glad of it to give me time to get my senses back. And as I got nearer to Woodview, my feet began to drag as if they would never bring me there, and as if the weight of guilt was bearing me down to the ground.

For now, all at once, I saw myself, with Maul's eye and the world's eye; and I could not believe how I had

69

been so bad a wife. Now all my debts and my philanderings came down upon me in one thump and crushed me.

Yet I could not make out even then how bad I had been, or how guilty. For I knew I had always loved Matt with all my heart and never thought wrong to him for one moment. And people use words so that you can never be sure what they mean. When the preachers used to speak of adulteries, it would turn out after all, in the thirdly or fourthly, that they were thinking of silk stockings, or women's bicycles, or mixed bathing; and again, for some it was Devil's work to play beggar my neighbor, with your own children and nurses, in your own nursery. Then one will say the act is all, and another, the bad thought. So that a cross word is as good as murder, but a kind man could kill kings and still be holy if his heart was pure.

"Oh," I said, "if only I had a glass door in my heart, like the new ovens, to see what was really there, and whether I am the worst of women, or just the common run of ladies in rich houses, with friends, who are guilty indeed of worldly living, but not of deadly sin."

But suddenly I heard Matt's voice, which scattered all my wits again. It is strange what a coward I was before that little man, but not so strange, for I knew him good and honest, when I was neither. The landau was at the curb and he jumped out and said: "You have been at the Jimsons' again."

"Yes," I said.

"Were you alone with him?"

"No, not today."

"But other days you were. Come, get in, we can't stand here."

I was glad to see the carriage was open, because he could not shout and wave his hands at me before all Bradnall.

But angry as he was, he saw that himself, and stopped and asked the groom to close it.

"But Matt," I said, "it's so hot." He would not listen. I could see his trouser legs shaking with rage, and my own legs were trembling. Yet I had to bow to several people and smile while the footman was shutting up the landau. I had to look even more friendly than usual to quite ordinary acquaintances, because Matt saw nobody. He would not have taken off his hat, at that moment, to the queen. His rage terrified me so much I could hardly get into the carriage when at last it was closed, and he was so furious against me and impatient that he gave me a great push behind which nearly threw me down. It was the first time Matt had ever handled me rudely.

"Why did you tell me lies?" he said. "What have you been doing with that man?"

"I only took his picture to the committee."

"You've been there every day for three weeks—don't contradict—don't tell me any more lies."

So it turned out that somebody at the Swan, probably the landlady, Mrs. Fogg, who never liked me, had told him about my visits. I saw that the man was quite mad with rage and that he believed I was in love with Jimson and had done wrong with him.

And now he began to talk about Mr. Hickson too, and even some man I had forgotten. He said that I had flirted with them all. "But it's my own fault for marrying you— I was warned about you, but I didn't listen. I suppose you were deceiving me with that fellow under my own roof, and laughing at me."

I was horrified at his thinking such things, but I could not say anything. It was not that I was frightened but I felt that all this had been prepared and that nothing I could

71

say would be any good. So I sat like a fool and looked at him while he raged and screamed and threw my arm about.

"You have always laughed at me," he said. "You have never cared one farthing for me, an old bald fool marrying a servant girl twenty years younger than himself. You and your friend Mrs. Balmforth think me the best joke you've ever seen. And nothing but lies, and bills and robbery and men ever since. There was that garden boy to start with and Hickson all the time."

The sweat was running down his face and he gasped as if he were swimming. "And now this wretched painter—I suppose he sent his wife to fetch you. Hickson tells me she gets any woman he fancies—he fancied you from the beginning. Why, I caught you together, when he was pretending to draw you."

Chapter Twenty-Six

THIS WAS the second time he spoke of Hickson and it made me wonder. And afterward I found out that it was Mr. Hickson had put the whole thing into his head that I was going to the bad with Jimson, and he had even given a hint of the freedoms he had taken for himself. All, I suppose, out of jealousy and spite.

And what a warning it is to us all, against jealousy. For here it made the clever Hickson do a mean trifling thing, which lost him my better friendship, and drove Matt mad. Yet I suppose those that are born jealous or envious will never be cured, for if you gave them a million in a bag, they would still be afraid of it bursting.

72

As for Hickson, I was sure even then he had told, because when Matt went on he said that he had always known about Hickson, and never spoke, for the children's sake. And that I must not think him jealous. "I don't mind what you do —a woman like you—why should I? I'm not such a fool as that."

He grew worse and worse, and when we got to the house, and I went up to my room so that the servants could not hear him, he followed me and began again. He said that this was the end and now he would summons me into our court and expose me; and Hickson and Jimson. He would divorce me and keep the children.

I wondered if he could do that. But I knew that the evidence would be black against me and that if I was appointed to have a fall it was no more than I deserved. It was no good my speaking to him so I took off my hat and went to go out. But he held the door and said: "Where are you going to now?"

I said I had to see about dinner.

"Dinner!" he shouted. "Do you think I can eat?"

I said I could not eat either, but dinner must be cooked and sent up or what would the servants think.

"And what are you going to do next?"

I said that I supposed I would go to Rozzie. She would always give me a home.

"And you will leave me and the children without another thought?"

I said that, of course, I would never leave him until I was turned out.

Then he stared at me and said: "If I let you stay, it will be the same thing over again. I can't trust you an inch— your whole life is a lie."

"I can't trust myself," I said. "I never meant to deceive you."

"And you expect me to believe that," he said, "that you're a weak, helpless woman, when after fifteen years you still do exactly what you like? Not one word I say has ever had the least effect on you."

"I don't know what I am," I said. I was too miserable to argue with him. I begged him to let me go to the kitchen.

But suddenly he sat down on the couch and burst out crying. I was always shocked to see Matt cry. He only cried two or three times in all those years, once when I refused him, and once now, and once when he was dying. So I sat down to ask him what I could do. But he jumped up again and told me to go to the kitchen.

I went and arranged for dinner, but when I came up to dress, I found Matt in my room. He said that he had thought things over and it seemed to him that he had been at fault too. He had left me too much alone, and as for Hickson, it had been his fault to introduce such a cunning philanderer into the house. Jimson, too, was not a fit person to know me. "Yes," he said, "I ought to have considered the difference in our ages. How could I blame you even if you did like the garden boy better—not to speak of Hickson?" So he blamed himself for everything; and I, seeing that it was to be peace between us, was glad, like a fool, and only tried to say that I, too, was greatly to blame.

But he would not let me speak and kept on crying: "No, let's have the truth—or I'll go mad. I can't bear any more pretending."

So I saw it was better to let him believe what he liked; even in the garden boy, and indeed, so he believed for the rest of his life, and gave himself peace.

And now I know that it was a bad kind of peace and that it brought our downfall. Not a great scandal or the loss of my home and Matt, as I had feared, but the ruin of the whole, which was the true punishment of luxury.

For Matt said that he had neglected me too long and that he could not bear to do business any more with Mr. Hickson, who was his greatest customer. So he retired from business and resigned from the council, and took me away to Paris to forget our quarrel.

All I had to do was to let him spoil me as much as he liked; and so he did, buying me all the newest clothes and a diamond bracelet.

Yet even then I saw how he was changed, and how he went back upon himself to the creeper time. He would scarcely cross the street without holding my hand; and never take any but the middle carriage of a train, in case of collisions front or back, or sleep above the second story in case of fire. He became as timid as a child, the poor lamb, and could not bear me away from him. So when the war came, it nearly killed him as it finished our destruction. For he sold out all his investments in the first week, for anything he could get, and we could barely scrape enough after to send Phyllis, our youngest, to school.

The war was truly a bad blow to Matt, for he had always been one for abolishing the Army and Navy, thinking that they were too warlike. And now he found that it took but one to make a war, and as we used to say: "One dog will drive a thousand sheep."

I had promised never to see the Jimsons again and this promise I kept, only sending Nina some work now and then for her fine sewing, when she gave me her address at a box number.

As for the competition, when the councilors saw Jimson's picture and found out that the committee was bound to accept it, because Hickson, even without Matt, had a majority, they called a full meeting and put off the decoration

75

of the lobby on the grounds of expense. Mr. Hickson made
them pay the artists a few guineas each for their waste of
time, but no one got the order. This was the end of all
my struggles to get the picture finished, yet so it was that
when the news came out a week after, I thought nothing of
it. I agreed with Matt who said that if Jimson had no success it was his own fault.

As for Mr. Hickson, I did not see him for a long time.
Matt could not bear the sight of him and said even that he
had cheated him in business.

But I met him one day at a party and after we had
looked at each other, I could not help smiling to see him so
nervous. He looked like a little boy afraid of a smacking.
So we talked a little and afterward we would meet now
and then, when I went for my hair, or for afternoon shopping, and walk across the new park. It was on one of these
walks that he pulled out his pocketbook and showed me the
drawing of a woman. I did not recognize it until he said:
"It's one of the best things Jimson ever did—because he
did it for his own pleasure, I suppose. I show it to you only
to let you know it's in safe hands. I'll destroy it if you like,
and I promise you it won't be shown to anybody without
your permission. But I hope you'll let it live because it is a
little masterpiece—a master's drawing of a magnificent
subject."

I was shocked and said it was very ugly. I hoped he
would burn it. But he smiled at me and spoke of false
modesty. It was always his idea that I had liked Jimson's
flatteries and that Jimson had made me value my shape.
And so, perhaps, it had been true, at the first surprise to
have an artist admire me.

But I insisted that the drawing be burned. I feared like
fire it might come around to Matt.

76

So at last Mr. Hickson put it back in his pocket and made a little bow and said: "It shall be as you please."

But he did not burn it. He even lent it to some publishers who brought it out in a book of drawings where it was called "English Portrait, from the Hickson Collection." He showed it to people, too, for even ten years afterward it was thrown at me by an enemy.

Chapter Twenty-Seven

MATT WOULD not forgive Jimson and would not even speak of him. From the year of the war I had no news from Nina, and I had forgotten the Jimsons, when one day the maid came to me in the kitchen and said a Mr. Jimson was at the front door. She had been afraid to let him in because he looked like a beggar. So I said: "Bring him around to the back."

For Matt was already failing then, and I did not want him upset.

Mr. Jimson was certainly very shabby, but gay and smiling.

"Don't be afraid," he said, "I won't come in. So he's still alive?"

"Of course he's alive," I said.

"I heard he was dying. He must be getting pretty old."

"Only sixty-two this year."

"But he was old for his age." So he went on as if we had not parted a day. He kept eying me too, and said: "You haven't changed, Mrs. Monday—I think you've improved."

"I'm fatter."

"Yes, you've improved."

I was afraid he would press me to sit so I asked him what he was doing. "I've got a commission to paint a Mrs. Bond."

"And where are you living?"

"I'm going to Bidlee for this commission," he said, which was a village not three miles away. "But I'll have to get some materials—and clothes."

"How's Nina?"

"Dead," he said as if it was nothing. "Flu."

I was shocked and said that he didn't seem to mind very much about his wife's death.

"I miss her a lot," he said. "I haven't done any real work since she died. She kept my time free and managed the housekeeping."

Then he asked me to lend him thirty pounds, so that he could buy materials and clothes for his visit to Bidlee. I said I had nothing to lend.

"I thought the place looked run down," Jimson said.

"I do the cooking. We have one maid for the house."

"I don't know what I'll do," he said. "I was relying on you. It's only for a few days till they pay me."

I had a soufflé in the oven that needed watching like a young child on its first legs so I gave him ten shillings to get rid of him. But he was back in three days. This time he let himself in by the back door and came into the kitchen before I noticed him. He made me jump when he said: "Good evening, Mrs. Monday."

But there he was and I couldn't tell a friendly visitor to go out of the house.

He sat down and kept looking at me, without speaking, while I was rolling out some scones. At last he said: "Mrs. Monday, I suppose it's no good asking you to marry me."

78

He said it so quietly that I did not feel the shock of it for a little while. So I could not be angry. I said only that I had a husband already.

"I meant, of course, after he dies."

I thought that this was a shocking thing to say and if Mr. Hickson had said it, I think I would have been disgusted. But the way Jimson said it, I felt that it would be silly to be angry. Because the truth was that poor Matt was dying. So I went on with my work and answered him that Matt might live a long time yet. There was good hope of it.

"I'll wait as long as you like," he said, "if you agree to take me in the end."

"The last man," I said. "Why, Mr. Jimson, have you forgotten that I was Nina's friend? Do you think I don't know how you treated her?"

"You don't think I would ever hit you, Mrs. Monday?"

"If you did," I said, "it might be the worse for you." For I was a head taller and my arm was as thick as his neck.

I thought he would laugh at this, but instead he looked very serious and said that I had not known Nina. "I may have given her a little slap," he said, "but she was a maddening woman. You mustn't think I'm a bad-tempered man. I'm very easy to live with."

"Mr. Jimson," I said, "I hope you won't go on like this, because it won't do either of us any good. Even if I were free to marry, I would never dream of taking you."

He went away then, but he was back again in a few days and though he did not propose, he kept looking at me as if summing me up. But one good thing was, now he was courting, he sometimes talked in quite a new way, seriously and quietly, not laughing at me all the time.

So he told me a great deal about himself, how he had been the son of a doctor, and sent to a good school. But

79

his father had died without a will and all the money had gone to the eldest son, who gambled it away on horses in no time. The schoolmaster had given him free schooling until he was sixteen and then he had gone into an office. Then when he was twenty-six he had suddenly begun drawing and painting and couldn't stop. He gave up the office simply because he couldn't bear to leave his drawing to go to work. "Luckily," he said, "I had some money saved—it kept me alive till I got married and then my wife kept me."

"Haven't you ever made any money?" I asked.

"Oh, yes," he said, "I made a hundred pounds this year—and I could make much more than that if I liked. Hickson will always get me commissions for portraits."

I could not drive the man away as long as he behaved himself. He was so pleased to come.

Betty, the housemaid, an old woman that had been the char before I was married, was my good friend and I knew she would say nothing in the house; and neither Matt nor the girls ever came near the kitchen. Matt, with his bad heart, could not leave his room and I did not like the girls in the kitchen, getting in my way, or spoiling their clothes and their hands. Nancy especially, who would have liked to help me, had a very nice young man who was interested, and I wanted her always to look neat and fresh for him and to practice her music. He was very musical and shy, and though he was plain and rather short, so that the girls despised him, he was in a very good business as a lawyer and very religious, and I knew he would be a good steady husband to any woman.

But Nancy hated music and so I would drive her to the piano, and Belle was too clever and proud for housework. She had always plenty of young men and she had been engaged already to one that was killed. And Edith had just

80

taken up her hospital training, and even when she came home at week ends, she would work at her books or learn at Chinese. For she always meant to go into the Chinese missions.

As for Phyllis, we had got her to boarding school at last, and there she was still, though doing no good with the books. So Betty and I had the place to ourselves and when Jimson came, Betty would go to the scullery.

I say I did not like his coming, but though I never liked the man, I liked his chatter and his jokes.

He was like a piece of the old happy gay times before the war, and he brought Nina back to me when I had forgotten the world at Bradnall.

Chapter Twenty-Eight

I THOUGHT very much about religion in those days, for God had punished me at last for our prosperity, and I was suffering very much with poor Matt. He kept quarreling with the girls, which was very bad for him and for them. He was all for me chaperoning Nancy with her young man, though I had no time and I knew the only hope for the poor child was to be alone with the fellow so that he might forget his shyness with her and talk about himself. So I would tell Matt that chaperones were out.

But he would shout: "What's that got to do with it? You used to be particular enough and you change because of a fashion. You don't seem to have any idea of right or wrong." Then he would say that I was teaching Nancy to behave like a Jezebel and he made me ashamed, for it seemed to be like the truth; yet I could not bring myself to spoil the poor girl's chance, a great piece of luck for her at last, by rushing in, and perhaps at the very moment when the young man was warmest.

And since Matt was at home now all day, which is not natural for a man, he grew difficult and quarrelsome.

He quarreled with Belle for her politics, because, like all young people with natural spirits, she did not agree with him and took up a little communism to have something of her own; and he complained of Edith because she was so set on leaving home. But why not? Thank God for the ones that know what they want and want something sensible. As for Phyllis, he said I had ruined her, and perhaps I had, for she was too like me in her love of pleasure.

But quarreling was bad for Matt and for the girls too. Nothing worse in a home, for it destroys all joys even among the richest. So that just when Jimson told me that I was happy by nature, I was at my wits' end with worry to know what would become of us all. It was no good warning Belle and Edith that a quarrel might kill their father. And if you think them hard, then you don't know what girls can be in the twenties, and yet ready to throw away their lives for any revolutions, or the Lord.

And when I tried to find out Jimson's religion, since he was so gay under all affliction, he answered me only: "Don't worry, it's bad for your figure and your hair."

And then again, and he seemed to mean it too, he said: "You're Mrs. Em and I'm Gulley Jimson and that fly on the wall has its own life too—as big as it likes to make it, and it's all one to God as the leaves to the tree."

But another evening, when all the girls were from home and Matt was asleep with his draught and we were sitting over the fire with some toasted ale, as Rozzie used to like

82

it, he seemed to be more serious and open as people are at that hour of a winter's evening, and especially before the kitchen fire. Believe me that is the sweetest fire in the house, for confidence and for lovers, and for consolation, and for religion too, I mean facing the world.

A kitchen fire is just the right height to look at, without going to sleep, and then it is a useful fire and not just luxury; and it is so made that it drops its coals and tells you, with every fall, that life burns away, and it has the stove top for a kettle to remind you that, at the worst, there is always tea, and that the best comforts are at everyone's hand.

So Jimson and I had at last some good serious talks by the fire, from time to time, in those sad months; and once when we had been talking about the war and its terrible weight upon artists, in stopping the sale of pictures, he said: "But what can I do? The great thing, Mrs. Em, is not to give a damn for all that kind of thing. Yes, to be all serene."

"Like Nina," I said.

But he said no, that Nina was always holding herself up and following a rule. "No," he said, "you need to live in serenity there where it grows. To be at home there, and not to swear."

Then I remembered that I had never heard Gulley swearing and from all I knew I think that this was Gulley's religion. Not to trouble about his ups and downs. But to get on with his work. And I liked him for this, too.

Chapter Twenty-Nine

OF COURSE the girls soon found out that Jimson was coming to see me and Nancy made a great fuss. She said that I had encouraged the man. It was strange how these young girls would abuse me, but the truth was, I had spoiled them. Belle, when she came into the kitchen one day and found him there, would not even shake hands with him or speak to him. She spoke only to me that she wanted tea early, and went out with her nose in the air.

Jimson was very angry with the girl. He said that she wanted smacking. But I told him that it was my own fault if she had no manners and that I could not complain if she thought little of me because I was not her class. She was a lady in all her feelings and it was no good pretending that I was one.

"Better than any of them," he said.

But I knew very well that I had failed to be a lady, even for Matt's sake, because I was too weak. I had gone back instead of forward and now sometimes I would talk broad, even to the girls. Only the week before, when Belle had a crowd of her friends, talking about literature, I had said that the old books were the best for the new ones had no religion. But I spoke broad and said "bestest" and "they'm."

I could see everybody looking at me and afterward Belle said that I had done it on purpose to make her look like a fool. But it was not so. I was quite as surprised at myself as she was. I could only think it was my own nature coming out.

So I could not complain if Nancy was ashamed of me before her young man, who was very polite and nice, or if Belle despised me.

At last Nancy came to me in tears and asked me not to have Jimson to see me. She said it was making a scandal and she was afraid it would reach her Geoffrey and put him off. She did not like me being so much in the kitchen either, or coming into the house with my sleeves rolled up and floury hands.

So I promised her to take more care with my appearance and to send Jimson away. But as it happened, before I could do so, while I was still wondering how to do so, Geoffrey proposed to Nancy. The engagement was printed in the paper and so I did not need to offend poor Jimson. Only I gave him the hint to come when the girls would be out.

Chapter Thirty

YET I, too would have been glad to see the end of Jimson because he had begun to pester me. He would not talk any longer. He would only sit and stare or follow me about the kitchen. He was as stupid as any man in that state, quite hangdog with love.

It drove me distracted because Matt was then at his worst. The poor man had gone behind all sense now and he was like a child, afraid of the dark. He would wake up at night, and say that he was smothering and catch hold of me and cry out that I must save him from Hell. He said that he had done such wickedness that God could never forgive him. All this, so the doctors said, because his heart was weak and could not put enough blood into his poor brain.

I told him a thousand times that he could never have done anything bad enough for Hell, but he said I did not know the great evils in his mind. Then I said that according to science there was no Hell, as he had often told me so himself. But he answered out of the Bible that he had spoken as a fool, for now he could see it opening for him; it was dragging him down by the legs. It seemed to me a cruel thing that Matt should suffer so in his conscience, who had never done any harm to anybody and only for the weakness of his body. But when I told Jimson of it, he said: "He is not suffering for his miserable sins, but for being a coward and losing his serenity. That's a certain way to be in Hell."

It was true, of course, that Matt had always been a timid kind of man, but then again, it was not fair. For it wasn't his fault that he was born nervous, and kept down by his mother and sister—and I still cannot understand why the poor man was made to suffer so terribly in his last days.

The worse Matt was, the more Jimson pestered me till I lost my temper and told him if he proposed again, I should turn him out and keep him out.

Then he went away and I did not see him for nearly a year. But when he had finished the portrait of Mrs. Bond, he sent me five pounds by post to pay his debt. He owed me much more, but I don't think he knew how much it was. He was always a man who counted shillings as nothing even up to thirty or forty shillings, but thought of five pounds as a big sum.

Chapter Thirty-One

MATT DIED in the spring of 1919, and it turned out that he had lost even more money than I had thought. And great debts. He had left two thousand each to the girls and the house to me. But the house had a mortgage on it and the lawyer told me that when the debts were paid, there would not be much left for me except the furniture. And he advised me to sell it and buy an annuity, however small, to have a regular income. I said: "No, I'll open a boardinghouse. For I can make double the income that way and keep out of investments."

But the girls were all against the boardinghouse. Nancy, of course, had to think of her husband and his grand relations, and Edith was sure I would lose all my money, feeding up the customers, and Belle was afraid she would have to live at home and help me.

"But what will I do?" I asked them. "I can't sit down and twiddle at thirty-nine, and the only thing I know is to work about a house."

"I'm sure you want a rest," Nancy said. "You can live very well on an annuity in very nice places."

"I see, you'd like me to be out of Bradnall," I said. Then the girl turned fiery red and said: "You're always saying things like that, Mother, but you know they're not true. If I were ashamed of you, I ought to despise myself. But I hope I'm not such a common snob."

"I never said so," I said, "and I wouldn't say such a thing. All I say is that you would be happier if I were away

87

from the place so you didn't have to be anxious for me not to say the wrong thing."

"You can say what you like, Mother," said she, "and I'll never be ashamed of you and never was."

"Not of me," I said, "but for me and why should you not?"

But she would not listen to me and we had another quarrel and did not speak for a week. Perhaps I was never tactful enough for Nancy. I never found the word to get past her school manners. But the truth was, she was too delicate in her mind. I couldn't complain of that—it went with her good heart. But those who said that my daughters had been spoiled with their good school education were foolish. Belle had a better education than Nancy, but she and I never had a tiff. "It's better for me to go," I told her, "because I don't fit in with your young friends and I'm too young for the sect of widows in the Upper Road."

"I think you're very wise, Mother," she said. "You'll be lost among those snobs and tabbies in the Upper Road. Of course," she said, "there's old Mrs. Benger and her literary circle, but I don't quite see you in that galley."

"No, indeed," said I.

"And that reminds me," said Belle. "Why did you plunge into the conversation yesterday when young Tonkin was here—about the new poetry?"

"Did I?" I said, and I thought: That's a new young man, and I thought, what a pity it is she doesn't stick to one, and fix him, instead of dodging about all the time. But it's no good telling her that there are no perfect men any more than a perfect woman. She wouldn't believe me.

"You did," said Belle, "and why on earth did you say your favorite poem was 'Now avening tawls the knell of parting day,' trying to imitate my broad talk."

88

"I don't know," I said, "unless it sounded more solemn."

"My dear mother," Belle said, "it's all very well with me but it does make things awkward for strangers."

"Of course it does, my darling," I said, "and that's one reason why I'm going away. To give you a chance." Then I asked her about young Tonkin. But she would never tell me how she was with a man. Belle was close and hard. She hadn't Nancy's tender heart. I often thought: If so be Belle does get a husband, and I pray God she may, he'll have to toe the line. She'll make him or break him.

Chapter Thirty-Two

SO IT was settled that all should be sold, house as well as furniture, and Belle would set up a flat where Edith could come at week ends, and Phyllis spend her holidays between Aunty Maul and me. But I thought her Aunty Maul would keep her away from the boardinghouse and so would her sisters, bless them.

For I was to set up house with Rozzie, who had been left pretty well off, nearly three years before, by Bill Balmforth. Rozzie had got a flat in Brighton and was longing to have me, and what better place for a boardinghouse?

But on the very day before the sale, when the house was like a secondhand store, full of upturned chairs, carpets with the tickets on them, and a lot of things brought into it that we had never seen before, in walked Jimson. He was terribly ill looking, just out of bed from the flu, but gay as a bird. "My fortune's made," he said, "and what is more important, I've got a wall without conditions."

I hardly listened to him, for all I had to think of. It was my first house and I thought it would be my last true home. Every last day was like another root pulled out of me. All was to be sold, for Nancy and Belle, if they agreed in nothing else, agreed that our good new furniture, which Matt and I had hunted for beauty and goodness through every shop in Bradnall and a special trip to London for the drawing-room suite, was not worth having. Belle laughed at it and Nancy hated it. "Vulgar yellow varnish," she said of our golden oak. She and her poor little manny would have nothing but antiques.

And as for the old Monday stuff, the few good pieces that Maul had not carried off, Nancy and Belle quarreled so bitterly about dividing them that I wished they were sold, too. For Nancy, who had just had her first baby, said her milk would be spoiled if she did not get the mahogany bookcase; and Belle, who was jealous of her for getting married, even to a man she scorned for herself, would not give way one inch. And as for me, I only wished I had milk myself for the poor baby who was really suffering in his stomach.

Old and new, all gave me pain; the cracks and cobwebs that shamed me; the dirt I had never seen before and jumped up now, like old sins in the angel's book, to cry down all my housewife vanities. They made me feel worse, for I felt: Poor house, you are to be despised by those who did not know your true character all these striving years.

So though I was glad to be busy, clearing out the rubbish and sorting the crockery, I was not so pleased to see Jimson and I showed him no great welcome. I wished him well away.

But on he went about his wall, fifteen by twenty, in a new village hall at a place called Ancombe, on the Long-

90

water, not twenty miles from my old home in the South. "A hundred pounds," said Jimson, "and no conditions—free living with the old woman who's giving the hall. She doesn't know a picture from the bath mat, but Hickson put her onto me. I'll do it in six weeks and then I'm off for the grand tour."

His coat sleeve was ripped at the shoulder, and I saw that it would be out tomorrow. But I wasn't going to say a word about it, for I didn't want to show my interest in him, now that Matt was dead and I was a real widow, without natural protection.

Talk away, I thought, but I won't ask you to tea. I'll give you no encouragement. But he went on talking about his great chance and the hole in his coat kept catching my eye until I said to him as coldly as a stranger: "Excuse me, but your coat seam is ripped."

"Oh, yes," he said, "it's been like that a long time," and he started again on his wall and his travels. So I said to myself, If you will ruin a good coat, you will, and nothing can stop you. Wives or coats, you're a born waster. But the coat kept on nagging at me. It was opening its mouth like a baby crying to be taken up and at last I could not bear it, and I said: "Mr. Jimson, for poor Nina's sake, let me sew up your coat."

"No, no, my dear Mrs. Em," said he. "Why should you take all that trouble? I'll do it myself. I can sew very well," and then back to his wall and how unlucky it was that he had sold all his paints and brushes.

So I went and got my workbox and threaded a needle before his eyes and said: "Now, Mr. Jimson, excuse me, but I can't bear to think of your poor wife seeing you in that condition."

"No, no," said he. "Really, it's too much—"

91

But what with the thought of Nina, poor helpless dead woman, and the hole, and my scorn for that poor feckless being, I fairly laid my hands upon him and took off his coat and sewed it up for him. Not only that, but two of his trouser buttons, which were dangling from him like a fool's bells.

Now when I found myself sewing his trousers and he in his sleeves, I thought: This is not fit for a new widow, and I looked severely enough. But he took no advantage then, but chattered about his wall and he was in a difficulty because he had no clothes and no materials and his last landlord had seized even his canvases.

"I've been sleeping in fourpenny dosses, Mrs. Em—till I remembered all your kindness."

Oho, I thought, so he's going to beg. True enough he asked for an advance of ten pounds on the price of his wall. And he brought out letters and a newspaper picture of a village hall to show me how he would be sure of getting the hundred pounds. But I would not look at them. I was not to be caught.

"I haven't ten pounds," I said. "We are very badly off. Where is Nina now?"

"Where is she?" He was surprised.

"Buried," I mean.

"Oh, near London. Mrs. Monday, do you realize that this is the great chance of my life and I may lose it for lack of a pound or two? I haven't even the fare to go south and claim the job."

But I thought of that bruise on Nina's cheek and I would give him nothing. "No," I said, "I have my poor girls to think of, and the lawyers are not done with me yet. I am a poor woman—ask someone else."

92

"There's no one else, Mrs. Em. Come now, only a pound
—I'll go part way in the train and walk the rest."

"Why did you beat poor Nina?" I asked him.

"What's that got to do with it?" He was angry at me and
went away. I felt ashamed, but still I said to myself: "Don't
you encourage that one. He'll stop at nothing. He doesn't
know the meaning of shame or common decency either.
You're well rid of him if he does have thoughts of you."

Chapter Thirty-Three

BUT JIMSON, if he was not a worldly man, was, for
that same reason, an abashless one. And back he
came on the evening of the sale, all among the moving and
the packing cases, and a winter rain of straw and dirt that
made me sneeze so much I could not tell whether I had
tears in my eyes for grief at leaving my home or only from
the straw dust.

"You don't believe in my wall," he said.

"I don't know what to believe," I said.

"Then come and see it," he said, "it's not so far—two
hours by train."

"What nonsense," I said.

"Mrs. Em," he said, as serious as a condemned man,
"it's life or death to me."

Then you must die, I thought, and yet I knew it would be
easy enough to see his wall and put him off my conscience,
after the furniture sale and before the house sale and fixing
with Rozzie, when I knew what money I should have. In
that week I had nothing to do, except I was meeting the

93

lawyers in London and having luncheon with Rozzie, just
to see each other and not for business.

For after all, I thought, I have seventy pounds loose
money for the furniture, and the house is to come. It
seemed a mean thing, with Nina's memory before me, to
make that poor struggler lose his best chance for lack of
a few pounds ready cash. And I knew he would pay me
back if he could.

So the end of it was I gave way to him enough to say I
might make inquiries if I had time, and I took the address.
And so I made time, and ran down to the old country before London and saw some old friends in Rackmill, and
dropped in at Ancombe on my way to the station.

I had written to Miss Slaughter, the old lady who ordered the picture, to be sure she would be in. No wall, and
no hall yet and Jimson had never been there. But the commission was true. Miss Slaughter had engaged him by letter. She told me she had subscribed two hundred pounds
to the hall on a bargain that she should have the end wall
for a picture.

She was a little pink-faced woman with a fichu, like
granny in a song, white curls all around her head and blue
eyes, with a sweet voice and sweetish ways. But I could see
that she had a will and so I noticed how she said twice
that the picture was to be paid for when finished. She said
the "f" so plainly, I knew that she meant it, and that she
knew artists, or perhaps Mr. Hickson had told her that
Jimson was a slippery customer. She showed me the room
she had for him, all white muslin and pink bows; and she
told me that she would like punctuality at meals, but if
Mr. Jimson could not manage it, then he must say so, and
she would arrange for him to get them by himself at his
own convenience.

94

The more I saw of her the more I thought: This one is no fool and not so soft as she looks. But then few old maids are. They can't afford to be soft.

I wondered how she would like Jimson's wall if she ever got it. But it came out that she had seen Mr. Hickson's wall, and he had told her that it was the latest thing and a great work.

She said to me: "I wanted the best for my hall" (she always called it her hall, though she had only given two hundred pounds for it out of a thousand it was to cost) "and if you want the best you have to take the best advice. I always consult experts. It pays in the end. I got my lease here done by the lord chancellor's own lawyer and I went to London for that electric fire. You won't see another like it west of Bristol. My roses too—I wrote to the president of the Rose Society and it cost me nothing."

It was spring and raining, so I could not judge her roses. But I liked old Miss Slaughter, for old maid as she was, she had branched out and kept alive. But I thought, too, that I would not like to live with her for she would have been the brass pot to any delf.

So I went away to Taunton, pretending that Gulley was to get his luggage, and come back at the end of the next week. But the fact was, of course, he had to buy paints and brushes, shoes and a suit, even pants and vests and a toothbrush. He had nothing except the rags he was in.

I wired his fare to Gulley that afternoon and down he came next day, and we fitted him out. It was strange to see that man of nearly fifty, already bald and gray, strip off his coat at the tailors and show his bare back through the rags of his shirt. I blushed for his shame and my own folly in not thinking before how he would be bound to have new holes. But he did not blush. He was laughing all the time

95

and making jokes with the shopman. "I've lost my ward-
robe and run a bit low," he said. "It's the great advantage
of being a duke that you need not mind appearances."

I never saw a man in such flowing joy, or so sweet in it.
He could not say or do enough for me. While we were sitting in the loose box waiting for them to bring suits to try
on him (for he asked for ready-mades, to be easy on my
pocket and quick) he took my hand, gave it a little slap,
and said: "I see you mean to make a good job of me while
you're about it."

So I said that he knew very well he had it in his power
to be a well-known artist and quite in the first rank, of
country artists, at least, if he would stick to his work, and
not quarrel with his friends.

I dared to say so much because I saw he was in so sweet
a mood, he was open to a hint. For he only laughed and said
I was quite right. He could have been in the Academy if he
had liked to keep up with the right people and especially
the right ladies, and tickled the freaks.

I asked him what he meant by that and he laughed and
said: "What did you think of Miss Slaughter and her idea
of being immortal?"

I said I hoped especially he would not quarrel with Miss
Slaughter, who seemed to me a very sensible woman, and
would give him a nice home.

"Oh, yes," he said, "I'll be good. But why do the freaks
always run after painters? I mean all painters, good or
bad."

I thought it might be because artists were also a little bit
in the freakish way, but I did not say so. I wanted to get
Jimson in a good frame for settling down. So I went on giving him advice, and looking very coolly on his smiles and
his philandering.

We stayed that night at Taunton in a temperance hotel, though Jimson proposed to me again, in the coffeeroom, with six commercials in the room, using the hotel paper. I set him down so hard, he was serious for all the next morning. I locked my bedroom door that night, but it was never necessary. So all went well. But I had been going to meet Rozzie next day in London for our lunch, and when I saw the trains would not suit, I sent her a wire, also wrote, giving the Taunton hotel for her answer. I wired: KEPT ON BUSINESS, WRITING. But the next morning, when Jimson and I were at lunch, waiting for his suit to be altered and the trousers turned up, who should walk in but Rozzie, as if she owned the place. Rozzie walked into all hotels like that. She could never forget that she had been in the trade.

Now though I loved Rozzie, she could not have come at a worse time, for she not only set me off, but Jimson. As soon as he saw her, he seemed to take to her ways, and began to make his chaffing jokes. Rozzie, of course, scorned him as she did all men, only more so, because he laid himself open and he delighted in it. He began to be so free with her that I thought she would box his ears, but she only glared at him and pushed out her front and said: "My God, you make me sick."

I could see she liked him, and both of them were at their best. Yet I was downright ashamed; a widow not six weeks, all in my blacks, and giggling till I choked. I knew it was wrong and that I oughtn't to laugh, but it was just as though I had a button in me, and every time Rozzie or Jimson touched it I had to laugh, if it hurt me. So it did hurt me. For I hate to laugh against my will.

There we were after supper in a little kind of snug behind the billiard room, with some bottled beer Rozzie had got in from a public; all of us in a row on an old horsehair

97

sofa with its springs burst. First it was when the springs made noises under us that Rozzie made remarks, and do what I would, she set me off. Then Gulley was such a queer sight, the little spindle, between us two big women, bulging out over him, that it made us laugh to see him. Rozzie would shoot me a glance over his bald head and roll her eyes over him with a face that made me laugh till I cried.

Then he, quick as he was, would chirrup "Mahomet between the Mountains" or the "Widow's Cheese Mite" and Rozzie would fill up his glass and say: "You're getting warm, Mr. Rat—it must be the heat, I suppose," and "Take one, Mr. Gulley, your temperature's going up. Don't burst anything."

It was true that the man was hot. He was fizzing between us like ginger beer. He could not stop laughing and chattering. He squeezed us by the arms and said: "The best pair in England and the finest four."

"Four," Rozzie said. "He's seeing things."

"I wish I could," he would say, for as I say, he had just caught Rozzie's note and, indeed, he always had that side to him.

Rozzie was bigger than ever since the war, and her clothes worse. She was all in crimson and mauve that day and when she asked me what I thought of her dress and I said it was striking, at least, she answered me that it was a mistake. "I got it on Monday in a fit of the cheerfuls, and I knew it was awful. But at least it makes a splash. And so ought you, Sally. What are you glooming at, you silly girl? Mind those blacks don't work into you and rot your guts. I'll never forget the time I was in my black. They ate into me till I was nothing but a dishrag; no appetite, no spunk, no nothing. Why, I couldn't even think and was a regular crybaby. You know, my dear, it wasn't for grieving over

98

my Bill after his being paralytic nine years—a happy re-
lease for all. No, I cried because I was so fallen away and
come down with those blacks. I tell you, when I went into
magpie even, I picked up half a stone. But I never had my
senses and my life again until the year was up. Colors are
my religion, and I always say, Sally, people had better
stick to their own religion for it always sticks to them and if
they try to throw it off, as often as not it will turn back on
their stomach and come out in spots. Well, believe it or
not, the only time I ever had spots was in my blacks. And
the doctor himself told me it was because my blood had
taken a turn."

Rozzie would say anything for a joke and she was free
and bold. It was always a wonder to Matty and the girls
how I could like Rozzie Balmforth; and often when I was
away from her, it was a wonder to me. For she often made
me angry as now when she pretended to think the worst of
me and Jimson. She would say: "I wouldn't blame any
widow for getting a bit of fun. Hasn't she had enough
trouble with her husband?" or "It's never too soon to be
happy."

She would never give me the chance of telling her that
I would scorn to live with a man, and when I said, "I shall
be glad when I can get the man fitted out and well at work,"
she would look at me with her bold eyes, which stuck out
of her head like a pigeon's, and say: "I'll bet he's good at
the work. The little ones are. The sap is tighter packed."

It would have done me no good, but harm, to be angry
with the woman or to go on my knees and swear that Jimson and I were no more to each other than brother and
sister. What she wanted to believe, so she would think and
say, and she always liked to think the worst. If she had had
her way she would have talked only that, and a few music

99

hall jokes, like those ones about the sofa springs, and a little about drinking. And yet I was always glad to see Rozzie and to hear her roaring voice. It wasn't that she made me laugh, for often it hurt me to laugh at the way she put things, but she warmed me up with her go.

I don't know how it was, but to do anything with Rozzie, even to buy a packet of pins, was a living pleasure. She made the sun warmer and colors brighter and your food taste better; she made you enjoy being alive. When I was with Rozzie, I would watch myself laughing or drinking or eating or cutting a dash and I would say to myself: "What a time it is."

If my poor Nina made me remember God and brought up my soul when it had fallen flat, Rozzie was the one to make me thank Him for being alive.

Chapter Thirty-Four

YET I was very cast down when the house was sold, and the time came for me to leave Bradnall forever and join Rozzie at Brighton. The house sold better than we had expected, for they were going to pull it down and build over the garden. I had twelve hundred pounds clear, over the mortgage, and good hopes to get well started in my new life. But I always misliked changes and I knew that from that time the children would go their own ways, and that it was time for them to try their wings.

For even Edith was all in the air and never thought of me unless she had washing or sewing to be done quickly, or talked to me of anything but Chinese diseases, which horrified me. True, it was partly from affection, for she wanted to make me feel her value, but it was scorn too, to triumph over my nerves. Edith had plenty of bravery and I often thanked God for her backbone and her true religion, which had given her life a hope, in spite of her plain face.

So though I was brokenhearted on the platform seeing Bradnall for the last time—and Nancy cried, and Belle and Edith, God bless them, both came to see me off, in spite of all their work and parties, and did not, for once, scorn Nancy's softness before me, and end up with a quarrel—yet I knew it was God's will for parents to lose and suffer in the forties, and perhaps His meaning is to harden them off for the terrors of the grave.

So though I was down when I got to Brighton, I knew I mustn't give way to it; and the first thing I said to Rozzie was that we must get to work and find our hotel. For Rozzie and I had agreed to take on a little hotel together, for superior visitors, and Rozzie was very keen on it. With Rozzie to manage the guests and the bar and me to keep an eye on the catering, I thought we would make a fortune. But now I made a discovery. So true it is your best friends have three sides in the dark to every one you see. For Rozzie always had an excuse from coming to see a place and when I dragged her to it she would always find some fault with it. It was too big or too small or a tied house or no proper snug or no room behind the bar; or too much room and a half a mile to walk for a double Scotch. It went on till I saw she didn't really want a place; she only thought she did, but when her brother-in-law, who was a sergeant major, and one of the finest men I ever saw, came down to see us, and I asked him to give Rozzie a little push, he said: "Me! I might as well push at a corporation bus. Bill could do it. Bill was the only man who could push

101

Rozzie into taking a chance. But it took even Bill six months to get her into a motor, when motors came in, and she wouldn't telephone now to save her life. She's nervous, Rozzie—she doesn't like responsibility."

So that was the end of our hotel. For who was I to push Rozzie if that man couldn't? Then I was indeed cast down, for how could I ever take a hotel or even a boardinghouse by myself. I had been leaning on Rozzie to play the man with agents and all those widow-eaters.

I wondered now how I would live with nothing to do. But Rozzie and I had already got into a kind of holiday life, and though my conscience would prod at me, yet I was enjoying it. It always seemed to me that we were busy and it was not till you took thought that you saw that you were busy with pleasures only. We got up late and ate a good breakfast. Then we went out to breathe the sea air and catch an appetite, to do our shopping and look at the people. Then we ate a good lunch and rested till three. Then we walked in the gardens and looked at the people and got an appetite for tea and dinner. Or we had tea out and got our appetite on the way home. Then we had a good dinner and afterward we went to a cinema or we played bridge with some nice ladies in the boardinghouse and we knitted and talked. Then we went to Rozzie's room and drank a little port for a nightcap and had a long good chat. Then we went to bed and slept till morning.

All this was a great pleasure, the sleeping, the eating, the walking and looking, the having nothing to do. I liked it so much that I thought I would never be tired of it.

The only fly was Jimson, for it turned out that after I left him at Taunton, he had got after Rozzie. He had tried to make Rozzie marry him and chased her all the way to Brighton and stayed a week pestering her.

102

"Yes," said Rozzie, "and he wanted to know my income too, to see if we could both live on it, and if my money was tied up. Talking of your widow-eaters, how's that? And no bones about it, the rat."

Rozzie had got rid of him only the day before I came, not wanting to have me bothered.

But I hadn't been there a week before he came to see me too, and lay in wait for me at the pillar box, not to let Rozzie catch him. I told him then I knew he had been after Rozzie, and he said that it was out of desperation because I wouldn't have him. And he would hang himself if I went on refusing him.

So I lost my temper and told him that if he did, it would be the loss of nothing but a rope, unless it could be used again, for hams. So he said yes, he deserved the worst I could say. But he did go off at last only begging me not to tell Rozzie he had been.

I had been angry with Jimson, but now when I heard nothing of him, I wished I had not set him down so hard.

Chapter Thirty-Five

I COULD NOT write to Jimson, for the one thing I feared was to bring him back to spoil my peace, especially in the fine weather we were having.

But he did begin to spoil it for me, only worrying if he had gone back to his work, and how he would live if he hadn't.

The upshot was I wrote to Miss Slaughter and asked her for a scarf I pretended I had left, saying that if she had not found it, then I had left it somewhere else and not to bother, and in a P.S. I wrote: "I hope your wall is going on well." Not a word about Jimson in case she told him she had heard from me.

When I had posted this letter then I said to Rozzie: "That's the last time I'll bother my head about the fellow. I've done my duty, I should think, and more."

"How much more?" Rozzie asked me.

I never knew a woman like Rozzie for turning everything. Yet she made me laugh and that was all I asked for. I suppose I laughed more that week than ever I did in my life before, and again I nearly laughed my hat off. I had to stop in the public gardens and lean against a tree. People must have thought I was drunk. So I was drunk, with laughing and something else; I don't know what, it was a feeling underneath like a big hiccup that wouldn't come up. It worried me, too, that feeling, and made me the quicker to laugh. I would laugh whenever Rozzie opened her mouth.

Even Rozzie laughed in those days, though not out. I never saw Rozzie laugh right out in her life but once, and that was when she lost all her money and her left leg in the same week. The best she would do in an ordinary way was a smile that came out just at the ends of her mouth, and you could see even that much was against her will. She would never do it unless she had had a couple of quarts. But in those days when we were both mad for some reason, with the sun and the great crowds and Rozzie had a new frock that fairly made the people point at her and call their friends, I saw her laugh three or four times. She would try to stop it, but up it came with a kind of choke. Indeed the first time she did it I thought she was going to be ill and I said to her quickly: "Rozzie, I told you the port wouldn't lie with the chocolate," so that she came back at me and said I'd called her drunk.

104

It was Rozzie's great pride that she'd never been drunk in her life. That and her foot and her hair and never being taken in or giving herself away, were all her pride.

I think she was ashamed of laughing and that's why she picked a quarrel with me about my hasty words. But she laughed again two or three times at the wild things we said and thought of, before the Monday when I came down for lunch and saw Jimson waiting for me in the hall.

Then I knew what the hiccup was lying on my chest, for I nearly turned and ran upstairs again. But I was the last to do a thing like that. I never had any presence of mind, so I just let manners carry me on to destruction and I went up to him and said: "What, are you back again?"

He said nothing, but he looked so wretchedly at me that I felt guilty and asked after the work. But still he was silent. And nothing could have worried me more; it was such a change in him. I took him out to the pavilion, not to see Rozzie, and then we looked at the iron palm trees which we both liked, and had a long quiet talk. He said he would never be fit for anything if I didn't marry him, and I said how could we be happy if he went on wasting his life.

So he said he would not waste it if I took him, and after all he had done some not bad pictures. "There are Hickson's and Bond's and the dealers have some more."

And I asked him what was that for thirty years of a man's life.

"What, indeed!" he said, looking sidelong. But I knew what he meant. "You blame that on the people," I said, "but why should they buy your pictures if they don't like them?"

"No reason at all," he said, "I quite agree—I agree with every word, Sally."

"Yes, but you think," I said, "that it's because they're too good for them, something new. But you could do them

105

in a new way and still please them. It's like the fashions. A hat may be as new fashioned as you like, but it must stick on a woman's head. You know very well my poor Matty would have taken that portrait if you had made it like. It wasn't because of the style he wouldn't have it but because of the bad likeness."

"I've got a commission for a portrait now," he said.

"But you won't do it or you'll twist up the poor man's face to look like a goose or a toad."

"That's true," he said, "I might. This one looks very like a Yorkshire White. He's even got the eyes. Yes, I might bring it out."

"But why will you do it?" I said. "Everyone says how clever you are. Don't you want to be a success, or is it just to amuse yourself?"

"That's perfectly true, my dear Sall," he said, "to please myself."

"Mr. Jimson," I said, "I'm sure I've no business to give you sermons but if there's one thing sure in this uncertain life, it is that no one can afford to please himself. I know it may seem to pay in the beginning, but where are you in the end?—without a friend or a crust. Especially for anyone in the arts. Because an artist lives only by giving pleasure."

"Perfectly true," he said. "No doubt about it. Would you marry me, Sally, if I got another picture in the Academy or painted a royal portrait?"

I could see he was chaffing me, so I said: "If it's a joke to you, it's nothing to me. A man who can joke about his own waste and ruin is not worth crying over."

"That's true," he said. He was surprised and kept looking at me as if I had pulled out a new feature on my face. "That's very true," he said, "and it goes deep."

106

Then we said no more for some time, and I saw that I had talked too much and abused him too much. For to abuse a man is a loverlike thing and gives him rights, which Jimson felt very well. For now he said that he would not press me, but at least would I come and stay over the week end at Rose Cottage as a friend, and perhaps give him my hand and my arm again. Miss Slaughter wanted me very much, and she would be my chaperone.

And the upshot was, how could I refuse? For I was doing nothing at Brighton. Though when I told Rozzie, she said: "You are done for, Sall; why, if you couldn't do without a man to fuss over, you must take that rat, beats me flat, which is another wonder in itself."

Now whether I knew that I was going to my fate at Rose Cottage, or I had brought it on myself, I can't tell now, for since that boardinghouse fell through I seemed not like a woman, but a truck, which goes where it is pushed and knows not why.

For, of course, the week end turned into a week. And Miss Slaughter was at me every day, saying that I would be the making of Jimson, and what an honor to marry that great man. And Jimson was as good and sweet and serious spoken as any man in love. Nothing too much for me and all truly meant, because of his state. And then we could have our own rooms at Miss Slaughter's, or take a half house across the road where, as Jimson said, there was the latest stove for hot water, and a new porcelain bath.

So at the end of a week we were engaged. And yet I could not say I wanted it, but that it had come upon me.

Chapter Thirty-Six

WE WERE going to be married at the Queensport registry office. Only Rozzie was to be there and Jimson didn't want even her. But I said I must have some real person at my wedding, if it was only in front of a counter.

I wrote to the girls, but only so that they should get it on the day after. I knew the trouble Nancy would make if it wasn't too late.

Now when at last the day was fixed, Jimson lost all his serious airs. He was so excited I had to laugh at him. He even looked different, you would have said he was full of clockwork, and when he walked his legs seemed to jump about as if he had St. Vitus.

The same night that we posted the notice, he came to my room at one or two o'clock and tried to get into my bed. I was surprised at his impudence and told him to get out, quick. So he apologized and said he had only come to say good night. The next night he was half in before I waked up, and I had to jump out and take him by the shoulders and fairly put him through the door. We made a bit of noise between us and Miss Slaughter came out of the bathroom. But she pretended not to see us. She was a sly one and meant Jimson to have me, like meat to a lion.

So I asked her next day for the key of my door, not that I was afraid of Jimson, but I wanted to show her that I wasn't giving way to his nonsense. She said there was no key. Yet I'd swear there had been a key a week before.

All that day Jimson was as black as night. No more

smiles and jumps. He wouldn't come near me. He wouldn't eat either, and he never went near the hall. Miss Slaughter was in a twitter and kept looking at us as if to say: "What have you done to my genius?" It was a miserable day and I thought: A nice lookout for a wedding.

But I put a chair against my door. I was having no more nonsense. I stayed awake till two, for I said: "I'd rather look like death than begin a serious thing like marriage and a holy sacrament by laying myself open to a villainy. My complexion will always come back to me, thank goodness, but not my self-respect, and this marriage is quite risky enough without beginning on the wrong side of God's law."

And I paid no heed to Jimson's sulks. But in the afternoon I saw that the weather was clearing and I thought: There's no good in spoiling the whole day, especially when it may rain tomorrow. So I said to him: "I hope that's the end of your madness until we're man and wife. Then you know I'll never stint you of your rights."

He swore it and I forgave him, and we were happy again just in time for the afternoon sun. We picnicked at the point and bathed and lay in the sun. Westerpoint is a lovely place, under the cliff by the lighthouse, but not where you can be seen, and the sand lies among the rocks so that you can have your private place and make a back and sit in comfort. It was June, before the trippers, and hot enough for August. The sun was as bright as a new gas mantle— you couldn't look at it even through your eyelashes, and the sand as bright gold as deep-fried potatoes. The sky was like washed-out Jap silk and there were just a few little clouds coming out on it like down feathers out of an old cushion; the rocks were as warm as new gingerbread cakes and the sea had a melty thick look, like oven glass. I love the heat

109

and lying in the sun and I know it makes me lazy and careless so I don't care what happens. So that my mind was laughing at little Jimson when he held my hand and told me he could make me so rich and give me furs and jewels; yet my flesh delighted in his kindly thoughts. So it grew sleepy and I forgot myself and he had his way, yet not in luxury, but kindness, and God forgive me, it was only when I came to myself, cooling in the shadow, that I asked what I had done. Then, indeed, I felt the forebodings of my misery, and punishment, and I was weighed down all the evening.

But though I jumped out of bed the next night when he came in to me, I thought it was not worth while to keep what little decency was left me, and to deny him what he thought so much of. So I got back again to him, as sad and mild as any poor girl that has no right to her own flesh and let him do as he pleased.

So it was every night. I even made it seem welcome to please the man, for I thought, if I must give him his pleasure, it was waste not to give him all that I could.

Chapter Thirty-Seven

SO ON the Thursday week we went off by the early train to Queensport. The time of the wedding was eleven, and the train got in at half-past ten. Rozzie was with us and as we walked along together, arm in arm with Jimson in the middle, we girls both noticed that Jimson was very quiet and pale and Rozzie kept on making jokes about the young bridegroom and his virgin fears. But poor Jimson

110

could not even laugh. Suddenly he asked us to come in with him to a public house and take a drink. He looked so pale and queer that Rozzie said: "It's not a bad idea. We don't want him to swoon on my bosom, and cut his face open. We'll all go in."

"Not you, Rozzie," he said, "I just meant Sall."

"Gooseberry," Rozzie said, "the giant gooseberry in his silly season."

"Just a quick one," he said, "to put some spunk into the ceremony."

"Go on," Rozzie said, "I'll pop into the public bar."

So we went into the saloon bar, and Jimson asked for two double brandies. Then he pushed along the counter till we were at the far end and said: "Sally, I've got a confession to make."

I thought he was going to tell me about some more debts or some of his models. Not a bit. He said: "I'm afraid there might be trouble about this marriage. You ought to be warned."

"What trouble?" I asked him.

"I may have a wife already."

"Do you mean Nina isn't dead?"

"Oh, yes, poor thing—but I had a wife before that, oh, a long time ago. In Glasgow."

"But you married Nina, didn't you?"

"No, we weren't legally married. We just said we were. It's quite easy. If you like to do that."

I was furious with him. I called him all the names and said that he had deceived me.

"I'm afraid so," he said. He was looking quite green in his misery. "My conduct is as bad as anything could be." And so he went on begging me to forgive and saying how his only fault was loving me so much.

111

At last Rozzie put her head in to tell us we'd be late. "There'll be no wedding," I said, "he's married already!"

"So he told me," Rozzie said, as cool as you please. "Well, I'm glad it's off. I congratulate both of you," and she began to make jokes about Jimson taking her instead if he would wait six months, saying she didn't mind bigamy in the winter.

I was too angry to laugh. I said we'd better get back to the station.

"You're not going to leave me," Jimson said. "You can't leave me, Sally, when all my fault is loving you so much. I told you I'll marry you."

"And get seven years," Rozzie said.

"I wouldn't mind."

"Why, how can you talk so?" I said. "Prison would kill you—you wouldn't be let draw there."

That made him think and he said: "Why should anyone find out?"

"I'll tell 'em," said Rozzie, "if Sara's such a fool as to take you on. All you want is her money."

We went on arguing, and presently Rozzie said that if we were going to make a parliament out of it, we'd better sit down, and take something. So we went to a table and ordered some more brandies. Now, in talking, the thing got to look more ordinary and Jimson was proposing, as bold as a pie, that we should call ourselves married. "No one ever questioned my marriage to Nina," he said, "and even her own parents never doubted that we were married. People don't ask to see your certificate—they take you on trust, unless, of course, you've got another wife or husband going about making trouble for you. And mine won't do that because she's pleased herself elsewhere."

"Why didn't you divorce her?"

"Costs too much money and too uncertain."

112

I said that if he got a divorce, I might think of him after all. For though I had not wanted to marry Jimson, yet so it was that I didn't want to go back to Brighton either, and that trolloping life. I felt let down as far as I have ever been.

They turned us out at last and we went to the hotel for lunch and had some beer with it. So we talked all day and kept on drinking till all at once I found myself so muzzy I was afraid to stand. Jimson, too, was quite drunk and kept on mixing up his words. Only Rozzie was solid as a rock, though her face got redder and redder and her voice louder. But though we were all shamefully drunk, we were sad and serious. Jimson kept on saying that he was a brute and a beast but that I was his star and his angel. He saw all the difficulties and the terrible position he had put me into, but he couldn't do without me. "Of course," he said, "I know I'm no good—and you've every right to say that I'm not worth saving. I couldn't blame you. No, I should only thank you for the joy you've given me already."

So Rozzie shouted that if I had given him joy, she hoped I had had some too, for that was all I would get out of this silly mess, and she kept on saying that all this love business made her vomit and that all lovers ought to be poleaxed. Love was the source of all the trouble in the world and she wished God had left Adam and Eve plain and not stuck the odd bits onto them.

At last they put us out and we went to look for a hotel. So Jimson went into the first. He jumped in so quickly that Rozzie said: "He's up to something. You look at the register."

We went in and sure enough he'd registered "Mr. and Mrs. Jimson" for a double room and "Mrs. Balmforth" for a single one.

I began to protest, but the clerk looked queerly at me

113

and Jimson said quickly: "Rozzie and you can have it if you like."

But I was dog tired and said at last I did not care what happened. So we went up to bed as man and wife and Rozzie said only that I was a bigger fool than I weighed.

Chapter Thirty-Eight

SO WE went for our honeymoon after all, not to Brighton, but Bournemouth, and it was a great success. Jimson had said that he could make me happy and I never knew any man so clever and pleasing when he chose. It was wonderful how little he needed to make me laugh with his stories and imitations.

It's all nonsense, I thought, to say he's difficult, and if he did beat Nina, she said herself it was only when he was driven mad with troubles. And no wonder with the way he's been treated by the world. All he wants is a little success and respect and money, which is every man's right, to ease his mind and take it off the stretch and please God he will have it now.

I was bold, therefore, remembering that Mr. Hickson was always the man of business, to write to him about commissions, and he wrote me a very nice letter arranging a meeting and saying that Gulley must have an exhibition. So I told Gulley one night when he was gamesome, and he laughed and said: "Go on, my dear, and make my fortune. I appoint you managing director and subscribe myself yours truly."

So he made a joke of it, but agreed with everything too.

He warned me only that the last exhibition had been a failure.

"What?" I said. "Did you have an exhibition?"

"Why," he said, "of course I did—in nineteen oughty four—it was the biggest joke of the year."

I saw that he did not like to remember that exhibition, so I said that his art had been new fashioned then, too new for the people, but now everyone was painting in modern.

"You're quite right," he said, laughing, "and if they laugh, let them laugh. You shall have your exhibition." He proposed even to paint some portraits. "I can always make money at portraits and they take no trouble—not the kind of portrait people want—and you and I could live like millionaires on five pounds a week and a couple of gallons a day—I mean we should have all we want."

"So we could," I said.

"And so we shall," he said. "I put myself in your hands and if I begin to get on my high horse and talk about art, give me a slap on the nose."

It was true that he never talked about art with me, or religion either. Except to chaff me for mine and especially for going to early service. For he always said I went to seven o'clock service only because I hated getting out of bed. "Like a woolly savage that cuts off his nose to please his idol."

God knows it may have been true, but I did not think so. For though I hated getting out of bed, yet I was never sorry when I was up and out, at that early hour, when the whole world looked as if it was new washed and waked and going to service itself; so quiet and calm. Even the sky, I thought, was like church windows. I mean the plain ones with glass like tapioca. And then, what an appetite for breakfast afterward. Bacon and eggs is my favorite

115

dish, but I can never eat it except on a Sunday when I have been to service.

I would have liked to take Gulley to service, for I thought a little steady religion might be good for him. But Gulley never talked seriously to anyone unless the fit took him. Then he would start off to any chance-met, in the train or a public, and often he would start a great argument. At Bournemouth he nearly had a fight in a public bar with a bus conductor, who held up the government. I must say I agreed with him, for Gulley was quite against all governments. He thought all the badness and misery in the world came from governments, and that there would be no peace or comfort anywhere till we all went back to live like Adam and Eve in the Garden of Eden.

This seemed so mad that at first I thought it was one of his tricks, because he wanted us to play Adam and Eve when we were bathing at the point. Just as poor Matty gave out the idea, and believed when we first married, that children should be begotten in the early morning, when their parents were refreshed with sleep. Because the truth was, Matt's nerves were so upset in his first months that he could do nothing at all with me, poor darling, unless he had been asleep first, and took his nature by surprise. So that he would be scornful of nature and say that it was a nuisance and a trap, and he would do the thing in a rough way that hurt me, snorting or grumbling as if he hated it, only because he had to be quick before his nerves spoiled him again, and shamed him. For he would almost cry with shame when he had to shuffle off and pretend that he had meant nothing but good night or good morning.

So I thought that when Gulley talked of going back to Adam and Eve, he meant only to get me to go naked before him, making his wish a religion. But I found out I was

116

wrong for he would talk in the same way to anybody, and get excited and shout against the laws. What I wondered at, after only three days with Gulley, was why he had not been locked up long ago. Not that he was mad with me. But he was mad to the world. So I noticed what a lot of mad people there were and what a lot of nonsense talked, quite as bad as Gulley's, and no one troubling their heads about it. Go you about with a man like Gulley and you will see what nonsense people listen to, as calmly as you please, and swallow every word, and then bring out some nonsense of their own.

Yet Gulley, though he always laughed at me before and after, as he laughed at the world, did sometimes speak seriously to me on our honeymoon. "Look how happy we are," he would say. "Why? Because we don't care a damn for the law."

And little as he was, and thin, Gulley never seemed to flag; you would have taken him for a young boy in his first hot youth, and the fiercer he was, the gayer and the more full of ideas. He would keep me awake half the night and have me up with the birds to bathe, or really, I think, to draw me. For though I hated to be seen naked, even by Gulley that was professional, almost like a doctor, and though I always refused to be his model, except for the head and arms and as much as a decent woman would show, yet he was always sketching at me and always inventing new tricks to spy on me and draw me.

Sometimes indeed he would rage at me when I would not sit and shout that I was a vulgar middle-class woman full of silly prejudices, still I felt that modesty was not given to a woman except for some good reason.

Yet at that time we had few fights and made them up soon and then we would be astonished at ourselves, so that I

117

caught myself laughing and thinking: Well, whatever is coming to me of trouble, I am the luckiest woman to have such gaieties and a new loving husband, at my age.

So trouble did come, in full measure. But I shall never forget our happiness at Bournemouth. For if Gulley and I agreed in anything it was in the same enjoyments, in laughing at nothing, in eating well, in bathing and sitting in the sun; we even agreed in liking to drive in an old landau they had along the front to Boscombe and back. I had always loved, from my rich days, the swing and jiggle of a carriage, and the clop of the horse and the back of the coachman and the shine of his hat, but I never enjoyed anything as much as driving there by the sea. For the sea itself, though gloomy from a boat, is always lively from the land. Even if it should be flat, on a hot day, yet it always has a sparkle. It never stops winking sunshine. But when it has waves, then it is like a whole ballroom full of heads bobbing up and down, and you would think the waves falling on the sand were the swish of skirts in the old grand waltz, not too quick, but always turning. The "Blue Danube." But even at night we had to walk along it by the sand and Gulley would model corpses or lions or dead horses. Then we would sit down against the horse or lion, between its legs, and watch the sun going down like a hot penny through green and yellow like snapdragon fires; you could see right through them into the sky behind, and above the sky was like a Dutch bowl, blue delf. Then the waves seemed to come up suddenly all glittering with hundreds and thousands, like cakes for Easters and birthdays, and try to go on forever, and only get so far and break themselves to pieces with a mournful noise, and fall back with a long sigh. It made me feel sad to see such waste of their work and to think of it going on forever, but then it was a comfort too, to think that they would always be

118

there, whether anyone was looking or not; such is the bounty of Providence, to pour out pleasures.

I daresay only looking at the sea was one of our great pleasures in that month, which was, I think, the happiest in my life. And I shall always owe it to Gulley. Not that Matt was not worth six of Jimson and not that he did not make me happy, but that we were young together and did not know how to relish the sweet joys of only walking and talking and looking about us, and eating and sleeping, in amity and kindness. Neither did we store up the memory of our pleasure, whatever it was, so that I have still but a confused notion how I felt as a bride, and how we passed a whole three weeks together with so little to talk about and so little to do; whereas Jimson and I caught up every moment, every bright day, every laughing face that passed, and every calm night, and rejoiced in it to each other and put it away in our minds. Even years afterward when we were at peace, we would bring out some trifle of that short time and admire it and enjoy it again, and live again by it in the time of our innocence.

Chapter Thirty-Nine

MY DAUGHTERS would tell you that Jimson took me for my money and robbed me of it and then left me on the streets without a penny, but it is not so. It only seemed so. Rozzie was shocked because I paid the hotel bill at Bournemouth. But Jimson had no money then. He said that he would owe me, and if he forgot, it was only because his head was so full of his work that he never thought of bills and debts. Even on our honeymoon, though

119

he made me so happy, I knew his eye was always picking something up and his mind was always turning over colors and shapes. So in the last days, when I began to ask if we would take rooms at Ancombe or board with Miss Slaughter, as she proposed, he would answer: "Just as you like."

"What will suit you best?"

But his eye would be on somebody passing, or on a tree in the gardens and he would say: "Did you see that old woman?—she had one eye half an inch higher than the other, and twice as big," or "You could do something with that pine—the red and green are the same tone as the sky."

But though, to be honest, up to the last day of that month, we were both on fire, and would even walk hand in hand like the children on the piers; yet as soon as we got in the train, Jimson seemed to forget all about me. Out came his book and he was drawing all the way. When we got to Queensport, he was still drawing, and I had to get the porter and find the luggage.

It was comic to see the change in him between one night and the next morning. For one day he had not been able to keep away from me and the next day he did not notice me at all. So he went on all that week, drawing all day, and whistling to himself, or at the hall, measuring, and trying new kinds of plaster to see how they would take paint. He would often draw all the evening too and come to bed at one o'clock yawning like a dog, and fall in beside me and snore all night like a horse, without so much as saying good night. The bolster was not less to him, something to lean against, or push into some other shape, as he wanted.

I was surprised but pleased, too. For it was as it should be. A honeymoon is one thing, and life is another. I was only surprised when I looked at it, because Jimson had turned so sensible and ordinary.

120

But as he couldn't bring his mind to look for rooms, we stayed on at Miss Slaughter's, and in the end we agreed to her plan and boarded with her.

Chapter Forty

I DID NOT like beginning another life in an old maid's house, who thought that an armchair was anything with arms; and though I had liked the idea of Ancombe since it was in my own country, I had never liked the look of it.

A long twisted street on a highroad beside the shore of the Longwater. Plain brick houses and a tin chapel; the church small and ordinary, and only two shops. Then it was close to the Greenbay and Westerpoint and Bluerock sands so that from May to October there was nothing but busses and cars, taking the summer visitors. Indeed when I first went to Ancombe the dust stood up all day so high you could see it from the fields, over the roofs, like a fog, and even at night when the moon touched it, you could see it like a fine smoke. But when the cars got worse, they brought one advantage, that the roads were tarred. Indeed, the tarred roads did good in all the country because the hedges were not smothered, as they used to be, as soon as the leaves were out. Even the may, in those old days, for all its glitter and sparkle, would look like dirty flannel long before it put out its flowers.

So in Ancombe we blessed the tar, in spite of its smell, which got into the very tea, for it meant that we could open our windows sometimes, even in the hottest weather.

Miss Slaughter's house was right on the road between

the new hall, which was still going up, and the doctor's. But though I did not like the first look, I thought better of the last for there was nothing behind the houses except the garden and Miss Slaughter's was on the south side, so that her garden ran down to the water. I have always loved a big peaceful view and I think this was the best I ever knew; first the garden, which was nothing but a few rose beds and then a strip full of gooseberries and cabbages. And then a slope down across a piece of meadow, which belonged to the garden; and then the water which was half a mile across, and on the other side good arable fields in all their colors, changing every year. I could see out of my back window just how it went with each of them, in roots and wheat and barley and oats, around again to the lea, and I could guess which was the better land and which was the farmer's favorite and which never got its rights, being too far off from the road or having awkward gates.

Morning, midday, and evening, except in a sea mizzle, there were the grandest skies you ever saw; and sometimes, even in a mizzle, if it was thin, I loved the view of clouds melting into it like suds in water, and the sky coming through on top like a touch of blue, and the Longwater like frosted glass, and the fields on the other side as bright as jellies, strawberry on the new plow, and gooseberry on the swedes and lemon on the barley. Then if you had it thundery over on the south next toward the sea, and the morning sun behind, you would have thought Longwater clear glass and the field bits of colored glass, in a black wall, with a light behind. They were as bright as my lamp shade in a dark room.

The other thing I liked at Ancombe was the yachts going past, often to race and often with girls steering. It was pleasant to sit and wonder if they were being courted by the

122

men, and if such girls, with their manly knowledge and their sports, would make better wives than us old ones. Belle's tennis, I thought, had done little enough for her, and Nancy was the happier woman, for all her silliness. But then Belle had been too choosy, and Nancy, for all her silliness, had never valued herself too high.

Then, too, though Ancombe had no shops, to call shops, there was a daily bus to Yeovil; and what was better, every year great steamer yachts came to Ferry for the regattas and brought ladies in the newest fashions. It was better than a visit to Paris to see them in the little village streets, coming and going from some party on shore. I never saw such beautiful coats and skirts as in that small place, fitting like a coat of paint. I knew, of course, that they had been measured by a man over a special foundation, and to fit the stays, and I daresay some of those smart women dared not eat butter, and I'm sure they could not lift their arms. But it was a great pleasure to see such a beautiful cut, and women turned out so smooth and polished that they had not a hair turned up, not the least speck on their shoes. You would have thought they had a new pair every day and ordered them by dozens, which perhaps was the truth. I liked to think it so, for I always liked a thing well done.

Chapter Forty-One

YET IN all the peace of the garden at Rose Cottage, I never had much time to sit down and think of myself or what I was doing. I did not read either, for I had forgotten to bring away my books and somehow they were put in the sale, or perhaps thrown away. I never liked any others but my Woodview books which I had from Miss Maul or which I bought for myself.

But I wouldn't have found time to read then, for, apart from the curtains and cushion covers, I was working up the exhibition. I had to write to Paulson and Robb, the landlords who had kept poor Jimson's pictures; and also arrange dates with Mr. Hickson.

I saw Mr. Hickson one day by appointment and he was very pleasant. But he had grown very old since the war and all the fire was out. He was like a father or uncle to me now, and liked only to be kindly and to gaze and talk, in his own sad way.

I asked him one question that had troubled me. "Is Jimson a genius?"

"Of course he is," Mr. Hickson said. "No doubt about that." But Mr. Hickson was one of those men who are so honest about some things that even business ideas and politenesses will not quite skin them over. And he was always honest about pictures.

So after thinking a minute, he pulled himself up and said: "To be quite honest, Sara, I don't know and I can't tell. I don't think anyone can. We're too close to him. In a hundred years perhaps or even fifty it will be quite obvious."

"Fifty years," I said. "But we'll all be dead. What good will it do him to be famous when he's dead?"

He smiled at me and said: "From your point of view, I suppose it's no good at all."

But I wasn't to be laughed at even by Mr. Hickson, and I said that I was thinking of Jimson himself. For it was very hard for a man to be happy in his work if he got nothing at all from it, not even a decent living.

124

I put it as low as I could because I knew Mr. Hickson, honest as he might be, had a business eye, and took but a cold notice of religion or people's rights. "I'm not too old," I said, "to be tired of my life and I mean to enjoy it if I can. But how will I enjoy it if my husband is always in misery and wasting his talents?"

Mr. Hickson liked that very well. He said: "You're a very sensible woman still, Sara, and I'll do anything I can to help you, that is, your husband, to establish himself and have a successful exhibition."

This agreement made me very happy because I trusted Mr. Hickson. That kind of cold man nearly always does what he says, and besides, I remembered what Jimson had said, that Mr. Hickson had invested in him and would like to see his stock rise. One way or both, I thought, Mr. Hickson would give us a push in the right direction.

Chapter Forty-Two

BUT THE money I had meant for the exhibition went elsewhere. Now on the very first day we came to Miss Slaughter's, she began to get after my money. She said what a pity it was the builders hadn't finished the hall yet, and that the subscriptions were so slow in coming in. Then she looked out of the window and said: "I believe you did subscribe to the hall—do have some more cake." Knowing, of course, that I had not subscribed anything.

The next thing was she left a subscription list in my room, and an appeal, and then set the vicar at me.

Miss Slaughter was mad about the hall; that is, she was

125

mad to get her picture done and it could not be done till the hall was finished. I don't believe she ever thought of anything else. I thought it was wonderfully kind of her to take us in, with our own bedroom and sitting room, and all board, for only fifty shillings a week; but I believe she would have taken us for nothing only to have Jimson well in her grip till the picture was squeezed out of him. She had heard that artists were sometimes very slow to finish a work; and so she was running after him all day. How was the design going? Had he everything he wanted?

Of course Gulley said that the picture was going to the Devil and what he wanted was a nice desert island with five thousand a year.

The poor body took it like a rock. She was ready to bear anything. But she tried a new plan. She said that she wanted the rooms in six months, for a married niece, so the picture must be finished then. The hall would be finished in a month and Jimson would have five more to put his design on the wall.

The next thing was she offered what she called a premium, of twenty pounds extra, if the picture was finished within three months after the hall was ready for it.

I used to dodge her to keep away from her hints and questions. Yet I was sorry for her too. She was old and she had nothing to show for her seventy years. Now somebody, perhaps Mr. Hickson, had put this idea into her head and it had changed her whole life around; she had got a fancy for doing something big and important after all. So she had come out of her shell, and pushed and schemed till, only for her two hundred pounds, she had got the right to put up a Jimson picture in the hall. I admired her for it. I know I could never have done such a thing, against the will of the churchwardens and all the parishioners. But I

126

suppose it is true that old age is a kind of madness in itself which either sends you woolgathering like a child, or makes you run after some crank as if there was a hornet behind you. Indeed, so there is a hornet, for you know you must die soon, and perhaps get nothing done after all. So I admired Miss Slaughter and pitied her too, while she fretted about Jimson's whims and the builders' strikes, and the subscribers who would not pay. I was told that she was going madder and that only a year before she had still kept up the garden and given tea parties to other old ladies. Now the garden was going so much to waste that she was glad to let me dig it and cut it, and prune her roses, only to get the flowers.

I say Miss Slaughter got after my money from the first day. But I told her that it was all in stocks and bonds, and that even if I wanted to sell them out the lawyers would make such a fuss that my daughters would come down upon me and stop it.

Then I saw another side to Miss Slaughter, for she went at me like a dog at a rat. "I'm surprised at you, Mrs. Jimson," she said, "that you don't think more of your husband's work. No hall, you know, no picture."

"But Miss Slaughter," I said, "if I pay for the hall and you pay for the picture, we might as well both keep our money."

"I'm not suggesting that you should pay for the hall, but advance some small sum to keep the builders at work."

Miss Slaughter was always a tiger after loose money. She would even watch the corn merchant's lorry go up the road to some farmer, and call on him the same day for a subscription.

She caught me at last on Oldport fair day, where so many girls have fallen. She was at me all that day, knowing I had drawn five pounds that evening for our expenses, and a car to and from, not to be squeezed in a bus which we both hated. But we dodged her then by going from the public house at the corner.

Oldport fair was always our favorite. For first the town is so pretty between the high Oldport hill, hanging right over it, and the creek. Then it has a garden full of trees in the middle as well as trees all along the promenade. And always some yachts and often some navy ships, small ones, in the creek; and on fair days they dress themselves with lamps. That year the navy ships had lamps from the very tip of the front, over both masts and down again to the stern. The promenade was gay with lanterns and there were hundreds of lanterns among the trees in the garden.

On the promenade it was quiet, only the couples walking and whispering together, and if you looked over the wall the water was quiet, rolling up and down against the wall just as usual, and not a sound from the yachts or the ship. Just one spark where a sailor was smoking his pipe on one of the yachts. Then you went through the trees and the crowds got thicker and in the middle there was a dance; young men in their shirts and girls in their new muslins and prints, dancing seriously and carefully as they do in the country. No romps. Even the drunks were keeping their bodies sober and you could see the madness only in their eyes, and the beer only when it poured down their cheeks.

So you came to the fair itself and the darts and the roundabouts and the shooting galleries with their pretty girls. There, of course, it is allowed to romp, and even the sober were bumping and tickling each other with feathers, or screaming on the horses. Five or six organs playing different tunes and all the boys blowing whistles and trumpets. It went to your head and made you mad. It's no wonder, I

128

thought, that nine months from Oldport is the time for sudden babies and hasty marriages. Had I not screamed and romped myself, as a girl, and been squeezed and kissed too, and felt myself go careless to all but joy? Was it not luck?—or only my mother chasing me home, that saved me, on fair days, from my nature. But then what I loved at Oldport, when feeling so mad and joyful, and on that night with Gulley we had both been drinking beer too, was to stand among all the music and lights, and to raise my eyes to the hill behind and see the hedges against the sky and a cow nodding along; and behind them the sky as deep blue as sugar paper, and yet as bright and clear as the water in a chemist's sign.

I said to Gulley as he hung on my arm, with his hat falling off the back of his head like any laborer's: "How quiet and peaceful it is—the cows don't even turn their heads at the rockets. You ought to paint it for the exhibition."

But Gulley only laughed and carried me off to the Noah's Ark, which was the fastest of all the roundabouts. It nearly shook my clothes off. So when we were coming home up the village street arm in arm, it seemed to us both that the world was not big enough for our joys. Gulley kept on laughing and squeezing me and calling me his fair girl, and my head was so full of lights and faces, and the quiet boats and the sky, and my flesh was so full of the dust and the warmth and the beer and the shaking, that I was like another person in my own dream.

So when we saw Miss Slaughter's light, Gulley said: "The old freak is sitting up for us."

I was angry and said that she would be coming at me again about the check. "She says if the builder doesn't get a week's wages by Saturday, he'll have to pay the men off."

"Well, why don't you let her have it?" said Gulley. "It's only fifty pounds."

"And she's only giving you a hundred for the whole picture."

"And if there's no hall, I won't get that. All right, you're the business manager. Come on, old girl—I'd rather push a horse uphill."

Indeed I was hanging back for fear of Miss Slaughter. I did not want my happiness broken in half by her mad look. But Gulley dragged me in and she came out in her blue dressing gown, with rabbit fur around the edges, and said: "Oh, Mrs. Jimson, I wanted to tell you there's another note from the builder."

"Go on, Sall," Gulley said with his hat still on. "Sign on the line and come to bed. It's all right, Miss Slaughter— she's just getting her checkbook." So, I don't know how it was, I went in and signed for fifty pounds. And yet I know it did not seem like weakness at the time, for I remember laughing as I wrote and thinking, So much for you, and signing my name with a dash. So I don't believe I gave it another thought, neither that night nor the next day, till I had a letter from the bank and another from my lawyer. Then there was a great fuss about selling out some shares. But the thing was done and I was not going to be pestered to death. I got up on my high horse and I told the lawyer to sell the shares and to pay the bank, and the bank to pay the check. I believe I was too happy to bother my head about money.

130

Chapter Forty-Three

NOW THE exhibition came on again. Mr. Hickson, seeing I could not take a gallery, offered to have the exhibition in his own house. At the same time, he got us a commission to paint a general called Foley, medals and all. But when next day I asked Gulley to fix dates with Hickson and for the exhibition, and a sitting with Foley, he always forgot. Yet he was mooning about again and doing nothing. Seeing that he had stopped work, I thought, here was a good chance to get him to attend to business. But not a bit. When I spoke of this at breakfast, saying: "Heavens, I've forgotten that letter again," he only stared at me and said nothing.

Then he began to follow me about. When I went into the kitchen he followed me there, and when I went to the village for stores he came after me into the very grocer's and stood staring at me.

I was buying a few sweets for myself, and I thought perhaps that annoyed him. I was still eating too many sweets, but I always found it hard to stint myself of sweets.

So I said to him: "You see, I still have a sweet tooth— what a monster I shall grow unless I take care."

"Go on," he said, "eat the shop."

So when we came out I said: "What have I done?"

"Nothing," said he.

"Why are you angry at me? Tell me what's wrong, at least, for I can't bear dumb bad feelings. They spoil the whole day."

"I'm not angry," he said. "Are you trying to pick a quarrel?"

"Good gracious," I said, stopping in the street, and the words popped out: "That's what it is."

"What what is?"

I had thought only that here was the flaw. For I had thought that Jimson had fallen out with Nina, angel as she was, because only she was not the type for him; too flat and too religious. But now I saw that I had been too conceited. It wasn't Nina, it was Jimson.

"What is what?" he said, so I answered him only: "I'm not going to quarrel about nothing—I have better things to do." For Miss Slaughter's cook had gone off and I was doing the work.

But he was determined to have his quarrel, and as any wife knows, it takes only one to do that. He followed me to the kitchen and tried this and that, my doing the cook's work, my being put upon by Miss Slaughter and so on. I said that I liked cooking and that we owed so much to Miss Slaughter that we could well overlook a little cleverness in taking small advantage.

So then, suddenly, he began on the portrait painting and said: "That was pretty clever of you to get me tied up with old Foley."

"You aren't tied to a day," I said, "there's a whole month for it."

"Yes," he said, "a good idea. Why shouldn't it work?" and he began to walk about the kitchen and say how he could paint a family portrait in three sittings. "Forty guineas a time—two or three a month—say, fifteen hundred pounds a year—and three weeks in every month for my own work. Do it all the better perhaps for coming at it with a fresh eye. I'm not one of those half-baked amateurs who

132

thinks he has to wait for inspiration. Inspiration is another name for knowing your job and getting down to it. I can paint anything you like any time, and why not. I've learned my job. I'm a painter, a workingman, a tradesman. Do you know, Sall, I wish the very name of artist was abolished. It's simply a bad smell, it's not even good English. Painter is the English word, or limner. Well, I'm a working painter. Tell me what to paint and I'll paint it."

So he went on until he carried me away and I forgot my doubts. I knew he had started in a bad mood, but I thought that he had talked himself around as anyone might, especially when his mind is in a loose quarrelsome state, not knowing what it wanted.

"It's not that we need the money just now," I said, to keep him smooth, "but it's always something to know where to find it if one wants it."

"I think I'll write to old Foley now and ask him for a sitting."

"But there's his own letter waiting for an answer," I said, "I'll get it for you." Floury as I was and the oven waiting, I ran into the sitting room to get the letter out of the table drawer.

Then I felt Gulley behind me and a feeling coming out of him; I did not know what kind. So I jumped around and then he was grinning in my face. "You brought that off pretty well," he said, "you and Hickson."

"But it was you said you wanted to write."

"My dear Sall, you've never had any other idea but to turn me into a money-maker with a balance at the bank and two motor cars. Well, I give you warning—stop it and stop it now. That's all I ask. Not to be nagged."

So then I lost my temper and said: "That's one thing I would never do. I'd scorn to nag—and I scorn a nagger."

"On the contrary, you've never stopped nagging at me —why, you nag me even when you're asleep. Your face says: 'Go on and make me money and be somebody in the world.' That's the word, isn't it? That's the way you think. Well, stop thinking. I won't be thought at."

"And I won't be talked to like that. I'll not stand it." I tried to walk out, but he got across the door. We looked at each other and I could see that he was blue and green with rage and shaking all over.

I tried to push past him and at once he hit me on the nose with his fist. I was so astonished and so furious that I could not say a word. I caught him by the wrists and pulled him from the door. I wanted to shake him and box his ears. But suddenly he jerked away from me and walked out of the room. I went upstairs in a rage. When I looked in the glass my nose was bleeding and I was afraid I might have a black eye, too.

"That's enough," I said, "no more of Mr. Gulley." So I packed a bag quickly to get away before he came after me with his apologies or before Miss Slaughter came to make the peace.

Chapter Forty-Four

YOU MAY say perhaps that I brought it on myself by interfering with Gulley. Now to interfere with any man of set ways is dangerous and stupid and I never did interfere with Gulley, for he himself wanted that exhibition and the portraits. He himself wanted to be known and to make money, for he had admitted that very thing at Woodview when he said he wanted to be in the Academy. And as for nagging, he invented that for an excuse.

"No," I said, "I'll never go back to be called a nagger." And as soon as my bag was packed, I went downstairs to catch the bus. I meant to send for my boxes.

I had half an hour to wait for the bus and all that time I was in a fever that Gulley or Miss Slaughter would come after me. But they did not. So I went to Queensport and took a room for that day at the King's Arms.

Queensport was a pretty little town going up on a steep hill with a church at the top and the Longwater at the bottom. There are quays there and lamps and some squares of grass; a ladies and gentlemen, and a cinema. A few ships bring coal to the pier. I liked Queensport and I thought that I might spend a day there while I decided what to do; whether to go to Rozzie or visit the girls, or to make some new plan. But I woke up so miserable that though the day was beautiful and the hotel better than most, I could hardly even bring up a smile for the girl that brought my tea and I ate nothing for breakfast. I don't know how it was, but I felt as if I had no business to be there alone in Queensport. When the bell rang in the hall, I jumped as if someone might be coming for me; not, of course, a policeman, but somebody from a church or chapel, a curate or a minister perhaps, to ask what I was doing there, as if I was a runaway from vows.

I went to send a wire to Rozzie, but when I had written it I thought: Rozzie will say, I told you so, and then how she will abuse Gulley. He's bad enough, I daresay, but not as bad as Rozzie makes out. She can never be fair to any man.

I thought too: And I can't go to Nancy's either, for what will she say when she knows that I have broken with my

135

husband after six weeks. Of course, she will take my part, the poor darling, but she will wonder at me.

But the worst of that terrible day was walking about and wondering what I would do. Every minute my mind was hopping back to the kitchen at Rose Cottage, saying: "Now's my chance to get a new colander," or, "Perhaps they will have a *bain-marie* in this place," or, "I must try Jimson with salmon in pastry." For though Jimson was the kind of man who could live on happiness and moldy crusts if you let him, he had a great taste for good food. He would even sit in the kitchen till a soufflé was ready, to eat it before it began to lower its head and sink from the height of its glory. It had been a pleasure to cook for Jimson. His senses were as quick as a girl's and he loved the art of it. He would admire my touch with the pastry and say that I ought to be a chef. Whereas my poor Matt had never liked to talk about cooking in case he might hurt my feelings or call to the girls' mind that I had been a cook.

But now when I saw something in a shop and said I'll give him lobster tails, or, what about a *bombe surprise* if I had a thermos to keep the ice in, I would be stopped at once by the thought that I had left the brute.

Then when I thought backward of those two letters lying in my drawer, and all that might have come from them, Jimson's success and happiness, and the use of his talents, I could have knocked my head on the walls.

Yet I hated Gulley. I hated his cruelty and spite. I was still raging at the man, and the very thought of his striking me in the face when I never even expected it made my bones freeze.

I made up my mind to go to Rozzie, let her be all-wise as she liked and use her nasty tongue on Gulley. I wired to Miss Slaughter for my trunks and went to get my ticket to

Brighton. But it was a lovely afternoon and suddenly I felt gay. I said: "I'll stop till tomorrow and take the early train. It's a better one. No fear of Miss Slaughter catching me because she can't catch the bus today and I'll be gone before the bus comes tomorrow."

So I had a good tea and afterward I walked on the quays. The seven lamps were lighted and there were about a dozen boys and girls walking up and down, in twos and threes, the boys together and the girls together, in their best clothes. They pretended not to see each other and when they passed they put their faces close together and laughed or talked loud, just like the boys and girls at Brighton or Bournemouth. But they were quieter looking, and had thick boots instead of fancy shoes, and they seemed happier too, in themselves and more enjoying. I suppose they had less amusement and did not expect so much, more perhaps than anyone could get.

There were three old men on one seat under a lamp, looking at the water and talking about fishing, and the old woman who looked after the ladies' lavatory had her arms crossed over the rail and kept looking at me as if to say: "I'm ready for you." I was the only visitor. It was like a real sea front, only so quiet and small it made you want to laugh and cry.

I didn't want to go into the hotel; I felt so full of this strange kind of happiness. My feet trod on air, and yet I was fearfully sad, as if I was saying good-by to my youth. I said: "It's the boys and girls playing around each other as I used to play when I was a village girl." But I knew it was not.

Chapter Forty-Five

AT LAST I went back to the hotel, and there, sitting in the hall waiting for me, was Miss Slaughter. The moment I saw her I knew that I had really as good as sent for her and if she had not come, I would have waited till she did.

Of course, she begged me to go back. She said that Gulley had been nearly mad when they found I had gone and she was terrified of what he might do to himself. She had brought a letter from him, but it was short and flat. It said nothing about hitting me, but only that he wanted me back and that he would have come for me himself if it hadn't been for an important engagement with the architect to discuss a new plaster.

Pretty cool, I thought, swelling, and I made a great to-do. But, of course, I knew I was going back, and so did Miss Slaughter. Yet I'll say of her: She was a lady and knew what was due to me. Though she saw (as I saw) from the first minute that I was longing to be home again, and knew perfectly well that I had sent for my trunks only to get her to bring me home, she went on apologizing for Gulley, and telling me that I had every right to leave him, for the next hour. She considered my pride and I needed it, for I felt low and mean. I am not a crying woman, but all the way back in the bus I was flooding with tears. They did not come out of my eyes, but my whole blood was swimming with their bitterness, and my heart was drowned under their salt. For I felt that I was leaving behind me the last of my youth and all good hopes before I needed. I was wasting my poor self, so healthy and strong and full of life, so ready to enjoy that my whole flesh would often seem waiting to laugh at nothing at all, only Rozzie putting on her stays or a man in a street with a long face and a pork-pie hat.

So I sat feeling like a martyr going to the torturers and slow hard death, and all for what? There was nothing religious nor any sense in it. God knows, I thought, you're a floating kind of woman; the tide takes you up and down like an old can.

I promised myself, at any rate, to put Master Gulley in his place. But not a bit of it. For when I came in, there he was sitting at his table ruling little squares all over a new drawing. He did not even get up for me, but called out: "Hullo, old girl! There you are, at last. You gave me a fright, but I felt sure you wouldn't do anything silly. Just a minute while I finish squaring off this sketch."

"So ho, I thought, is that his line? I'll show him," and I answered in a sulky kind of voice: "No hurry at all."

He began to hum and swing his foot. He was full of his drawing and he always hummed ruling off squares. So I said: "I see you've got started again—perhaps that will improve your temper."

"Started!" he cried. "I never stopped."

"Isn't that a new drawing?"

"I put it down today, but it's an old idea of mine."

But I meant to take a strong hand and I said in the same voice: "And what about Foley's letter? I suppose you never answered it?"

He gave me a look as if to say: "She dares to bring that up again," then he laughed and said: "To be honest, I

139

forgot about it—but you're the business partner, aren't you?"

"It must go off now."

"There's no post."

"It must catch the eight o'clock tomorrow."

"All right—tell me what to say and I'll say it."

"And the letter to Paulson."

"Won't that wait?"

"No, it won't. That's more important than the other. How can you have an exhibition without pictures?"

He went on ruling and said nothing. He had a kind of smile and I knew that he meant to get out of the letters if he could. But I was hard and bitter still. I thought: If I'm to be hit, at least I'll stand no more nonsense. If he treats me like that, I'm not going to treat him like glass.

When he drew the last line, he jumped up and came to me where I was leaning against the wall and threw his arms around me as far as they would go. "Welcome home," he said, but he was still laughing at me and he kept looking at my nose and laughing at that, too.

"Yes," I said, "but things are going to be different."

"How's the old potato?" he said.

"If you mean my nose, it's no better for being punched, and it won't be punched again. That's one of the things that is going to be changed."

"Punched," he said, "who punched you on the nose? Where is the brute that raised his hand against a woman? But I thought you might have knocked it against something when you rushed into me like that. I felt a distinct blow."

"It's not a joke," I told him, "as you'll find out if you do it again. I'm a great deal stronger than you are and I have a temper too."

"The elephant never forgets," he said, laughing.

140

"How could I forget?"

"You won't, anyhow," he said. "Trust a woman to keep her mementos. Come, Sall, aren't you going to be nice to me? I've missed you fearfully. I couldn't sleep last night with the drafts all around me." So he went on half chaffing and half serious. He could not make me laugh because I was too sad, knowing what was in store for me. But he went on buzzing about me with his compliments and his jokes till I could not go on using a sulky voice, for it would make me ridiculous. He insisted on helping me to undress and when I was at the dressing table brushing out my hair, he perched himself on my knee.

I knew what this meant and I was in two minds to refuse him what he wanted. But he was so clever, so gentle, so quick, that he made it seem that I would only be a sulky kind of fool keeping up a quarrel for the quarrel's sake. So I had to do as he wished, and since to do so without kindness and kisses is a mean dirty thing, I let myself be friendly. And when I had no guard on myself and no dignity, the words popped out: "Why did you hit me?"

"Because you asked for it," he said, and that was all he would say. And he would never admit that it was because he was stuck; still less that it might be his liver. For Gulley was a yellow man and took no exercise, and I always believed his sticking and his tempers came from his liver. But that was a great and bad difference between my dear Matt and Gulley. Matt lived upon the honest ground and you could say anything to him, except about the bills, and he was never shocked by the quirks of his own nature. He knew that constipation made him cross and so when he was cross and I said: "Perhaps you need a pill," he would receive it as a good idea and thank me and say: "Yes, I don't believe I did my duty yesterday at all. No, I missed

141

it running for the train," and he would take a pill and wait to see if it improved his temper.

But if I had said to Gulley: "Next time you are stuck and feeling miserable, why not try a pill or a tonic," he would have laughed at me and raged at me. For he was up in the air always, and I don't think he ever asked himself, all his life, what our poor souls may owe to the flesh or how often the greatest heroes must dance to its comical fantods.

I caught him again at the good moment, the next evening, after the Scotch salmon in pastry, and he wrote off the Foley letter at last. But the exhibition contract he would never sign. He said he had no pictures good enough to show.

I did not try to bring him to a better idea, because he was working again, full steam, and so in full happiness.

But though all seemed peace and comfort, and I found myself singing over my pots, delighted every day to be back in my own home, I knew very well that I had given myself up to a bad, uneasy life. It was no good my telling myself that Gulley had learned his lesson and would never strike me again. I had seen and felt his cruelty, and I knew he would always beat his women. He had beaten Nina, gentle as she was, and he had beaten me.

A beaten woman that goes back to be beaten again can never know the same happiness or hold up the head of her soul. She feels a disgust at herself that works into her flesh. I was a worse woman for going back to Gulley. But who knows? if I had gone to Rozzie I might have taken to her way of life and thinking, which would have destroyed me altogether. For I was not made of that battering stuff. I never had Rozzie's art not to care for anything and to keep myself going on, like a horse, without any kind of happiness or hope or proper object in life.

Chapter Forty-Six

NOW I don't know whether it was a reward or not, but Gulley was so pleased to see me again that he said, all by himself, he would agree to the exhibition at once. "It won't do any good," he said, "but Hickson will have to buy a few quids' worth because it's in his house and we'll have a binge on it—good old Brighton."

But I think it must have been a reward, for the same week I got a letter from the man Robb, who had kept Gulley's old pictures. He had changed his address, but he had the pictures still and Gulley's bill was only nine pounds and a few shillings. So I paid it and had the pictures sent straight to London, to be framed and taken at once to Mr. Hickson's house in Portman Place, in case Gulley should mislike them and say they weren't to be allowed.

Mr. Hickson arranged them in the drawing room, and advertised the exhibition in the papers. Though he charged me with the cost, that is to say, I owed him for it. Also he got a famous writer to write a notice in the catalogue explaining why Gulley painted in new shapes. He and I did all the arrangements. But I could never get Gulley to fix prices, and then when the catalogues got sent to me, I found he had put mad prices on them, no painting under a hundred pounds, two more three hundred, and one was five hundred. But when I went to tell him that he must be mad, he said only that the National Gallery had just spent fifty thousand pounds on pictures much worse.

"Yes," I said, "old masters that are dead and famous."

"Why shouldn't I be famous when I'm dead?"

It must have popped out by accident, but it was a give-away too. Because Gulley always made out that he scorned fame. I saw him turn red and furious, so I said quickly that of course he would be.

"Not that I care, for I won't even be here," he said. "Dead men can't read the papers."

I said that he would be famous alive too, if he went on giving exhibitions. But five hundred pounds was too big to start with. "My dear Sall," he said, "you won't sell them anyhow, so why not put a fair price on them. Those people have no other standards but money. If I put down fifty pounds they would say these pictures can't be much good. I wish now I'd told Hickson nothing under a thousand pounds."

So I thought: I'll have to tell people that I'll take less. But when I went up to town, the week before the exhibition, I got another great shock. I had not seen any of the pictures before, and all the ones from Mr. Robb, eleven in all, were of the queerest kind, with the red women and the green men and purple trees, and the flowers like butter-cups about three times their right size. But what was worse for me were four great new pictures that he had done from me myself, though I never knew it. Mr. Hickson had got them from him without telling me. It was a plot between them. It gave such a terrible feeling to see myself naked on those walls that after one look I ran out of the room. I felt that God would strike me and at first I said that I could not bear such a thing. So I went to find Mr. Hickson and I wired to Gulley himself. But Mr. Hickson was not at home and Gulley did not answer my wire. It was all in the plot. Then I told Mr. Hickson's servants not to open the exhibi-

144

tion until I saw Mr. Hickson. But when I went in next afternoon, it was open and there were a hundred people in the room, drinking tea and making such a noise you couldn't hear yourself speak. And there was a crowd of men around my pictures, staring with all their eyes, as they well might.

Then suddenly Gulley stood before me. He was laughing and I thought he was laughing at me. So I said: "It's no laughing matter. Those pictures have to come down." But he answered: "No, why, let them laugh. Why shouldn't they?"

"They're not laughing," I said. "It wouldn't be so bad if they were—look at them."

"Oh," he said, "I didn't mean the nudes—they don't matter. I meant the pictures from Robb. Look at that woman over there—she's laughed so much that the tears are coming down her make-up. I'm told she's a duchess too—Hickson has spent a month trying to get her."

"What should a duchess know about pictures?" I said. "I think she's laughable herself, old fowl dressed like chicken. I think that the exhibition is a great success."

"You bet it is," he said, laughing. "Look at that old man over there shaking all over. It's the joke of the year."

It was true that people were laughing and that they seemed to be laughing more and more. Well, I thought, I've heard a lot about London people and their great knowledge and up-to-dateness, but I think you are no better than a lot of silly children and well behind the fashion, too. And as for the crowds still around the pictures of myself, I was disgusted with them, for if the others were children, what were these? well up in years, and gentlemen from the best part of the town, staring and staring at a fat naked woman. For that was all those nudes were. I could

145

not have stayed in the room with those pigs of men if it had not been I was so anxious about Gulley. For though he was laughing, I could not forget that other exhibition, when the people had laughed him out of the room.

I knew that however he might laugh and keep up a bold front, he had suffered then so much that he had never wanted to show his pictures again, or perhaps even sell them; and that he was suffering now. No wonder. The people were getting worse and worse and I could see the exhibition was a terrible failure. I could not keep my temper and I said to him: "Come away and leave them, dear. I can't stand them another minute. A lot of silly children and worse."

But Gulley was never so grand. "Go on, Sally," he said. "What's wrong with you? This is nothing. Better they should laugh than cry. Come on, you're in the profession now, you must learn to take it on the nose. This is nothing."

And he said over and over again, what was true, that we couldn't expect people to understand his pictures. They were a new idea and just because they were new, they surprised people and made them laugh.

"No, my dear Sall, I can't complain that people don't understand me—I ought to be damn glad that they don't hang me or shoot me. That's what a lot of them would like to do."

This was really true, for one man wrote to us and called Gulley a Bolshevist and said that if he dared to exhibit again, he would beat him up. "What we want in England," he wrote, "is a few Black Shirts to deal with scum like you."

But Gulley laughed at him too, and said that it had been the same with William Blake, some people wanted to put him in jail, and after he died one religious man burned nearly all his work. And now Blake was in all the poetry

146

books. "It's only that some people don't like anything till it's a hundred years old," he said.

Gulley was always reading Blake, who was a poet about a hundred years ago, and illustrated his own poems. I think Gulley agreed very well with Blake when he told me Blake used to play Adam and Eve with his poor wife, and draw her too. Once he threatened to take two wives and he always claimed the right, and this was like Gulley, who used to argue that it would not matter to me if he had another woman as long as she did not interfere with me or my pleasure. So I would tell him that if he meant Rozzie, he might try, but I didn't think he would succeed, and if he did, it would be the end of him. For Rozzie was a man-killer and had killed her own husband.

Chapter Forty-Seven

THE EXHIBITION, as I say, was a failure. Only one critic wrote about it and he said that Gulley was not an original artist at all but an imitator of two other artists, French artists, who were not only old fashioned, but quite different from each other. The nudes were like one and the other pictures like the other. Gulley only laughed and said that the critics always wrote so after they had stopped abusing you. "If they can't say you are bad, they say you are not original."

But I was very cast down. There were only two people in the rooms the whole of the next day, and none on the day after. I sat there moping at my little table and when anyone did come in, I kept my head down and my chin in my hand,

147

and pretended to be writing, so that they wouldn't recognize me on the walls.

But as if to show me how wrong I was to complain about my luck, the exhibition took a good turn. For on the day before the last, a very nice young man, with a little fair mustache, came in and looked at the pictures. I was sure he was an officer by his beautiful suit and his shoes. Then a little dark woman came in too, older than he, but very pretty and lively. You could see there was plenty in her. They met behind my back and I think they kissed then, because I could feel it on my skin. I felt too that it was a true case. So I went out and the woman gave me just a glance through her veil to say thank you. But the great surprise was when I came back there was a note left to apply for one of the pictures of a hundred pounds. It was one of me, the best, as I thought myself, and what was still better, with my face bent down and not well seen. The note gave an address at the Albany. So I telephoned and I had a check the next morning. I could not believe my eyes. A hundred pounds out of the air, for nothing. Then the next thing was, on the last day, two dealers came. One was a dirty little man with a gray beard who had been there on the first day, laughing and joking. I hated all those who had laughed, so I was very cool to him. But all at once he offered me a hundred and fifty pounds for the exhibition, the whole lot as it stood. I was just going to say: "Yes, indeed," when we both heard someone else coming through the hall. I thought it was the young man back and I thought, perhaps he wants another of the nudes if that's his taste, which it might well be. I didn't mind so nice and clean a young man having the pictures of myself. For I thought that it was all in nature that he should have that taste.

So Graybeard, seeing me hesitate, said: "Take it or leave

148

it, Mrs. Jimson. I have to go to Paris today and I couldn't repeat the offer, because I shall spend the money over there."

But I held out till the other man came in, not my officer, but another dealer, a tall dark man, who as soon as he saw Graybeard burst out: "I hope you haven't sold the nudes, Mrs. Jimson!"

"No," I said.

"Because I want them," he said, "if we can agree on a price."

"But I've got them already," said the other.

"No," I said, "you have not. You made me an offer only!"

"How much did he offer?" said the other.

"Two hundred," Graybeard said quickly, "for the whole show."

"I'll give that for the nudes alone," said the other.

I thought they were going to have a great argument and put up the price and so I said quickly that of course the real prices were much higher and I did not know if I could take less without consulting the artist. But to my surprise, they did not say another word. They just looked at each other. Then Graybeard walked out of the room and the other, after looking all around, gave a sniff as loud as a pig and followed after. I was so cast down I went to Jimson and told him my folly and said "Now hit me as hard as you like." But he, good man, said I was a hero and bought me pearl earrings out of the check. "You see," he said, "I can make money with the best. Now for dear old Brighton." And when Graybeard wrote and offered him a hundred for the whole exhibition, he took it and thank you.

I saw I didn't know how pictures were sold and, after our holiday, I went to ask Mr. Hickson, for I thought he at least would know the business part. But he repeated my question: "What is the value of a picture, my dear Sara?—nobody knows, not even the dealers. A picture has a price but not a value. The price is anything you can get—the value is a mystery, like all the things of the spirit."

So I asked him if he thought Gulley's nudes were things of the spirit and he said: "Yes, indeed—don't you make any mistake, Mrs. Jimson. They're his best things," and he tried to persuade me to get Gulley to paint only nudes. But I could see he knew very well who the model had been, and so I thought: I know why you like them, and I didn't encourage him to go on.

When I told Gulley of what Hickson said, that a picture is worth what you can get, no more or less, he was delighted and said: "He's quite right, and there you have him to the life, the dirty little money-changer." Gulley did not mind even when two days later we saw one of the pictures of me in a Bond Street window with a ticket: NEW WORKS BY GULLEY JIMSON, and inside there were four more pictures at a hundred pounds each. What's more, we found out that the dark young man, who had no gallery of his own, had gone shares with Graybeard, and then sold his share to other dealers, at a profit of about ten times, especially for the nudes. One of them was bought by a rich newspaper lord and Hickson said he had paid five hundred pounds for it.

I own that when I heard this I cried from pure mortification, for this was a year after, when we were so poor that we didn't know what to do for money, and when my poor Gulley was in despair with his work, and when, to tell the truth, he had beaten me so cruelly that I thought I could not bear another blow. For he had broken my nose and loosened my teeth, and though I never cared for my nose, which

150

would have been vanity for a woman of my age, yet I valued my teeth, for my health's sake. But what was the worst, when I tried to have another exhibition, even Mr. Hickson said it would be no good; and when I even went to Z., that is Graybeard, to sell something, he would not buy even a nude. For he said that no one would buy Jimsons and the old ones from the first exhibition were still on his hands. "If Jimson would only paint some modern pictures," he said, "it would be different." So I asked to see some modern pictures and he showed me a thing like a patchwork quilt, with a piece of a fiddle worked into it.

I told him Gulley would never paint like that. Yet I did suggest to him once that it would be easy to paint a few patchworks for Mr. Z. But he only laughed and told me that he was too old fashioned. "I'm out of fashion," he said, "before I was ever in fashion. But don't worry yourself, Sall, even if I did paint quilts, no one would buy 'em. It's not the quilt they pay for, but the name." Then he began to laugh, for he was in one of his good moods, and said: "Do you remember the time when I was going to make our fortunes?" and he began to tell the story of that exhibition. He acted Mr. Hickson, and the young man buying the nude, though he had never seen him, and the duchess, and the dealers; even imitating their voices and waving his hands about; and then himself and me cashing the check at the bank and going off to Brighton to stay at the Albion. Gulley never forgot that we had stayed at the Albion, with two lords and a cabinet minister, and paid a bill of over seventy pounds at the end of our holiday. He would tell it to everybody and make a joke of it and say that I had flirted with the lords and that we had sat two nights in the bow window, for all Brighton to admire my dress and my figure. It was one of his pet stories, part true and yet all made up.

151

He told it differently every time. Sometimes the dealers were Scotsmen and sometimes they were Jews. Either it was Lord Lonsdale at the Albion who complimented me on my figure or it was the Prince of Wales. But he could always make me laugh with it, and yet I wanted to cry too. We had been so happy then, and I had really thought that our fortune was made, and that we should have many such holidays, in the best hotels, with the best of everything. For I had thought even if the dealers caught me this time, next time I will know better and charge proper prices.

And Gulley knew my feelings, for if any of his friends were in the room when he told the story, he would imitate me in the bow window, pushing out his chest and patting himself in front and he would say: "And Sally there, you should have seen her playing up—she spread herself over Brighton like a million pounds. Poor girl, she thought she'd caught a real money-maker."

"Well," I would say, "it was good while it lasted. I'm sure you enjoyed the food too, and the champagne." For the truth was that Gulley had been the spender at Brighton. It was he who had said that we must go to a good hotel and live like millionaires, and he who had ordered champagne for dinner, and all kinds of expensive dishes.

What I wonder at in my life with Jimson was how much happiness we had, with all our ups and downs. For it was not only that I lost all my money at Ancombe, and got my nose broken, but that we never had a day's full peace from the picture. And let me tell you it took five years.

There was always some new hitch; either the plaster was wrong or the paint wrong or no money.

Miss Slaughter said the vicar was against us, and hated him. But I always put my hopes in the vicar. It was not only that he was a good man, and preached good sermons,

152

but that he admired poor Gulley's work. First he helped us with the churchwardens when they wanted to write to the bishop against us, and then he would say often: "Yes, Mrs. Jimson, you may count me among your husband's admirers," or "The color is really excellent."

Gulley would laugh at him and say we were a pair of devil-dodgers, but Gulley laughed at everything, and the vicar did me much good, especially his sermons. Because they were aimed always at selfishness and self-indulgence.

Every week he would tell true stories about those who had given way to their faults and come to ruin and misery by them. "For the desire of the body infects the soul," he would say, which I knew well to be true. His name was Rodwick. He looked always sleepy and I was told that he did not like the country. He had been a famous slummer in some big town and his health had given out. He lived with his sister who was a little square woman with a red nose like a finch, a great visitor and gardener. She was gay and lively and she would bounce on Miss Slaughter's sofa so that the springs sang and Miss Slaughter would draw herself together like a cat at a dogfight. She could not bear Miss Rodwick's strammaging ways.

Miss Rodwick was a good soul. She would bring me daffodils and tulips, and if they were the short ones or the little ones, as Miss Slaughter said, why should I poison a gift with looking beyond it, especially in the country where, God knows, a bad thought about a neighbor is as good as grease in your own soup. Miss Rodwick gave many a start of pleasure and asked nothing in return but a few recipes and now and then a day's helping at the vicarage, when she was giving a party.

Miss Slaughter said that the vicar was worn out; and that the bishop had thrown him upon us only to die. "They

153

think any rubbish is good enough for us in the country," she said. But I thought it must be hard enough to be a clergyman in these days when, for all you do, the people care more for the newspapers than the gospel; and people get sober and clean in spite of you, only because they have better houses and better wages. It is a hard time for all clergy and I used to feel sorry for the poor vicar, with his wasted life.

And even if he had pushed harder at the architect and been firmer with the builders, so that the hall had been finished, Gulley would never have got on with the work. For he would give himself a holiday as he wished it, and make me sit for him. "Come, Sall," he would call, "give me your back." And he would say it was like a holiday to paint my flesh.

So it was, for when he was happy, so was I; and then, as I say, we had great joys. We would go up on the moor perhaps, and bathe in the dam, where the waterfalls poured down on your head, and you could stand inside them and see the sky itself melting down like blue copper flames. Then the water was like gold, with the peat, and when I sat in it, my legs were like ivory, like that old master of Hickson's. I was always surprised to see my beauty in that golden water.

But it was cold and we came out as pink as cochineal; and so hungry we would eat a dozen scones apiece and a whole plum cake. Then, if the day was warm, we were sleepy and Gulley would put his head on my stomach and go to sleep and I would think of sleep too. But I did not want to sleep, either, because it seemed waste to sleep away such an afternoon, with the sky full of clouds like old pillows, gone yellow, and the smell of the grass like new cider and the waterfalls ringing like a peal of bells, from the little

154

one high up to the big one at the dam. And a waste, too, of the memory of our sweet bathe and the good tea; and the weight of Gulley's head, enjoying his peace, poor manny, while he had it.

Chapter Forty-Eight

IT WAS HARD to come back from the moors or the beach and find Miss Slaughter in a new fit about the vicar, or the builder wanting a new check, or only in terror that the picture would never be finished. She would speak to me sometimes so madly that I thought she would soon forget herself in the village and be locked up. She would say she was ruined with our keep and that Gulley was cheating her. "He promised me my picture in six months and it's not finished after four years." It was always her picture. She would say to visitors: "Yes, my picture is going on very well. It is going to be finished by next month. A wonderful conception, don't you think, the Garden of Eden?"

Of course, all the people in the place were disgusted at the picture. Ugly was too good a word for it. It was an outrage, an insult to decent folk, a Bolshevist plot. Why they thought it Bolshevist, I never could find out, because it was only naked men and women in a kind of garden with queer flowers and trees, and some of them speaking words out of their mouths, written on colored puffs. None of the words were to do with bolshevism, which Gulley hated like poison because, he said, the Bolshevists tried to make artists paint for the government.

One of the women, with very short legs, was saying in pink letters on a blue puff: "Love is my name, on death I stand." A tree with white flowers was singing out of one of the flowers: "I sleep in this joy, do not wake me with admiration." A goat was saying in white letters on a green puff: "Chain me or I shall eat the world bare." An old man with no ears or arms or legs was saying: "You do not speak my language—I can't hear your voice." A big strong black man with his legs like tree roots was saying in black letters on a big white puff: "I am death, from life I grow. Maids, take my seed, and bear."

No one liked the picture, not even Miss Slaughter, who was shocked by the puffs. She was terribly upset when she saw Gulley painting them on, in the very last month. I heard her catch her breath. But as I say, she was tough, and she always stuck to her principles, which were that Gulley was a genius and that a genius is always right. So she even praised them to him. But all he said was: "I think they look silly."

So I thought too, 'and I hoped he would change them. But he never did. For one day he came in and told me that the picture was done; he never wanted to see it again. He agreed only to stay for the opening day, which was to be after harvest Sunday.

Miss Slaughter couldn't wait even as long as a month. She turned us out as soon as the picture was finished. Not that she was rude. She said that her niece was coming, but no niece came and it was only to get rid of us. I don't blame her after five years. But as it turned out, we had no money, at least till Gulley finished a portrait down in Queensport; so we had to take the cheapest room, over the blacksmith's.

It was small, but that was no drawback when Gulley was happy. So he was, glad as always to be finished with a picture; and full of a new one, for Mr. Hickson's drawing room, twenty feet high and forty feet long. Mr. Hickson had not ordered it and we both knew he would never take it; but it kept us both happy in that week. For as I say, when Gulley was happy then we were both gay.

Chapter Forty-Nine

WE WERE LAUGHING together, I don't know why, and I was only in my petticoat, when Miss Slaughter came to us with her white hair blowing like fleece on a bush and her eyes red like the windows of a house on fire, to tell us that there would be no opening day for the picture. No one would open it and the vicar would not take down the stage. Now the vicar had put a stage against that end of the hall for the dramatic society to rehearse, and a curtain over the picture, till it was opened, and to keep it from harm.

But now, according to Miss Slaughter, the stage was to stay and the curtain was down, and holes knocked in the picture already. It was all a trick, she said, to get rid of the picture. "But they won't get around me like that," she said, as fierce as a snake. "I've written to my lawyers and I've warned the vicar that he will have to pay the damage."

So she wanted Gulley to come and patch up the holes. Gulley, I say, was in a good mood. So around we went to the hall. There, just as she said, was the stage all fixed and bolted to cover the bottom of the picture, and a piano stood against it, and piles of chairs and ladders leaning against it; and a hole knocked in the woman who was saying:

157

"Love is my name, on death I stand." Her nose and half her forehead and a bit of her balloon had been knocked off with a ladder. There were nails, too, driven into the black man.

Now I'll own that though I had never liked that queer picture, when I saw those nails, and how they had been driven in malice, I broke down and cried. I went beyond even Miss Slaughter in denouncing those murderers. "It's a wicked thing," I said, "and God will punish it if the law won't."

But Gulley was looking on with his hands in his pockets as cool as you please, and even whistling to himself.

"Don't you be sure, Sally," he said. "Perhaps God is on the other side. The vicar would tell you it's a wicked picture."

"But he got his hall by allowing the picture."

"He would say that he has brought good out of evil."

I could not help being angry with Gulley, taking so coolly what was his own ruin and the waste of five years. So I said to him: "It cost you enough, at least."

"I suppose I enjoyed it while it lasted," he said. "At any rate, I'm sick of the sight of it now."

We both begged him to fight, and I was going to run for his color box that he might patch up the woman's face and the nail holes. But Gulley caught me by the arm and squeezed it so hard I knew he was determined. "Don't trouble yourself, Sall," he said. "It's not worth me doing anything to it. If I started on it, I'd never stop. You can't fight against the whole village."

"I'll fight them," Miss Slaughter cried, "if I have to shut the hall. Such creatures are not fit to have a hall."

"You can't shut the hall because it isn't yours. It's vested in the parish."

158

"But I have the vicar's signed letter to allow the picture to be painted."

"He didn't say he'd let it be seen, did he? Besides, it's not the vicar only, it's all the churchwardens and the whole parish. Why, Miss Slaughter, don't you see—what between you and me and the churchwardens, the vicar was in a nice jam. But he's got out of it very well. He's a smart chap, the vicar, though he does look half asleep. Yes," said Gulley, "I admire that chap. I'm ready to bet that there won't be anything left of my picture within a year, and no one responsible."

"I'd die first," said Miss Slaughter.

"Yes, perhaps you will," said Gulley. "I daresay the vicar counted on that, or his sister put him up to it. That's more in a woman's line."

The poor woman looked shaken at that, as well she might, for I suppose it was true that her whole idea was to be immortal, which was why Gulley always despised her and pricked her on that score. And there now was her immortality with a big hole in it before the first week was out. She turned as red as if she had a stroke and it was half a minute before she pulled herself up again and said that her lawyers would take care of the vicar, if only Gulley would mend the picture. "I know you wouldn't like your masterpiece to go down to posterity in a damaged state," she said.

"Posterity will have plenty to think about without me," Gulley said, "and to tell the truth, I don't think much of that picture. If I had to do it again, I'd do it differently. My ideas have changed a good deal in five years. The balloons are not bad, but all the early part is rubbish."

Then when she went on at him, he said: "Paint it yourself, Miss Slaughter. Anyone can slap on a piece of plaster

159

and rub a little paint on it." So he came away, whistling.

I say I was more upset than Miss Slaughter. So I stayed to promise her that I would help her and do anything she liked to save the picture and get it properly opened. For it was only Gulley's due to have an opening. A wall picture, as you know, might as well be thrown into the sea without an opening, for you can't send it to an exhibition. It never gets in the papers, or even known, without an opening, and a party.

I was resolved to have my opening if it was only by Mr. Hickson; and I promised Miss Slaughter, too, that I would bring Gulley around to mending the holes.

Now I daresay I was so angry and so upset that I didn't pick my words, or consider how Gulley might be feeling. For he might whistle and make light of the thing, as he had made light of the laughers at his exhibition. But no man can see his life and work thrown away without a pang, and Gulley was already gray. All this I should have thought. But whatever I said or did I upset him, for as soon as I began about mending up the holes, he told me to say no more. "Don't pester me, Sall—the picture's done for and you know it as well as I do."

"It's not done for if only you will fight for it."

"I'm not such a fool," he said. "Fighting is a fool's job for me. Painting is my job, not fighting, and if I start fighting, I won't be able to paint. That would be one up for the churchwardens, wouldn't it?—to smash the picture and stop me painting too—and worry myself to death on top of all."

So I said if he would not fight, I would.

"That's the same thing," he said. "If you get into fighting and bitterness, then so do I. The only thing for us, Sall, is to keep serene and spit on the lot of them. Come

160

now, old girl, you don't want to get gray hair and wrinkles from knocking your head against a wall. You did your best on the vicar. Well, then, let it go."

I said I was not going to let us be ruined and wasted, all for want of a little spirit.

So then he turned savage and told me that if I said another word, he would hit me. And I daresay I said the word, for he gave me the worst beating of all. I was so obstinate, indeed, that even while he was punching me with all his might, I was full of bitterness and anger against the dramatic society and the village and the churchwardens, and all the world; and I kept on saying that he could never knock me out of it. So I drove him mad. The upshot was that he knocked me out against the bedpost so hard that I cut my head open, and put me into a faint, the first time he had ever succeeded in such a deed. And when I came around he was gone, and I didn't see him again for years.

Chapter Fifty

AT FIRST, of course, I didn't know that he had run off and I hurried up to get lunch, for he had made me late. I was giving him for a treat, and at our worst I never gave Gulley cheap food, a schnitzel and a cheese soufflé which he greatly liked and though I say it, I would cook either of them against the Ritz. But I would not start cooking the soufflé till I had him under my hand, and so I waited for him. Then I put on my garden hat to cover the cut and went out to see if he was at the Brethren. But no. And then the smith told me that he had seen him jump on the twelve o'clock bus with a bag and a color box.

The smith was goggling his eyes at me as if he was full of news. The smith always knew when I had been beaten. He would hear our feet shuffling and me falling, through the floor. So though he had been my friend, I had come to hate him, and I would not speak to him now or ask him why he looked at me so tellingly.

I went in and waited and when Gulley did not come I put my veal away and the bowl of eggs for the soufflé and made myself a cup of tea for lunch. I never could be bothered cooking for myself, and then having to wash up my own plate and my own pans.

When he did not come back that day I began to think perhaps he had run off, and I remembered there was a girl in Queensport he had been painting in a portrait, a big buxom girl, his very type, who was playing at art too, and made a god of the poor manny.

Sure enough, in came the post girl with a telephone message from this girl to ask for me. I went to the phone and the girl's mother, as calm as you please, said that the girl had gone off with him. She had just wired from such and such a hotel in London. Would I go up and take him away from her?

How could I get him back if he wanted to go? I asked. I was told: "You have great influence over him, Mrs. Jimson, and I feel sure that this is only a passing infatuation on my daughter's part."

I thought that even if I could bring Gulley back, I would not, to beat me again. But I said only that I was afraid I hadn't as much influence as that.

Then I went back to my room. I was in a great rage at Gulley and I think if I could have got at him, I would have beaten him. Though indeed I might have been afraid of doing him a real injury, for I am a very strong woman

162

and he was so light built that the wind of my skirt would make him stagger.

I raged at him all that day and the next. I could not sleep, and what was the good of eating? I think that next day was the worst in my life yet, for I was full of hatred against him and the girl, and hatred is always bad for me. It makes my head split. So I thought: I mustn't go on in this rage or I shall do myself an injury and perhaps turn my hair gray and have a stroke from the pressure of my blood. But as soon as I tried to turn my mind from Gulley and get on with my work, I found there was nothing reasonable to do. For I did not want to cook and so there was neither cooking nor shopping; and why should I mend for a man that wasn't there?

So I was putting the room straight and the shelves, and smoothing out the covers on Gulley's canvases and portfolios, which he had left all behind him, to worry me with wondering what to do with them, and dusting and cleaning and washing, for no purpose at all but only as a duck will kick after its throat is cut—when I felt something wrong. I wondered if it were milk left in some bowl, but my nose, if ugly, has always been good for its work, and I soon tracked down my feeling to the meat cupboard. So I opened it and there was the piece of veal, bread crumbed as I had left it two days ago, ready for Gulley's lunch. But when I opened the cupboard the stink came out with the door as if it had been a coffin lid. The thunder weather had been too much for it.

I took the plate up to throw the meat away, when suddenly it carried me back. When I remembered the busy day when I had gone into Queensport by the bus, to get the meat, and been so happy to find just what I wanted, tender and prime, and then getting it ready and thinking:

163

This is going to be a grand success. Suddenly I began to cry. And I threw it in the dustbin and banged the lid enough to bring the village running. For I did not care though all saw me there bloody and weeping.

It made me cry and it made me rage when I threw that lovely piece of veal into the dustbin. Waste and nothing but waste. I thought: I have wasted five of my best years, and I hope I'll never see him again.

But, as they say, the worse the grief the better the heart to bear it. When the ball hits the floor, it must bounce or burst. I was knocked so low I couldn't go any lower and there was nothing to do but get up. So I got up and no credit to my quality or my religion for, God forgive me, I had not been to church since Christmas, and I had my hair curled over the cut and I went to a little public in Queensport where I was known and put down my name at a registry office for a cook's place.

I left all Gulley's things with Miss Slaughter and she was my reference, and she agreed to say that I had been her cook-housekeeper, as indeed I had been. For the last four years of the picture I had done the whole work of the house for no wages.

Chapter Fifty-One

I WAS LUCKY. There was a place waiting for a cook-housekeeper at seventy-five pounds—good wages in those days, and I would have got it if it had not been for my trouble with the police.

This was my first police trouble and it did me so much

164

harm at my other one that I must say it never seemed to me as bad as they made out. It happened so. When Gulley left Ancombe, the bills were falling like May flowers in June, unlucky to all they touch. But I had nothing except my fallback, that is, nine gold sovereigns sewn up in my stays, which Rozzie had told me to put away at the time Matt died. For, she said, a widow never knew when she might need gold, if only to bury herself.

Now I would not touch that money—for the rule with such a fallback is that you must pretend it isn't there and count it nothing—for bills. So I had only checks, and I paid with checks, though I knew we had nothing at the bank except a debt; and got a few pounds change for ready cash.

Now I cannot tell why I did so foolish a thing. I could not believe how I had done it when the policeman came to the hotel and took me up. "You surely don't think me a robber," I said, "for you see I haven't run away." It was true that the bank manager in Queensport was a friend of mine; indeed he had often come through his counter only to see me and chaff me and pat my arm. So I had thought perhaps he would cash my checks, and let me owe him for a little. For goodness knows he had had plenty of my money.

So I may have thought, but the truth was I was in such a hurry to be away from Ancombe, I did not care what I did. So I was had up before the bench and it was a near thing I did not go to assizes and prison. There was still a lot of feeling about the picture and bolshevism, and somehow, I don't know how, it was known that Gulley and I had not been married. Then the checks had come to seventy pounds and that was a big sum. I was lucky indeed to get off with a probation order, and a promise to pay as I could; and a word to my character from the vicar and Mr.

165

Hickson. Mr. Hickson, too, took back his own debt which I owed him for the exhibition frames, thirty pounds, and he paid the bills at the colorman's only for a letter saying that I owed him so much.

I was lucky in my friends, and I was lucky, too, that they never searched me and never found the gold in my stays.

I was lucky, too, in getting a place, having lost my character. For when I went back to the registry office the other place was filled and the woman shook her head at recommending me, unless, she said, I would go to Tolbrook Manor.

"Why not?" I said.

She shook her head again and said that it was not really on her books, for she could not recommend it to any respectable girl. But perhaps it was all I would get. When I heard this I felt myself turn over within. It was the first time I was made to feel like a criminal, not just to the police, but to the world, and to know what it is not to have a character.

Yet I was due for a check too, not only from the police. For I had gone downhill with Gulley, not only from his beatings but his spoilings, which had brought me to pamper myself. I had grown soft to my sins.

Chapter Fifty-Two

WHEN I asked the registry woman what was wrong with Tolbrook, she told me as if it pleased her. A big country house, with only two maids indoors, no gas or electric light and three miles from a village or even a bus.

And it had a bad name, too, that is to say, Mr. Wilcher, the owner, had a bad name, deserved or not. He had difficulty with keeping servants, specially female servants, and once or twice he had nearly been had up with his goings on.

When I heard all this I said I would never go to such a terrible place and I held out two more days. But I saw I would get nothing better from the registry office with my character, and I had pawned even my clothes to live on at the Crown.

So I took the place at Mr. Wilcher's. For I thought: If it is bad, perhaps it is meant for me. And bad as it may be, it won't kill me. For thank God, I had my health and my strength, all my teeth, which, though I say it, were the wonder of every dentist that ever saw them, only to clean them, for I never had a stopping, and not a gray hair. No one would have taken me for forty-six, nor yet thirty-six. For if I was plagued by my heavy body, yet I had this for a comeback, that my fat kept my skin tight and firm. My skin, which was always my consolation and my best friend. Indeed, when I gave the police my true age, they were surprised and the sergeant said that I had the complexion of a baby. So I might have called myself less and saved myself another fall if I had not feared to keep anything back from the police, in case it came out. But I found that I was down for thirty-five at the registry, and so when my true age came out in the papers, Mr. Wilcher's agent spoke to me about it as if I had been telling lies.

He ought to have known, I thought, that just as twenty-five in a cook means nineteen, so thirty-five or forty means not her years, but that she is strong and fit for heavy work. As middle aged means doddery and fit for no work, except eating and sleeping, poor things, if they can.

Chapter Fifty-Three

TOLBROOK MANOR was a rambling kind of place in a field with a ha-ha fence. It had no park to call a park. The gardens were behind and the field in front, and outside the ha-ha there were meadows and hedges. The house had good rooms and very good furniture, but in sad repair, both up and down stairs; holes in the roof and the floors and half the windows with no cords. I was surprised to find a good double sink in the scullery, and the range gave all the hot water we could ask. Rats and cockroaches, yes; but a girl who is frightened of cockroaches had better not hope to be a cook in the good old places. The Tolbrook rats, I'll admit, were something special, as big as jack rabbits and as fierce as boars. I used to tremble at them galloping in the passages and jumping on the stairs.

The house, too, gave me shivers, for it was all under the trees, and even in broad daylight there was a green shade over everything so you would think the kitchen table had the green sickness. The fields were small, and the hedges full of great elms and oaks: the sun never could get into them except by streaks like the gold on a green tomato.

It was a lonely place, too; only the two other indoor servants and a daily help, the gardener's wife, who slept at the lodge, and two outdoor men for the gardens in their own village half a mile away. The head keeper had a man under him, too, but we never saw them at the house. They took their orders from the agent. The first nights at Tol-

168

brook, lying all alone in that dismal place and listening to the rats, I thought I had been a great fool to come there. For though it might be my deserts and a fair punishment for so many years of luxury and gaiety, yet I thought it would do no one any good if I went out of my head. I was always a good cook, and though I say, a good servant, and I set that value on myself. Our Lord Himself claimed the name and gave it for an honor. Martha, too, was praised in the Bible, and I always thought that she was perhaps a better woman than Mary, if we knew the whole.

As one who has been both mistress and maid, I will say that both have their tasks laid upon them and their rewards; and I could not tell now which I had liked better. For if the mistress has more glory, the maid has more peace in herself. She always has her profession. Then, too, the ladies, if they are better clothed, have great trouble to get husbands, while a good servant is never without her followers.

Yet in those first days at Tolbrook, for all that I knew I could not have got a better place, after the loss of my character, I pitied the waste of my talents. I will admit that when I stood in my bath and looked down upon myself, I have cried to think that I was done for, and thrown away upon a living tomb, pitying my flesh as well as my skill.

So I was surprised at myself when, after a month, I had a letter from Gulley saying that he wanted me to come to him in London, and I found that I did not want to leave Tolbrook. True, I was in the middle of the biggest house cleaning I ever did; a job that still gives me satisfaction, and I had been to the agent about the roofs and I was expecting a plumber and the plasterer, tradesmen that you can't get in the country when you choose, but only when

169

they like. I scarcely left the house for a fortnight, so fearful I was to miss them when they came and not fix them for the jobs I had waiting. Gulley couldn't have chosen a worse time to send for me, as I told him. So I looked into my mind and I saw that the truth was my grouses against Tolbrook were just a habit from the first days. So I stopped them. I always hated a grouser, for one of them will spoil all the pleasure in a house and spoil you too. If I ever loved Gulley, it was for his never grousing and never spoiling a joy in hand with yesterday's grief or tomorrow's fear. And if I have called him a sparrow for heat and the fidgets and his stick legs, I say he had the pluck too, and nothing would put him down. I'll own I nearly packed up and ran to him, like a wet hen into the coop. But I thought to myself: I can't go now with the cleaning here and the agent's letter coming, and the sink ready to flood the whole kitchen story. So I sent him three pounds advance on his commission, which was all he asked, and half a ham, to be sure he had food in the house. For I thought that woman must have left him already, if he was wanting me so soon.

Chapter Fifty-Four

SO I FOUND myself quite grown into the quiet of Tolbrook, and even the shade. I thought here was the very place to remember my faults. I had had a great fright to find myself in the hands of the law: a warning to stop in time, and seek grace. So at Tolbrook I first took to saving, as a religious duty, to keep out of extravagance, and of giving checks, and put money in the post office.

170

And though when I first came I thought Tolbrook a poor sort of house, I grew to think it the sweetest of all with its old gardens full of yew hedges and old statues of the women goddesses. When I saw them I knew why Gulley had called my figure good, for they had just such thick waists and wrists and ankles, and heavy chins. Not that I was so cocked up by that, for I had known a hundred country girls with the same limbs, and the boys used to call after us all: "Beef to the ankle."

But the sweetest sight of all was from the scullery window across the fields in front, which should have been a lawn, and the ha-ha, into the meadows with the high trees in the hedges, elms and limes and chestnuts; and the Devon cows grazing, as red as port. The meadows were so shaded that you would say the house was gloomy, but I never minded a shady garden or a shadowy field as long as it was green. So at Tolbrook I liked to see out of the scullery windows when I was washing up, the banks under the trees as fresh green as angelica, right into June, and the elms rich like cucumbers halfway through August. Then there was a pond in the first meadow that they called the fishpond, and from the housekeeper's room I could see the tops of the trees in it hanging down in a row as clear and sharp as a plush valance on a looking glass, except when it was raining or blowing or the cows went in to drink. But I liked it just as well then, when it was covered with the rain like sequins or crinkled up with wind like a watered silk, or trod by the cows into great smooth rings, like slices of watermelon, green and pale green and clean gold and dirty gold.

Everywhere you looked around the house you saw nothing but peaceful harmless things, like the trees and the cows, and if the fences were rotten, then you felt at least they had been left in peace to go their own way.

Inside the house was another thing, for I was shocked to see the dust and the cobwebs. It was plain that Mr. Wilcher had been badly served, just like all bachelors, for the top of everything, furniture, paneling, tallboys, door frames, was like a chimney flue.

But it was a real pleasure to rub up that furniture, and indeed I felt angry with Mr. W., old bachelor as he was, that he had let it get in such a state. Furniture like that had a right to be properly looked after. And when I asked Aggie, the housemaid, if he was the kind of man to let things slide, as long as he was easy, she said no indeed, and poked his nose in everywhere, and his fingers too, she said, giggling. But I pretended not to notice this last turn. Aggie was always hankering to tell me tales about Mr. Wilcher's philanderings with girls about the place. She would throw out a hint and giggle till she was swelled like a boiling tomato, ready to burst.

It was Aggie who told me about the last cook but one, Mrs. Frewen, who had, so she said, let the master come too near her. Then he had turned around all at once and put the police on her box and run her into jail.

"I daresay she got too cheeky," I said.

But Aggie said it was only because she sat down one day in the drawing room when the master was there. "He's a funny one," she said, ready to go on for a week. But I thought that I was the cook and in charge of the house, and I had no business to hear tales against the master. It would do no good to anyone, him or me or Aggie. So I cut Aggie short. Besides, I knew all the story from the gardener's wife, which was that Mr. Wilcher had sometimes squeezed one of the maids a little or pinched her, or perhaps shown her something that he had better have kept to himself, and that he had been warned by the police, more than once,

172

magistrate and churchwarden though he was, to let the girls be. And as for Mrs. Frewen, she had flouted herself in the village and said that Mr. Wilcher was going to marry her and that she would make him. "So no wonder he ran her into jail," I said, and the gardener's wife, though stupid enough with a duster, had plenty of woman's sense, and she agreed with me that if a gentleman like Mr. Wilcher, who was so strict about churchgoing, went so far with the girls that it came to the police, then he could not help it and ought to be pitied, or, if mad, locked up, or married.

Not that I didn't feel the wrong of it in a gentleman like Mr. Wilcher and the foolishness too, but I thought country people were more uncharitable than they used to be and less reasonable in their thoughts. The schools gave them too many books and not enough Christian sense. Yet, I admit, I was all on fire to see the new master, when at last he came down, in the latter end of September.

Chapter Fifty-Five

HE WAS NOT at all what I expected. He was a little man with a bald head and round black spectacles. His nose was very short, just like a baby's, and he had a long blue upper lip, like a priest, which made me say: "You're one of the arguers." He had long thin red lips and the under one stuck out and curled over, which made him look obstinate and sulky. His chin was blue as if it had been shot full of gunpowder and it had a very nice split in the middle. His neck was blue too, and there were scars on the back and I could see, too, that the poor man, like Matt, had suffered terribly from boils. His face was pale yellow all but a little mauve, rhubarb color, over the bones of the cheek. I thought with these colors and lips and something in his eye, he had hot blood still, and sure enough within the month the poor man had a boil on his behind which gave him no peace. But he wouldn't lie up and he would just sit on a rubber cushion and bear it. I don't know why men should be so afflicted in this way; perhaps it's because of the hotness of their blood which my mother used to say was an affliction God gave them to balance that stupid thing which is such trouble to women and which nearly frightened me out of my soul when I was a child, not knowing to expect it and thinking it was God's punishment for some sin. And indeed I suppose it was for the sin of Eve and if so, she was fairly caught, as I was, for I too was one of those who can put their conscience to sleep when they like, just to please themselves.

As for those who said Mr. W. was a hypocrite to make so much of church and then run after young girls, I thought of his boils and his hot blood, and I thought, too, of my past deeds. And it seemed to me that I might have been called a hypocrite, when I was going to church in my best, knowing that Hickson and several more men were looking upon me with lickerish eyes. So that I could not have told you whether I was laced and dressed and scented to an inch of my life, for the honor of God, or the lusts of the flesh.

I thought, too, how often I had gone to church only to repent of some sin, and to keep myself from another as bad. If Mr. W. is even as bad as they say, I thought, he may be better than most, having greater temptation and a harder fight.

174

Chapter Fifty-Six

NOW, FROM the very first I'll admit I took to Mr.
Wilcher, and he seemed to take to me. Whether it
was because I was sorry for the neglect he lived in, or for
his pain, I felt quite a flutter when he first began to send
for me, and to ask about the larder and arrange the dinner.

Above all, I liked him keeping up family prayers, and the
way he read the Bible, as if it had been about real people.
He said the prayers, too, better than anyone I have ever
heard, and on Sundays, when he read the lessons in church,
it was as good as a play. I never enjoyed anything so much
before in any church, and I thought: Oh, that some would
take example from him and then there would be no more
sleepy heads in God's house. For he would read like a lion
and change his voice, too, in the speaking parts. So, indeed,
when he spoke like Ruth in the cornfield, he made his
voice so like a girl's that the tears came into my eyes. For
I had always loved that story and, indeed, it is easy to
know how poor Ruth felt, so low one day and so raised up
the next. Boaz, too, you can see him, the good manny,
doting on his nice young wife. Yet she would not mind his
being so much older, in those days, for girls were brought
up differently, to value a husband, however old. I often
wished to know how many children Ruth had and how
happy she was with Boaz, after that good beginning.

Mr. W., as I say, seemed to take to me too, for he would
send for me often to do little things for him, and he complimented me, too, on my good work in the house, and
thanked me for bringing the others to church, even Aggie

175

and the gardener's wife who had not been for a long time, and he found out, too, that I was a reading woman, and he would talk with me about the books.

For at Tolbrook I found books again and time, and my reading came back to me. I must not say that I would have come back to that duty of reading good books by myself, but only that it came back to me, or God brought it back by way of Mr. Wilcher.

For one day when he had gone out to tea, and came back earlier than we expected, he found me sitting in the little patch of garden behind the kitchen with a book. It was only a paper book that I found in the kitchen, about a girl that had had come into millions and left her poor lover for a rich one; but even a poor book will give you good ideas.

Now Mr. Wilcher, going in at his own little back door into his study, was so surprised and shocked he did not know what to do, but stood on one leg beside the door and pretended not to see me, until I had gone away, which I did quickly enough, for, of course, I had no business to be in the garden while the master was at home.

But the next morning when he called me in about a luncheon party, he asked me if I liked reading, and what books. So I said Yonge was my favorite. Then he was very pleased and cried: "You could not do better, Mrs. Monday. She was my father's favorite." Then he told me how his father, who had been a colonel, had taken the *Heir of Redclyffe* with him to the Crimea, and been shot in it. "When you come to London, Mrs. Jimson," he said, "I'll show you the bullet. It went right to chapter sixteen."

"Is that where the young baronet is suspected to be a gambler?" I asked.

Mr. Wilcher was surprised to see I knew the book so well and said that he did not remember. But that if I wanted to read, I could always sit in the garden, even when the family were at home, unless I thought it might upset the staff.

"The best place I think for you to be quiet and undisturbed is in the corner by the yard well. No one will trouble you there."

The corner near the yard was behind some laurels, so I thought his real idea was that I should not be seen, should anyone call, and his slyness made me laugh. He was still a regular old bachelor, full of his tact. Anyone could see through him. Yet I mustn't say he was sly, for I daresay he didn't know why he did just so.

But then, when I had put my chair in the patch, he came to me and asked about the book. And I said: "It's nothing of a book, sir—but it makes you think—and I haven't got my own books here."

"Nothing has a better influence than a good book," he said. "I must look you out some."

So he did, and filled a shelf with good old-fashioned books, some on religion, and some by Yonge, and Braddon and G. Eliot and J. Austen; some from his own library, though not in leather, of course.

Chapter Fifty-Seven

NOW THIS was one of the kindest things he could have done for me, and what I can never forget. For perhaps if the good books had not been brought to me, I would have gone on with Aggie's paper books. It is easy to read bad as well as good, when you get the habit, and please yourself. But the good books take hold of your mind, too, and in the end, you have double the pleasure and twice the profit. Going back to my Yonges was like going back to my first service and the time of my sober conscience. For the thoughts that came to me out of the pages were the same thoughts, as if they had been pressed between the leaves, only to remind me of my simple days, when my highest joy was a ribbon or a half day to the fair.

Yet I was wiser too. I knew more of the world and its temptations, and how much better off I was, in this quiet corner, with a good place and a good book, and the afternoon to myself, than the richest in the land, who had no time to feel or think or wonder at themselves, wasting their days like flies on a cow pat.

It is easy to say so much, but not so easy to know it, or believe it. For what is deceiving is that the rich are often gay and happy. So was I at Woodview; I would not have changed places then even with Nina Jimson, for all that I loved her. I pitied her poverty.

But my gaiety was not the happiness I had at Tolbrook, in the garden corner, nor yet what I had left, when I married Matt. So it was really waste of my days and their proper delights.

Chapter Fifty-Eight

THE NEXT week was the first of the shooting, and the London staff came down, Mr. Felby, the butler, Mrs. Felby, the housekeeper, and three maids. Mr. Felby was the finest man you ever saw, like an archbishop, as

178

clever as a lawyer and a beautiful waiter. But his eyes
swimming in drink and a bad sly tongue. He made game of
Mr. Wilcher's boil and said: "Serve him right, the dirty
little swine—I wish it was a carbuncle."

"Why?" said I. "That's a cruel wish for the poor man."

"Poor man," said Felby, "he has a million if he has a
pound, and look at the way he lives—meaner than a rat
that eats its own tail."

"That's right," said Mrs. Felby, who was a sharp cross
little thing with a hump on her back, "with all his locks
and his double locks—the one thing gives me a happy
feeling when I get my pain and can't sleep is that he's
going to be shown up."

"Not a bit of it," said Felby. "He's got off before and
he'll get off. He'll buy himself out of it. A rich man can get
away with anything."

Indeed, they both hated him, but I think they were the
kind that hated anybody unless those that were only fit to
be scorned. Felby hated the world because he was not a
millionaire himself, and it was true he was born for it. A
man like that, so handsome and strong and clever and well
mannered. I often pitied him in servitude and married to
that wasp who would stab him so that you could see him
swell up weak and blue like a sting on your neck.

"To hear you talk," she would say, out of nothing at all
and like a hornet on a summer day, "you'd better tell
people how I took your trousers down last time and gave
you toko, yes, and made you kiss the stick and say thank
you, mamma," and she turned to me: "If a man behaves
like a dirty little boy I say I'll treat him as such—drink
is no excuse."

Sometimes she brought Mr. Felby so near tears that I
couldn't look at him, and I was in a hurry to change the

179

subject. I daresay it was her back made her so mad at him, but no woman has a right to bring her husband to public shame; it is too easy and my mother used to say: "Never spoil a man's dignity, for he's a poor remnant without it, and don't think yourself so good a wife either if you do so much. It's only common sense and your own best interest." My mother was a true Christian woman and I never forgot her teaching. It was in my blood, the best part of me, and, I daresay, the only good part I had, so it was shocked by Mrs. Felby's cruelty.

But she hated all men, not like Rozzie for the joke, but in good truth.

"You know it yourself," Mrs. Felby said. "Men are rubbish and dirty to boot."

So I said that we couldn't do without them and that God had His purpose for them, trust Him, as for the worst of us.

But Mrs. Felby was fierce and careless. "Oh, that God!" she said, rubbing her hump. "Poor thing, don't bring Him in. I've no patience with Him. But it seems that He was a man too, or He wouldn't have stuck His image into the world to be an everlasting pest to a decent woman. We never asked for Him and only want a little peace and quiet."

So I dared to remind her that if there were no men in the world there would be no babies either, and no girls.

"Good riddance," said she.

"Well," I said, "you wouldn't have the world come to an end?"

"Why not," she said, "it'll last my time and what then? It won't be anything to me either way for I won't know."

I was shocked at this at first that anyone should care so little for the whole world, but then I thought: Ah, the

180

poor thing, she hasn't children to carry her spirit forward. So I turned back and said: "If we don't need men, they need us, and I wonder Mr. Wilcher has never got him a wife. With all that money he could have had the pick. And they say he needs one."

"You be careful," she said to me. "I hear he's throwing an eye on you already. Has he been pinching you?"

"Good gracious, no," I said. "How could he?"

"And what was he doing in the upper passage last night, when you went to bed?"

"I never saw him," I said. For the truth was that just when I was going up to bed, I had seen the master come out of the attic with a candle, and with only a towel around his neck, as if from his bath. So he walked toward me, but as if not seeing me. And I had pretended not to see him and turned my back to go into the linen room. But I wasn't going to tell Mrs. Felby that tale with her bad mind. For I thought still that if the master had that whim, to show himself, it was no harm in the world, except to idle heads and bad tongues. If he had been a drunkard, or spiteful or cruel, then I might have misliked him, but not for being simple, like any lad in his teens.

But Mrs. Felby had nothing to do but nurse her rage and feed her pain. She went on at me: It was as much as my place was worth to give way to the master. "You know what happened to Mrs. Frewen."

"I hear she tried to frighten him."

"And so she could have, the fool. But he's a bold one, the master, I'll admit. He told her she could send it to the papers if she liked and when she spoke of the police, he sent for them there and then and put them on her box."

"Had she taken anything then?"

"She said no, that the master had given her the things.

181

But then she began to howl and wouldn't say anything more. She was quite beaten flat, the silly sheep. She got eighteen months and serve her right for being such a fool. To think she could have brought the master into court and shown him up before the whole country. May she rot."

Taken all around, I was more shocked by the Felbys than any couple I can remember. To think how they lived in daily bitterness. You wondered they did not die of the poison. And I thought: I wonder did my servants when I had them talk about me so, and thought: Ah, my girl, you don't know how well off you are back in the kitchen with the good honest flags under your feet. For a drawing room, comfortable though it be, may only be stuck on the roof of envy and backbiting and no real peace in the whole mansion. See how I live now without an enemy in the world to poison my sleep, and good food and fires of sweet-smelling wood, and it seemed to me that it was Providence Himself that had taken me by the hand and led me back to the kitchen. For where could a woman find a better life, I mean in a good house with a good draft in the chimney, and double sinks and really hot water, as I always had at Tolbrook.

Then it came back to me about what poor Jimson had said about my true home being in a kitchen and that I was a born servant in my soul, and my heart gave a turnover and I felt the true joy of my life as clear and strong as if the big round clock over the chimney mouth was ticking inside me. So here I am, I thought, mistress of my own world in my own kitchen, and I looked at the shining steel of the range and the china on the dresser glittering like jewels, and the dish covers, hanging in their row from the big venison one on the left to the little chop one on the right, as beautiful as a row of calendar moons, and the kitchen table scrubbed as white as beef fat and the copper on the dark wall throwing

182

out a glow to warm the heart, and the blue delf bowls like pots of precious balm.

And then beyond where the larder door stood ajar you could see bottles of oil and relish and anchovies and pickles and underneath the lid of the big flour bin as white as its own lovely flour; I call it a treat for queens to sink your hands in new wheaten flour. And next the larder, the dark scullery door with just a wink within the brass taps to say: "Your servants, madam," and a slow drip from the one or other to tell me: "We are ready this minute and never will fail," and next the scullery, the kitchen pantry. I could not see its glass-fronted cupboards as fine as the British Museum, or its china and glass in thick heaps like the treasures of Aladdin. I could not see them, but I felt them like kingdoms in my charge. And, indeed, I felt bits of myself running out from the grand kitchen into pantry and scullery and larder and beyond into the passage and the stillroom and even to the wood cellar and the boot hole as if I was really a king or queen whose flesh is brought up to be the father of all his countries, and not to forget the little bye-lands even when they are on the dark side of the sun. You would say I was putting out in buds like a shallot with my big kitchen heart in the middle and my little hearts all around in the empire of those good faithful offices, all fitted up as they were, even the cupboards, in the best of country materials. The very shelves in the boot hole were oak, and the fruit racks were sweet apple.

How many women, I thought, can sit before a fire like this one among such a noble property of bowls and pots and cups and plates and knives and forks and whisks and pestles and colanders, bottles and kegs and jars? Why, I thought, the mustard pots alone would make a regiment, and a kind of awe came on me at all these many things put into my sole charge. Well, I thought, if you tied a knot of all the roads and railways and pipes and wires in the world it would come to a kitchen in the middle of it. And so close and neat, there wouldn't be room in it for a single piece of useless nonsense or vain furniture. For the great beauty of my jewels was that every one of them was needed and of my treasure chests that all this silver and gold was new-minted flour and fresh-baked cakes and my shining armor was to keep dinners warm and my regiments were cut up chickens and ducks and to stick their bayonets in chops and steaks for the glory only of conquering hungry stomachs and bad tempers. It's after a good dinner, I thought, that the lion and the lamb lie down together and let out their top buttons (as poor Matty would do) and put their feet on the hob.

So I looked around me that night and many more afterward in the Tolbrook kitchen, and prayed: "Let me only live cook in this dear place and not die too old for the work, and I'll never want another heaven."

This was my prayer and it seemed a judgment on me for making it when not three months after I was sent for to come up to town in place of Mr. Wilcher's town cook.

This was the first work of my chief enemy, though I did not call her enemy then, and she meant to do me good.

Chapter Fifty-Nine

THE NAME of this woman, when I first knew her, was Blanche Hipper. She came to Tolbrook that year in September, with her elder sister Clarissa, when the first party was made up, to play tennis with Mr. Loftus Wilcher, the master's eldest nephew. Mr. Loftus was a soldier, a pretty man, fair as a girl, but sleepy. He would often dawdle about the kitchen at Tolbrook for mutton fat for his boots, or oil for his flies, or only for something to do, and though he spoke little, he was easy and friendly. I liked him well and wished him joy, which I thought he would have, for the girls were mad for him, with his looks.

This Blanche was nineteen, daughter of the vicar in the next parish, plump and pretty enough, though too short in the neck and high in the shoulder. Her prettiness, to tell the truth, was only in her skin and eyes.

Even then I liked Miss Clarissa better, for though she was not so pretty, she always treated us servants like human beings, with souls, and Miss Blanche was hoity-toity even to the butler. Yet I could not feel angry with Miss Blanche because she was so gay and full of life and ready to enjoy everything and to make things go. Indeed, I always felt a liking for her and I could never be her enemy. I thought then that as she came from a poor family she had not learned how to treat servants, and had not enough sense, like Miss Clarissa, to think it out for herself. Miss Clary was three years older and working in London at an office for a whisky company. She and Mr. Loftus were childhood friends and we were all sure they would make a match of it, a good match for both, for he had money and beauty and she had brains and kindness.

I wished for the match more than anything in the world, for, as I say, Miss Clary was friendly with us all, and from the beginning she was my special friend. Of course, she came to me, at first, to get something out of me, special sandwiches for her lunch in the train, to save her pocket, or coffee to dye her stockings, but she did it so sweetly, it was a pleasure. Then to reward me and make all seem

185

friendly, she would always talk, and she talked so freely, I was surprised. I had not known how the new girls that had come up in London since the war would talk about anything to anybody. It shocked me at first to hear Miss Clary, mentioning Mr. Wilcher's boil, speak of "poor old bottom" and say that Aggie behaved as if she were in the family way again, and she hoped not because the girl was so careless in choosing her sires.

But though we servants could never have talked to each other as Miss Clary talked to me, and some were offended, I saw it was only the new way. For the new ways always begin at the top and go down; so I remember, when poor Rozzie went to the workhouse at last, she complained there was an old woman in the next bed who called her a Jezebel because she tried to powder her nose with plaster off the wall and tooth powder. As Rozzie said, she would rather have died before the war than paint, but now even the vicar's wife powdered. And the poor-law nurses, as grim a set of crows as ever picked among old bones, painted and rouged; for all she knew, so she said, they dyed themselves pink behind like the monkeys.

I never could get used to paint, and, thank God, I never needed powder except in the time with Gulley, to hide a black eye or a swollen nose. But they were in fashion, even for ladies, and I saw that Miss Clary's free talk was all in the fashion too. So I did not mind it, for I thought: The world must move. I even got to like it, for, as I say, it made me friends with Miss Clary, and I saw very soon how it was with her and Mr. Loftus. For she did not speak freely of him, or if she tried, her voice would change and her color come up. So she would say of a dance which Mr. Wilcher didn't want because of the expense: "I'll get Mr. Loftus to ask him—he'd do anything for Mr. Loftus."

186

It is true that Mr. Wilcher liked Mr. Loftus and it was said, too, he wanted him to marry Miss Clary and often asked her out, in London, to meet him.

Not that Mr. Loftus was so certain to be the heir and to get Tolbrook. For though he was the true heir, the only son of Mr. W.'s brother, Mr. W. liked better another of his nephews, who was the son of his elder sister. This was Bobby Brown, who was still a boy at school. His mother was dead and his father was married again, in India, so he often went to Mr. W.'s for his holidays.

I say Mr. W. looked upon Bobby almost as a son; yet whenever Bobby came here, he always managed to fall out with him. He would come to me and say: "Mr. Bobby will be here tomorrow, Mrs. Jimson—his favorite pudding is suet with jam and we will have a goose for dinner. He likes goose."

Master Robert was just sixteen, but small for his age, and not needing to shave except once a month, with scissors. He had a young voice still and he would call out like a child. But he would talk at anyone like an old man, about anything you liked. He was at the age when boys begin to read and think they know everything because the books make it seem easy. I suppose they must, like a cookery book, for how could they put the hard parts, like real life, which are different every time; your cream all turned that morning, or a hole in the stockpot; or the kitchen boiler to be cleaned. I dearly loved Master Robert, who came to me the very first day of his holidays, to make toffee in a soup plate, and abused me for not knowing how to cook.

"Now then," he said, "come along, and I'll show you."

But the toffee stuck to the plate, which broke in getting it out; one of the best china service. "Oh, lord," he said, "what will Uncle say?"

"Perhaps he'd better not know," I said.

"Oh, I must tell him," Bobby said, putting out his lip just like Mr. W. "Oh, lord, aren't I a fool not to remember to butter it? I could kick myself. Oh, well, come on, what's the next thing? Get a move on, old lady. We want our tea." And he would take me and push me around the kitchen like a Bath chair.

That was when Mr. W. was not at home. For Bobby, having no home and no place to go, often came to Tolbrook for his holidays, and was alone there for a week or more. Of course he had his friends and would go off fishing or sailing most days. But he was often in the house too, and then he would always be in and out of the kitchen, chattering or whistling, or watching me work, and picking it up too, in a wonderful way. He always made the coffee and he could turn off a sweet omelet, too, to beat the French. And it was always: "Come on, old lady, what's the next item in the program?" He was as familiar to me as if I had been his own nurse; and so I felt to him. For all his roughness was the kindness of a good young soul that had nothing to spend it on and did not know how to come close to those he loved except by running into them or slapping them, by hand or word, as little children do.

Bobby even wrote to me from school, though it was only to send his cricket trousers, or some toffee. But he would put in his love and remain your affectionate.

Mr. W., as I say, loved Bobby well and I'm sure he knew the lad's true goodness. Yet I dreaded their coming together in the holidays, because it always meant putting the master out, and upsetting him, including his appetite.

It upset him to be so upset over arguing with a boy, and because he would often find himself turned right around, as arguers will, and arguing against his own mind.

188

So when Bobby would say that the coal miners ought to have better pay because it was a dirty job which he wouldn't like, Mr. W. would smile and answer: "Perfectly true." But, of course, the matter was not quite so simple, for what about this and that, the steel workers and foreign competition and so on.

But then, Master Bobby would say: "Wages come first," and Mr. W. would say: "Not so. What if the country were ruined? Then Wales would starve too."

So then they would argue until Mr. W. would be telling Bobby that his pets, the miners, only wanted to ruin the country, so that they could start a revolution, having begun by saying they were good fellows, as all know, and only sometimes misled.

Then he would send away his plate and eat nothing more for dinner, nor even breakfast. For Mr. W. took everything to heart and didn't get over his troubles like the lighter kind, all in a moment.

Chapter Sixty

MISS CLARY and Bobby were very good friends and Clary often made peace for him with Mr. W. Mr. W. really loved Miss Clary for her gentle ways and her good sense. We all hoped for the romance between her and Mr. Loftus to have a happy end, as soon as might be.

That September, Mr. Loftus and she came down together by the same train and we were all sure that he was going to propose. Indeed, the housemaid found a new ring box, done up in tissue, in his collar box, a lovely sapphire with diamonds. Sapphire was Miss Clary's color, to bring up her eyes, which were blue, a far better blue than her younger sister's, but not so strong. She wore spectacles for work and she could not play tennis.

But just when Mr. Loftus was going to propose and they had danced one evening together to the gramophone, Miss Clary being a beautiful dancer, her aunt fell ill in London and there was nothing for it but she must go back to nurse her, because Blanche would not. Indeed, her own father said she was not fit to nurse anybody, being too noisy and selfish. For so the post office told us, which was the Hippers' post office, too, and knew all about the family.

Miss Clary went off on Monday and Mr. Loftus drove her to the station in the trap. We were told she was in tears on the platform as if going to a war, to throw away her life, and saying good-by to all the joys of this one, and so she was, poor child. Mr. Loftus came back looking very cast down, and did nothing all that day. He was a young man very easily bored, like many horse soldiers, when there's no hunting or races or horses either. For we had none at Tolbrook then, but trappers and the cart horse. So Mr. Loftus was quite worn out with nothing to do, and having to make talk with Mr. W. who, talkative as he was, could never get up a real conversation with Mr. Loftus. He would speak about the Army and about the lessons of the last war, and Mr. Loftus would say: "Yes, Uncle," and "No, Uncle," and hardly be able to open his eyes for boredom. He was a young man who hated conversation.

Then Blanche came along for tennis, and when Mr. Loftus said it was too hot, that he had no things, that the court was not fit, she said: "Nonsense." So she made him roll the court himself and tie up the net with string, and she borrowed the agent's trousers for him and lent him

190

her second-best racket; and she showed him new strokes all the afternoon and fairly abused him when he could not do them. I heard her myself call him an ass, the very first day. Of course she had known him for some years too, but not since her hair had gone up, for she had been at school until the last two years. And I'm sure she had never been familiar with him before.

So she bullied him and made him run about, and the next day it was riding in the field, because she wanted to practice her riding. Mr. Loftus had despised riding about on a cob, but he did not mind when Miss Blanche made him take her out. Then it was picnics to Longwater, and sailing, and the end of it was, after only a week, that they were engaged, and she had on her finger the ring that poor Mr. Loftus had bought for her sister.

It was said that she proposed to him; but I think it more likely she only led him up to it, after a little kissing and perhaps only one kiss. For to do her justice, she was very particular and no flirt. Perhaps she had set out to catch Loftus, but if she did, it was not by philandering with him; never more, at least, than putting her cheek close in front of his eyes, at a gate or in a gig. Any girl who knows that her complexion is her chief beauty might do so much, without knowing her own artfulness.

So Mr. Loftus married her and she had Clary for a bridesmaid. I never saw a girl so green at a wedding, and I thought she would faint. We all thought it the cruelest thing that she had to stand up there and hear her man say that he would love and cherish her sister. Some blamed Miss Blanche for it and said it was a piece of her spite, because she was jealous of Miss Clary's brains and goodness and her being loved more by their father. But I thought it was only the way it happened. Miss Clary could not

191

stand out, or people would have said that she was bitter and unforgiving, in her sister's time of joy. I think it had to be and that Miss Clary was to suffer that cruelty. But she did not faint, and when that night she wanted to go to bed early, because she said her head ached, but really I think it was because she could not bear daylight any longer, she asked me if I could make her some tea. And this was the beginning of my friendship with Miss Clary. For when I said the tea must not be too strong, to keep her awake, she said that she did not hope to sleep "this night of all nights."

It was a slip and she colored up when she had said it. But the truth was that she had got, even then, into such a way of chattering with me that she never thought before her tongue spoke. Then she looked at me and smiled in a way that almost made me cry, and said: "I've shocked you again, Sara," for she always called me Sara. "But you shouldn't be so comfortable to talk to."

I thought then that she might be going to cry but if she might cry for joy, she was not one to cry for grief, and it was just as well, seeing her appointed fate. For she never stopped suffering from that disappointment and the ruin of her whole life; and if she had been a poor-spirited girl, she would have gone to pieces and turned into a misery, fit for nothing but to drag upon other people. But not at all. Miss Clary never dragged on anyone and stayed what she had always been, her father's right hand and, so Mr. W. told us, the prop of her whisky office in London. It was my only consolation when Mr. Wilcher, that November, sent for me to London, that I might see Miss Clary there.

Chapter Sixty-One

THE LOFTUS WILCHERS had used the town house in a part of their honeymoon and the cook there was to make arrangements. But it seemed that the new Mrs. Loftus, full of her wedding ring, had found the place dirty and quarreled with the cook.

So the cook went out at a day's notice, which was always Mr. W.'s way. He would never keep a discharged servant in the house one night, but handed her a month's wages and a bit over and sent her off. A regular old bachelor, I thought, who can't bear to sleep on so much as a crumb. But the Felbys, of course, had another tale. That the woman had something against the master and gave Mrs. Loftus some hint of it. And that she went off with a hundred pounds to keep her quiet.

I thought I would break my heart going from Tolbrook to London; and to make me feel it more, it was snowy weather. There was no place prettier under snow than our Tolbrook with its old garden walls and the yew hedges, its small fields and big trees, and the pond and streams. When I went out for the eggs, before breakfast, by the cart lane, the fields were like icing sugar and the pond as gray as eels with the snow water; the sky was like new-cleaned window glass full of its own shine, the very weeds and old docken were like silver and velvet cut for a wedding. Then when I was going away, the sun was up and all was like a pearl, pink and blue, and you saw the snow at the roadside full of bubbles like white of egg beaten up, with rainbows in every one. The air, too, was so clean with all the dust brought down that you couldn't believe that there was such a thing as dust in the world, to spoil all, and waste our lives away, only cleaning it away.

And then to come to London, as dim as a cellar in midafternoon, with a sky like a coalhole ceiling, even to the black cobwebs, which were their clouds, and the roads like cold gravy, and the snow like marzipan piled in the gutters, and the trees in the gardens weeping down black as if their sap was only soot.

The town house, No. 15 Craven Gardens, was what you would expect; a slice of a house, seven stories from basement to attic. I felt squeezed sideways as I went in and going down to the basement was like going to my grave. A real old-fashioned basement with long passages and dark holes off them, a great low kitchen with the ceiling hanging down as if it would fall on you; a fog of blacks and gas and smoke like the old underground, and a cold smell of cockroaches and mold and mice. If it hadn't been for the other servants I would have sat down and cried.

My bedroom too, I would never have put my own kitchenmaid in such a place. A cupboard with the ceiling falling down on the floor on one side, dirty matting eaten away by rats, an iron bedstead with a tin jug, one chair with a hole in it, and when I had a fire lit, the chimney smoked me out. "No," I said, "I'll go. I can't bear it and I have no right to bear it, with my quality as cook and housekeeper. I'll give in my notice tomorrow. I know that with my nine months' character, I could get a better place." I could have picked and chosen.

Now why I did not give notice, I don't know, for I certainly meant to, or get my lot bettered. But I think it was only my rolling way. For when I got up there was the

194

breakfast and then the looking over my battery and the larders, and then the cleaning, and before I could think of notice again, the master sent for me.

Chapter Sixty-Two

M R. W. put me on a chair in the corner. He looked so queerly, jumping about the room, I remembered all the stories I had heard and went cold with fright. Well, I thought, if I don't struggle he won't kill me and the worst of such wickedness is only the thought of it.

Then he sat down and drew up a chair till his knees were nearly touching mine and said in a voice, like his church voice, that seemed to pray in my mind: "Mrs. Jimson, I am at your mercy."

I was too frightened to speak. But he was too excited to notice it. And the whole thing was that he wanted me to be housekeeper instead of Mrs. Felby. He was going to put out the Felbys, and I was to manage both houses.

When I said it was above my degree, he said: "Mrs. Jimson, you have been mistress of a household much larger than my modest establishment, and as the wife of a distinguished artist, you cannot plead that the housekeeper's room is above your degree."

Then I begged for Tolbrook only. But Mr. Wilcher was one of those who will not take a no. Hadn't I seen it in his lip and his nose too? "Mrs. Jimson," he said, "I mustn't press you but as you see I'm in a terrible difficulty. I must get rid of the Felbys and they'll have to go at once. Who is going to run this house? I could go to my club, but I can't leave it with servants only—you know what they are as well as I do. They'd be up to mischief as soon as my back was turned. And I have my work to think of, important work. It's waiting for me now, at the office. How am I to work when things like this go on happening? Never settled for a moment. The place is like a madhouse."

He was so excited with his wrongs that he jumped up and ran about the room as if he were really mad. I could see indeed that the houses were a perfect pest to him, as you might expect, in a wifeless man.

"Mrs. Jimson," he said, "if you desert me, I don't know what I shall do. You understand the Felbys are going today. I had to give them notice in case they heard anything from other sources."

Mercy me, I thought, and I wondered at the poor man's faithlessness. No wonder, I thought, he's half mad with it.

So, I thought, I could do with extra money, especially if Jimson should write for more advances, as I expected, and I agreed at last to be housekeeper, town and country. But no sooner had I said it than Mr. Wilcher was up again and crying out, what could he do for cooks?—two cooks. Where could he find them? And he asked me to do the cooking too.

No, no, I thought. It's too much—it would be killing work. Then he was in despair again and when I said I could get cooks, he said that he only wanted my cooking. But if I went on as cook, who would be housekeeper?

"Of course," he said, "I'll consider it in your salary."

So he went on at me till I found that I had agreed to all. Only I held out for a kitchenmaid. And he said I could have one, if I didn't give more than sixteen. It was all he could afford. But where could I have got a kitchenmaid, at that rate, in 1925?

When I went out, I was to do four women's work, for less
196

than the wages of one. For I knew Mrs. Felby had seventy-five for her own part, and he was to give me sixty-five.

Of course he was full of his thanks and compliments. I did not know quite how I stood, until I was downstairs again, in my own place. Then I was angry, for I thought I had been done out of my deserts. But I would not say now that Mr. Wilcher meant to take advantage of me. He was a man so worried and pestered by everything in his life, by the houses and the nieces and nephews and the times and the world, and I suppose his own nature, too, that he was like three men tied up in one bag and you never knew and he never knew which of them would pop out his head, or something else, or what it would say or do. True, all of him was of a saving disposition, as I was; though he had given away thousands, too, as I heard, to missions, and he had doubled the seating in Tolbrook church.

So I came to see that if I had been done, it was my own fault, for giving way to him, and as for my deserts, it was what they say:

If I had my deserts, I should ride a King's coach
With bows to my back should the courtiers approach,
Flogging and whipping as court shall devise
And coach to the gallows to give me a rise.

Chapter Sixty-Three

AND THE place was easy. In London Mr. Wilcher lived like a clock. It was a pity to see how little he had of a life, with all his money and his houses. Up at seven, cold bath, a cup of tea and a walk around the gardens; then house prayers in the dining room and breakfast in his own room, and off to work.

It seemed that he was a lawyer in a very old firm, which had been in the family since George III. Every evening except Saturday he came back to tea at five, drank a cup of tea, and read the evening paper. Then a long bath and dinner at seven. After dinner he often went to a concert or a theater. But often he read the whole evening, heavy big books from his own library, so quiet you would not know that he was in the room. His room was a small study next his bedroom and bathroom on the fourth floor. He really lived there, for he never went into the dining room only for prayers and dinner. He had that in style, with four candles and flowers and plate, and dressed for it; but he ate very little and did not stay long. He drank only soda water or one glass of port.

On Saturday he had a Turkish bath and tea at his bath; and he went out to dinner with an old friend and often stayed till two or three in the morning; or all night. But he always came in to No. 15 early to change and bathe before he went to the office. On Sundays he went twice to church, often to early service too.

Not much entertaining and always at dinners, which I prefer. A party of five or six about once a month, and much talk and sometimes cards after. But they talked at cards too, and I don't think Mr. W. cared for cards. He would rather talk, especially to clergymen. There was always one or two clergymen at our parties, which I liked too, for the rich ones are always so pleasant and the poor ones could always do with a good meal.

When the captain came with his new wife, we would have young people, but these were always the quietest and saddest of all. The only one to talk was Mrs. Loftus, and if she did not get anyone to talk the talk she liked about tennis or golf, she just ate. The footman, Billy, who waited,

198

said they would all sit mum like corks on a wire, waiting for a wind to make them sing.

As for giving Mr. W. satisfaction, that was easy enough. He wanted only simple food and he never noticed how the house was kept up, except now and then when his fidgets took him into some shut-up room and he would find dust on the mantelpiece and ring and say to me that no doubt the housemaid had forgotten the mantelpiece and he had no wish to worry me with trifles, but look at his finger. This to show he was keeping his eyes open, when he had not seen the great black cobwebs which the Felbys had left on every cornice.

But I liked him for trying to do his duty by the house, although it was not his born work. He tries to keep things up, I thought, and give them their rights, when he might let them down and let himself down.

Chapter Sixty-Four

I HAD BEEN afraid of a town life; that it would drive me mad, boxed up among houses; but not a bit. It was true I still liked Tolbrook best; but I got to love No. 15 too. I loved the peace and quiet of town without hens and calves waking you up at four in the morning; and the company. For I had many friends and went out to tea or to cards two or three times a week. There was my first cousin married to a grocer in Ealing, and my two old aunts at Penge. I went to them and they came to me in my own room, which was prettier than any of theirs. Then I would walk in the park, which is better than the country for company.

199

I would go often to sit by the Round Pond where the nurses take their prams and the children sail their boats. I can't tell you the pleasure I had there, all for nothing. For first there were the prams and the babies and I always knew some of the girls, so that when they sat down to rock the pram, I could talk with them about their babies and mistresses, and their young men. Then there were the little boys and girls running about mad with the water so near, for water always goes to a child's head. And the other people enjoying the sight and the children, such people that you know are a good kind of souls; and then there was the breeze, and the open sky, and the trees full of the breeze and the water itself glittering and jumping like a child's sea, as gay and happy in itself as any child. And the boats, and the wonder would they get across; and last but not the least by long ways were the grown men with big expensive boats and long beautiful brass polished hooks to catch them with. There was one there, quite old and bald, with fat weak legs, who would run after his boat and pant until you were afraid for him, and if he had been a child you would have told him to wait and gone to catch his boat for him. But since he was a man, in a very good suit too and gold watch chain, you could not help him; you could only hope the boat would not turn away from him before he ran himself into a fit. I don't know why to see this man so anxious about his boat made me feel so pleased that I would be gay all the evening, as if I had been a young girl coming from a party or from the Communion; not knowing yet my own self or the traps of the world.

I remember the feeling because I needed it just then. It was the first time we all noticed what a grip Mrs. Loftus had upon poor Mr. W. Now her husband's regiment was in London, she came around almost every day and used the house like her own. Indeed, it surprised us all how that girl had changed in one single year from a lumpish sort of kitten into a touch-me-not kind of cat. She walked as if the floor was hers, and spoke as if the rest had only ears. Especially after her boy was born, she would tell Mr. W. himself how the law was and what must be done. As for us servants, she treated us like dirt; even me whom she still liked. She told me that when her husband got the property, she would continue with me as cook at the manor; for though my cooking was not up to London standard, it was good enough for the country. But she would do her own housekeeping. "For I hate waste," she said, "and I never allow perks." She was not yet twenty-one and had engaged her first servant less than a year. "They're quite unnecessary," she said. "I don't mean that you would ever take anything, Mrs. Jimson, but then you're an exception."

She meant, of course, that she was sure I did take as much as I could get, and that I had better stop it, before she caught me.

But what troubled me and Miss Clary was to see the power she had over Mr. W. We had seen how she swallowed up her poor husband, so he could not blow his nose without her. Not that she was rough with him. She was never out of temper and always ready for anything. But that was it. She was always with him, whatever he did, shooting or hunting or sailing; they say she had gone to the parade ground with him till the colonel gave her a hint, through his own lady. She was like a slave to him and yet she was his master too. For he could not do without her. At Tolbrook, it was "Where's Blanche?" all day; or if he was asked to shoot or fish or ride, he would say: "I don't know what we're doing today. Ask Blanche."

She kept him on the go, and I never saw him bored, but

201

I never saw him laugh either in his old way and sometimes I thought he would have liked to dawdle again and talk nonsense with Miss Clary.

But how was it that Mrs. Loftus had such power over Mr. W. that it seemed she would take anything out of his hands and rule his house, and get the property for herself and Loftus, in spite of all he could do and his natural feelings toward Robert? Miss Clary said it was because Mr. W. was so shilly-shally in himself that any woman could do what she liked with him. She said that Mrs. Eeles, who, it seemed, was his Saturday friend, had always turned him around her finger; and it was lucky for him that she was so stupid and lazy she did not think of marrying him or robbing him of all he had. "She takes hundreds because she can't think in thousands," Miss Clary said; "and besides, she doesn't need jewels or clothes because she hardly ever leaves her room. She used to go out on the streets and take pickups to the park; but now she gets the drink sent up and won't be bothered with men."

But I did not think it was all shilly-shally with Mr. W., because he would often refuse to take Mrs. L.'s advice. He would come to me about a dinner party. "I'll ask Mrs. Loftus—she understands these things." But he would change her plans too and cut off half her guests and all the champagne.

He used to say of Mrs. Loftus, like Miss Clary: "She's young—and it's a young world. Perhaps it takes youth to understand it." But though he often took Mrs. Loftus' advice, he never listened to Miss Clary. She was too free and too much for politics, or too much for Bobby's and my Belle's kind of politics, which I would have thought young. But Mr. W. seemed to think the other old Blue kind could be young too, in Mrs. Loftus.

202

Chapter Sixty-Five

I HAD not heard from Gulley in three years except when he wrote for five pounds and offered to sell me all the pictures left behind in Ancombe, for a hundred pounds, paid in installments. I said nothing to that. Where was I to get a hundred pounds, even if I had thought of buying pictures with it? But I sent him three pounds and after that he had written only once more for another three pounds. And put in a kind of account showing that I had paid six before.

When one afternoon at Craven Gardens, the footman Billy came down to say there was a gentleman for me in the drawing room. "He says he's your husband."

"In the drawing room," I said. "Why did you put him there?" Billy was only a boy, not yet seventeen. He said that he had pushed past him, and wouldn't be stopped.

It was just time for Mr. W. to come home from the office; so I ran upstairs as fast as I could, and asked Gulley if he wanted to lose me my place. But he answered only that I looked younger than ever.

I thought he looked much older and shabbier. He smelled of whisky too. But he would not tell me anything about himself or where he was living. I knew it was in London, somewhere near Finchley, because he had given his box address there, at a tobacco-sweet shop. But he would not say the address, or come downstairs.

"At least if you came down, I could clean your shoes," I said, "and save that coat button."

"No," he said. "I want to see this Mr. Wilcher."

I saw that he was in a bad mood and I was terribly frightened. "You don't want me back," I said.

He didn't answer but looked at me more slyly than ever. I saw he was in a bad idle mood and I was frightened. For I thought I could not bear any more beatings. "Pretty comfortable," he said. "Housekeeper to a single gentleman, all found and bed and board. Especially bed."

"It's a lie," I said. "Mr. Wilcher would never do such a thing."

"That's not what they say about him at Queensport," he said. "So you don't mean to come back to your lawful husband."

I was terribly cast down, for I knew I would go back if he asked me, and be beaten and lose all my comforts. I dreaded it and yet I knew he had only to say the word. For cruel as he was, he had yet a hold on me. I don't know how it is but when you've lived with a man, and cooked and cleaned for him and nursed him and been through troubles with him, he gets into your blood, whoever he is, and you can't get him out. Besides, there was no doubt Gulley was the most of a man I ever knew. For he carried his own burden, which was a heavy one; and even if he was cruel, it was only when driven mad.

"The only thing is this," I said. "If I come back to you, how will I be able to pay you your installments?"

"I don't care about the money," he said, eying me over. "My God, Sall, I believe you've improved in these years," and he caught hold of my front with his hand and squeezed me. "Just as firm as ever. By God, Sall, we had some good times, hadn't we?—and what a model you were. Some of those drawings were first class, though I say it. Well, so

204

you'll come back to me. Better clear out before Wilcher arrives. I'll order a cab, shall I?"

But he did not order a cab. Instead he kept on looking at me sideways, in his wicked mood. I thought that probably he had been stuck and suddenly had the idea of coming after me.

"That reminds me," he said. "Where are the drawings? I sold you the canvases, not the drawings."

Now Gulley had written of the drawings, the time he asked for the three pounds, but, of course, I knew nothing of them or the canvases except that I had left them with Miss Slaughter, and when she died, Mr. Hickson had said that he would take care of them; and pick out two canvases in exchange for our debts which he had paid. I had signed a paper to put me right with him, and glad I had been to throw that weight off my conscience, in exchange for pictures that no dealer would look at.

But I dared not so much as speak the name of Hickson to Gulley, who would rear up at the word; he had so made it a hobby to hate him.

So I pretended to look stupid and said: "What drawings?"

"All my drawings," he said; "about five hundred of you. Come, be honest for once, Sall, and own you've pinched them."

I denied it for I was in terror of his picking a quarrel. But Gulley could always see through me and now he said: "What will you bet your box isn't full of my things?— I know your old cook's box with loot twenty years old." For he had always laughed at me for keeping some old things from my first place, only in memory of it, a velvet ribbon someone had thrown away and a trumpery bangle, a fairing from the man cook there. Then he took me by

205

the arm and said: "Come on, Sall, where's your room? Show the bridegroom into the wedding chamber—and welcome him with sackbuts."

Then I was in terror, for the truth was I had a few of his drawings at the bottom of my box, and one pinned up on the wall, a head only. I had packed them at Ancombe in the hope some dealer would give a pound or two for them, since I could not pack the canvases; but Mr. Z. had offered me only five shillings each; and I said I would rather keep them. For one thing, they were all of me and I did not want to see myself naked in a shop window, only for five shillings. It would have been a sin to bury a lot of money in my box; but if only shillings, it was better not to expose myself and risk the master seeing me, and knowing me, by the name and the figure.

Besides, I did not want to take him up to my room, for I was afraid of him, in his wicked mood; I had got too soft for Gulley in my comforts. So I began to say that my room was too untidy and that Mr. Wilcher was just coming in.

So he came close to me and said: "Are you coming back to me, Sall, or aren't you?"

"Of course," I said, "if you want me—haven't I always been ready?" But I knew it was my death.

"You think I can't support you," he said.

"For God's sake," I said, "if you want me, call your cab and let me go and pack my box. But don't go on worrying at me."

"Worrying at you?" he said.

So then I lost my hold on myself and said: "I suppose it's only because you're stuck and ready to quarrel with your own shadow."

"Stuck," he said. "I'm never stuck. Thank God I'm never

short of ideas. What do you mean, stuck?" and he came at me. So I told him not to dare to hit me, for I wouldn't bear it. I was too old.

"Stuck!" he said. "What do you mean, stuck?" and bang, his arm came out so quick, you couldn't see it. It was like a snake striking. And so hard the blood flew over his own face. I saw a drop on his own forehead.

He called me names, too; names I couldn't write; and I never saw him in such a rage. But though I was in such terror, my bones were melting, yet I would not run away, or give ground, but stood there and took his blows and told him he was a brute.

But suddenly we both heard the front door open and steps in the hall; Mr. Wilcher, and Billy come to take his hat. "There's the master," I said, and flew out of the room and past Mr. Wilcher, and up to my room, to put my poor nose into cold water.

So I heard no more till I came down to make the dinner and Billy told me that Jimson, all bloody as he was, had come into the hall and introduced himself, and shaken hands with Mr. Wilcher. And then they had talked about art, Mr. Wilcher complimenting Jimson. Mr. W. had even asked him to stay. But he would not, and went off. And Mr. Wilcher had even gone down the street with him, talking all the way.

Now I think that if those two had begun about art, they ended about me, for though Mr. W. never said a word to me, and only once looked sharp at my swollen nose, yet he began to show me new little kindnesses from that day and told me I could spend a pound on the garden patch behind the house where I sometimes sat, if I thought I could improve it. He even sent a pot flower.

But I hardly noticed the change at first because I was in

207

such terror of Gulley coming to take me away. I was grown such a coward I would lie awake at night in a sweat to think of his beatings. I could not believe how I had been so happy with him, and I wondered at my strength in those days and thought how I had fallen off, and was the more exposed to a letdown in my old age. Savings in the post office were something, I thought, but the better ones were in the soul. For even the rich are wretched without them.

It was from this time that I began to pay Gulley installments every week, but whether to keep him in some comfort and please my conscience, or only to keep him away and please my flesh, I never could tell.

Chapter Sixty-Six

BUT I KNOW I was glad when he did not come, and indeed my only troubles in the rest of that year were my weight and sometimes cook's eye from living too much over steam and smoke; and of course Madame Loftus. But for two years about the time that skirts began to get longer and figures were coming back, she never came to us at all because of a great quarrel with Mr. W. about his Saturday friend.

Now, though I rejoiced that Madame Loftus left us alone I was troubled, too, about this friend of the master's. He was not growing younger and every winter he began to have lumbago. He did not sleep so well either and would often fidget about the passages half the night; or read, not in his room, but downstairs in the library, as if he could not bear his own place.

Now I happened to know that this Saturday friend of his was also getting old, and she had been growing into drink; and with one thing and another, she was a great nuisance to my poor master, and had been so for years. Miss Clary also told me that she had never been good to him and had caught him young and kept him only because he was too polite to hurt her feelings and break with her.

This was what Madame L. and he had quarreled about. For she always wanted him to give the woman up. And even after two years, when they were friends again, Mrs. L. kept at him. To do her justice, she never considered her own interests when she had something on her mind. She would have called down an archbishop before the whole county, to please her conscience.

Whenever Mrs. L. had another wrestle with the master, he was upset for a whole week and fidgeted till we were all on pins and needles.

Now he had got into a habit, which pleased me very well, of coming to the housekeeper's room every Sunday evening to look over the bills and tell me his plans for next week. Then he used to say: "Sit down, Mrs. Jimson," and make me sit down by the fire, and he would say: "You don't mind if I smoke," and he would light a cigarette and sit on the other side of the fire and smoke it out and talk about the great cost of everything since the last war, and the changes in the world which we had both seen.

So we went on till it was a settled thing; our talk by the fire, and I think he would have missed it as much as I did. After two or three years, we got so far he would smoke two or three cigarettes and stay an hour; and sometimes he got off the changes in the world to his own changes. He spoke even once or twice of Gulley, respectfully saying that he did not understand modern art, but showing to me, too, that he thought I had been taken in and misused, that he knew my story. Now one Sunday night, when he was only just over the fidgets from a quarrel with Madame L. about his woman friend, he sat so long with me, and so quiet, that I wondered what was coming. He sat till nearly one o'clock, never speaking. Till all at once he said: "Mrs. Jimson, how long is it since you came to me? It must be nine years."

It was only seven, but I myself was surprised at the time; it had gone so fast, but I thought, if he makes it nine, then he has something to say upon that, so I did not gainsay it.

Then he said: "I hope you have been as comfortable as you have made me."

I said that I couldn't ask for a better place.

"In fact, I don't know what I'd do without you."

I said it was very kind of him to say so, but he answered: "No, yours is the kindness; you've made a home for me that I never expected to have. For when I decided to be a bachelor, I knew that I should have to make some considerable sacrifices."

I said I was sorry for any bachelor that had to be at the mercy of his servants.

"And not that only." He stopped a moment and then he said: "You are a woman of the world, Mrs. Jimson, or ought I to say Mrs. Monday?—I have never known exactly which was right. Not that I would dream of hurting your feelings by recalling anything painful to your memory. Yet may I ask if you are free from that unfortunate entanglement with Mr. Jimson?"

I said that, to be honest, I had never been married to Jimson.

"So I understood," he said, "and I admit that it is a great relief to me to have it confirmed from your own mouth. That you are free. But now I have my own confession to make. I believe you probably know that I have had an arrangement in a certain quarter that takes me out now and then in the evening, often till rather late. Now that's all very well for a young man, though I'll tell you in confidence, I never liked it. It means going out on wet miserable nights which make the whole thing a perfect penalty. And now that I'm getting older and have a touch of rheumatism, it is really quite ridiculous. To undergo such a disturbance and such misery just because one has made a certain arrangement, and to pay a considerable sum for it, and on top of all, to risk lumbago, is a perfect humiliation."

When Mr. W. said this, I felt quite delighted. For it was really what I felt myself. So, though I knew I was on delicate ground, where I might easily offend his manners, I said that I would be very glad indeed if he didn't have to keep such late nights, come all weathers.

"I'm very glad you do," he said in a pleased voice, "but I thought you would, and if it could be avoided, by any possible way, I will gladly stay at home. So the question is, how can it be done?"

It had been on the tip of my tongue to say that he only had to pay the woman off and stay at home, but I knew in that last minute that this would be just the very thing that would upset him. So I said nothing.

"How can it be done?" he said again, looking at me.

"That's the only point," I said.

"If you could help me to answer it," he said, "I should think myself a very lucky man and a completely happy one."

Now when he said that, all at once I had the feeling that he was going to propose marriage. I couldn't believe it, for

I knew that Mr. W. was not the man to marry his house-keeper, and yet for all my surprise, I felt it was coming. But before I could think, he went on: "You and I know, Mrs. Jimson, at our age, that the really important thing in life is living together in amity and mutual respect and we have that already. Anything more is not really of great importance. As they say, those that have it think nothing of it, and those that have not, think much too much of it. So if you feel that you wouldn't like to go any further in the matter, you'll never hear any more from me. We'll forget that we said anything about it—I'm not going to throw away the solid good fortune I have with you just for the little extra. Pleasant as it would be and convenient, since we do inhabit the same house, and I won't hide it, a great addition to my comforts, I'll think no more of it. What do you say, Mrs. Jimson, shall I drop the subject?"

So I, still thinking that he was making a proposal, and that he was only not wishing to give me too grand ideas about his feelings, I said to him he knew very well how much happiness it gave me to be with him.

"And you think you could give me this other addition to it? Of course," he said, "I'll see that you don't suffer. I'll see that your position is secure. Though, if you wouldn't mind, I'd rather not have any settlements for family reasons."

I thanked him very much and said that he was very generous. And then he said: "Very well, we'll shake hands on it."

So I shook hands with him and then at once he said that it was time we were in bed, and went off.

I thought all this very well done; a very dignified kind of proposal. Only I was sorry to feel that he did not like me better than to make it all so much a matter of business.

212

What was my surprise when I was brushing my hair for bed, when he knocked at the door and walked in.

"So here I am," he said, "my dear Sara." Calling me Sara for the first time. I was so confused that I did not know what to say. I went on brushing my hair while he walked about impatiently. At last he said: "Come on, my dear. I don't want to be too late. I've got a board meeting tomorrow."

So then all at once it came upon me what he meant and that his whole talk had been nothing to marriage. Indeed I had been a great fool to dream it, for I knew what he knew about me. So there was I brushing my hair and wondering what to do.

For I thought: If I turn him out, he'll be bound to be hurt. Whatever he says, he's a man and though I've no doubt he is not so delicate as my poor Matt, he has a great sense of what is proper, and is easily hurt by anything unexpected. Here he is now, so sure of himself and if I tell him it's all a mistake, won't he feel like a fool?

So after I had waited as long as I could bear him waiting, I said: "You don't think it's a little soon?"

"Why, Sara," he said, "if you think so, it is so. This is my usual day, you know—but I'm not so tied to routine, and I wouldn't for the world do anything to hurry you, or bother you. For I know when I'm a lucky man and have got a woman that I certainly never dreamed of. Yes, my dear," he said, putting his hands on my shoulder, "a good woman." But then he was taken with his manners again. For he jumped away from me and said: "Tomorrow, then," and went out of the door. But when he had half closed it he put in his head and said: "Or when you like, my dear Sara, for it's for you to say. Remember that I am fully aware of my extraordinary good luck."

He did not come the next day, or the next, and he behaved as if nothing had happened. I might have thought he had given up the whole thing. I almost believed it, but I knew in my mind that he had not. I knew very well that he was holding to his word and that it was for me to say.

I'll own I found this a terrible difficulty. It was bad enough to take him but worse to ask him. Yet I don't know how it was, but I felt that I must. Again, I thought, if I don't have him it will be, at the best, some late nights, more of that coarse rough woman, and more lumbago too; and at the worst, a chill and double pneumonia on top of it. For a man is always more exposed to chills after it, and indeed it is the most natural thing for him to stay warm in a double bed, and that, I always thought, was why Nature had suggested that kind of bed till the modern unnatural customs were brought in.

Now I have to confess that I was quite confused between my conscience and my duties, and indeed I prayed one night, and cried over the whole thing, since I thought that even if Mother could have been alive, she wouldn't have been able to guide me, yet all the time, I knew I would give way. For I liked my happiness in Craven Gardens and my comforts and my peace and my dear Mr. W. himself far too well to do anything to lose them, or do them any injury. So that (I'll confess) more than half my grief was simply the perplexity how to tell him that I would do what he liked, without making myself ashamed, and without giving him any offense. For goodness knows, it is easy enough to offend a man at these critical moments.

So while I was puzzling one night, after dinner, it came to me in desperation that I couldn't wait any longer. So I took in the savory myself and put it on the table and said: "I'd rather you said, Mr. Wilcher."

214

"Said what?" said he, surprised to see me in the dining room, and not too pleased.

"When you wanted to come to me."

So I blurted it out and I was fearful at once that he would be put off forever; as Matt would have been. But there was the difference in the men. I couldn't have done a more sensible thing with my honest Mr. W. if I had studied him like a skeleton leaf under the magnifying glass. He answered me at once: "Very well, Mrs. Jimson, as you wish. But, of course, you must turn me out if it's not convenient."

So he came along that night, and what was strange and unexpected, he was most gentle and respectful. Though I should not say so, yet I must be honest and confess his way was a real pleasure; he was so thoughtful and attentive.

Now although in the next years I often suffered in conscience, and wondered at myself, while I walked in the gardens and thought: How is it that I can go about like this, like an ordinary person, and not be found out, or sink into the ground with shame? Yet the truth was that I was very happy.

So we went on three years without a single cross word, and the most perfect understanding. The only thing that gave me grief was that Mr. W. would never allow me to show him any kindness, or rather, I saw that it upset him. I must never allow a dear to slip out, and if I had to touch him for any reason, I must do it as to a young nervous creature, with a quiet movement and a steady still hand. For if I seemed to pet him, he would jerk away and say something cool and businesslike. "Come now, it's late," or bring in some conversation about the house. At first I thought he kept me at a distance for fear that I would grow conceited and make myself a nuisance to him, as I daresay

215

other women had done. Afterward I saw that he was nervous of kindness; and perhaps indeed he was afraid of women. He had learned one way to deal with them and so he could not risk any other. For I know he was happy with me; he told me so many times.

Chapter Sixty-Seven

NOW IT was said at the trial that I got Mr. W. into my clutches and drove away his own family; and did what I liked with him and robbed him of everything. It was made out so, or nearly so, by the evidence, but it is very hard to get truth into evidence, as I think it is hard enough to get it in life, about human people, or even yourself. It was Mrs. Loftus' evidence went against me; and she believed every word of it, for she was always very truthful. Yet I think she was wrong. She took a dislike to me and could never get over it.

The first time she quarreled with me was at the time of the great slump. Bobby Brown had finished school that year, and he had won a prize at Oxford, forty pounds a year. So, though he had not meant to go to college, now he was eager. Mr. W. was pleased about this, and delighted about the prize. But then it turned out Bobby's father would not pay for him. Mr. W. would have to pay.

This, coming on top of the slump, upset Mr. W. very much, and this was the first time he talked to me in a private way, about his affairs and told me his troubles. Even then I don't think he would have forgotten his manners, if it had not happened one night that he fell asleep in my arms; our first night that year, at Tolbrook.

Indeed we had both been very sleepy and both of us fell asleep. I don't know how it was, but waking up like that in a strange bed at a strange time, for it was dawn and the birds were singing, he seemed to forget himself and instead of getting up and going off, as he usually had done all these years, with a polite "Good night, I hope you will sleep well," or "It's very good of you, Mrs. Jimson. I hope I haven't disturbed you too much," he began to talk freely.

"Is this Wednesday?" he said, and when I said it was, he burst out: "Then it's the day of the lawn meet here." So I said yes to that too.

Now the hunt had always upset Mr. W., for he did not hunt himself. Indeed, he had meant to be a clergyman, before his elder brother was killed in the war, and he had to look after the property and the nephews; and this was another reason why he hated all the burden of the houses. He said they had spoiled his life.

"A perfect nuisance," he said, "and more expense. I'm sick of it. It's a damnable life."

I was surprised to hear him swear in my presence. For though he had burst out at Bobby and even Mr. Loftus, he had never forgotten himself with a servant. So I said that so long as he didn't let too many of the hunters into the house and kept the whisky back and pushed the three-shilling sherry, I hoped it would go off under five pounds.

"Five pounds," he said. "Twenty guineas subscription and the chicken fund. It's the life of a convict—a life sentence."

"But you see the neighbors and they like to come." So I said how everyone admired Tolbrook.

"I wish I'd never seen it," he said, "or No. 15—a couple of white elephants that are eating me into the bankruptcy court. And now I'm to pay out a thousand pounds for

217

Master Bobby, because his father has some crackbrain prejudice against the universities."

Now here comes in what they said was influence. Miss Clary and I were both fond of Bobby and we wanted to see him get his rights. Miss Clary had been at Mr. W. already, many times, to get him pocket money, or clothes, when, poor lad, he had grown out of his suits like a charity boy, and now it was my turn. For both of us knew the poor boy was looking forward to Oxford like a birthday party. He was expecting wonders from Oxford, not only enjoyments, but discoveries, about the way the world really worked and what he should do to help it on. Of course he wanted to row too, and to drink beer, like any boy out of school and why should he not while he was young? But he truly wanted knowledge, which is like a boy too, of that age. I really loved Bobby at eighteen. He was little and ugly, but good all through, not a speck of meanness in his whole body. If he was noisy and sometimes seemed to be rude, it was only that he did not stop to think, or know what it was like for old people to be old. Why should he know the pains of that state, not only the rheumatism, and the not sleeping, but the great heavy cares and the wondering: What shall I do in this or that, and Have I done right or wrong, and also all the memory of all their mistakes and sins to confuse them about their duty.

If Bobby was sometimes rude to Mr. W., it was not out of unkindness, or socialism, but only because of what he could not know, which makes all the young ones impatient with our old dillydally.

So finding Mr. W. in so soft a mood, I spoke to him about Bobby's hopes, and I said also how much he looked to Mr. W. as his father, since his own father was so unnatural.

218

Mr. W. was surprised, and perhaps I made a little more of it than was true. For I was carried off by my hopes. And he agreed that Bobby was a good lad in spite of the nonsense he picked up at school.

Yet as for influence, no sooner had I got him to that, than he fell away again and said that good lad as Bobby was, Oxford might spoil him. For as Mrs. Loftus had said, it was full of Socialists and playboys, a disgrace to their class.

Then he got quite furious again, and when I had turned him off Bobby, he cursed at the hunt, at the farmers, at the Tolbrook roof, which was leaking in twenty places, and even the collections. He meant all the things collected by his grandmother, china and jewelry and stamps and medals, which were in glass cases about the house or packed away in the attics.

He said it cost him two hundred pounds a year only to insure them and they were nothing but rubbish. So I got up my courage and said that I thought Captain and Mrs. Loftus were wanting him to sell No. 15 and let them live at Tolbrook.

"Captain Loftus is a very useless person," he said. "Why, he's a rich man at the rate he lives—doesn't need to spend anything. But of course he's a regular miser." So he went on at the captain for ten minutes or more, that he was a disgrace to his order, and a parasite on society, till I had to stop him for fear he would say too much and be ashamed before me.

"It's quite light," I said.

"So it is," he said, surprised. I think he must have had his eyes closed before. Then he noticed that he had his arm around my neck, and he gave a little cough and after a moment said: "Bless me, where's my handkerchief?" for

219

an excuse to take the arm away without hurting my feelings.

Then he blew his nose and said in his old voice: "I'm afraid I went to sleep, Mrs. Jimson. I hope I haven't been a great nuisance to you."

"Oh, no, sir," I said.

"I didn't keep you awake?"

"Oh, no, sir. I slept very well."

"Then perhaps I had better be going. Good night, Mrs. Jimson," and he went off. But his voice had been getting more and more polite and I thought that I had been too late after all in calling him to his recollection. I was quite right, for he hardly spoke to me for a month and never came to visit me at all. On the other hand, he was very kind in his messages and would send down after every meal to say he had appreciated it.

Now, of course, I had a new idea of Mr. W. and I saw how the poor man had cause to be troubled about expenses; for whether reasonable or not, he felt them a burden. So I went to him and told him some ways he could save; on the coke, for instance, and on the laundry, by doing away with the tablecloths which he used in the dining room, cloths three yards by two, three times a week, for his own use only. He thanked me very much, and we cut down the coke, but not the tablecloths, because the Loftuses had done away with theirs and he could never bear to follow them, even if he took Mrs. L.'s advice. For she got her way, for all our economies, and Mr. W. said he could not afford Oxford. And Bobby was to go into a bank.

But the poor boy would not go into a bank. And the end of it was the Queensport Estate Agency, which, indeed, I advised, to get him used to managing property.

Then Bobby liked the work so much and did so well that

all were delighted with him and Mr. W. began to consult him about the Tolbrook property.

Now when, next year, Bobby was to come of age, it seemed he would be made heir. We gave him a hint of it, to mind his arguments with Mr. W. and make no trouble about names, if Mr. W. wanted him to change his. Miss Clary said it was snobbery to take any notice of names at all. The thing was to study what was right and what was wrong. And he was the only man to do right at Tolbrook.

Miss Clary was always my stand-by with Bobby and Mr. W. She could bring them around to things I dared not touch. She was clever and besides, she was a lady and understood the minds of that class, as I never could. For one minute you would think it was all religion with them, and money nothing; in the next, money was all and religion nothing. But, of course, money for them often comes out as duty, and so religion, while for the poor, money is always money only, because there is not enough of it to be duty. So Bobby agreed that if he had the property, he would be Wilcher Brown, and yet, as I said, it was not against his religion, because the property was so big that it was his duty to get it and improve it.

Chapter Sixty-Eight

BUT THEN he got out such a plan for improvement, as he called it, at Tolbrook, as frightened Miss Clary and me into fits. For half the house was to come down, or be turned into barns and byres; and all those elms and oaks in the shady fields were to be cut and sold; and the little fields themselves to be drained and turned into very big fields for the tractors.

But we knew it was no good talking to Bobby about the look of things, so we went at him about Mr. W. If he saw such a scheme as that, we said, turning Tolbrook into a farm, all among the smell of cows and pigs and manure, with the fleas hopping out of every man's trouser-turns, as soon as he came into the house, and the flies blackening the ceilings, then good-by to his hopes.

"Get the place first," I said, "and then try your improvements—a little at a time. For you know Tolbrook's is as much your uncle's home as 15, and he loves every crack in the plaster like the face of a friend."

"I wouldn't take the place," Bobby said, "except on my own terms. As it is, it is good for nothing and doesn't even pay its way."

And I told him he was an obstinate, foolish boy. "I'm sorry, Sara," he said, a bit put out, "but what else can I do?"

So we told him again to keep his scheme back for a while for all our sakes and his father's too. That made him think, and he pondered for a moment or two, but then he gave a sigh and said: "No, it wouldn't work." Then he pinched my chin as he loved to do and said: "It's no good, Nanny, you can wangle your way through a brick wall but you couldn't wangle me out of this. If I took Tolbrook on your terms, it would soon come to a real split with Uncle, and I don't want that, for after all, he does mean well—though he is such a footling old fossil."

So he sent in his scheme. And what was our surprise when Mr. W. said it was just what he wanted.

"Tolbrook will be a real manor again," he said, "the center of country work. Making its own bread and its own

222

beer, and the squire of Tolbrook will be a real country-man, as in the old days of Domesday, when lords could not write their name. And he said how wise he had been not to send Bobby to Oxford.

So off he went to the West, to see Bobby and go over the place with him. For Bobby was to do what he liked. No money spared till it began to come back again. Bobby was to be the manager and bailiff so that when he came into the property, he would know all about it.

Chapter Sixty-Nine

THE NEXT thing we knew was that Tolbrook had been let for seven years to a rich young man called Few-less, who had made a fortune in wireless sets. He was to pay a very big rent and put the whole place in order, and a new floor in the ballroom.

It was Madame Loftus who had found the tenant and made the agreement. As for Bobby, he knew nothing about it. He had not even quarreled with Mr. W., who still liked the scheme greatly. But he had said: "Now this tenant has turned up, who will mend the roofs and put the gardens in order. Perhaps we had better see how the old place shapes with plenty of new money before we undertake any new big change."

Bobby was disgusted and I don't blame him. He went off next year to Canada and worked his own way up to a farm and we did not see him again for years. Mrs. Loftus was in triumph. And in the same month she took Tolbrook rectory for herself, and her husband out of the Army, to have her finger in all pies there and to get the poor captain into playing the squire. Indeed, she was like the squire from that time, for Mr. Fewless, not being born for that troublesome work, could not be bothered with it, and never learned even the names of his own workers.

And when Mrs. L. next came to London, she walked into my kitchen one day and said: "Let me give you a little piece of advice, Mrs. Jimson, to mind your own business. You fancy yourself as having influence with your master, but a woman in your position had better be careful, or she may end in very serious trouble. I believe you have been in prison once already."

I was going to say that this was not true. But then, I thought that perhaps it was not worth making so much difference between the dock and the prison, and besides, I was so startled by the woman's fierceness, for I didn't know how I'd deserved it. So I went on with my ironing, not looking at her. I was ironing Mr. W's., suit, which I had cleaned too. I saved ten pounds a year on cleaning.

Now whether she thought I was being rude in not answering her, though it was only that her tone of voice took my breath away, she burst out again and said I had better give in my notice. "If you had any sense, you'd get out while you can do it quietly, without a scandal. And if you think you have Mr. W. so much in your clutches that he can't escape, you'll find yourself very much mistaken there, too. Mr. Wilcher may have his faults, but he is a very religious man at bottom, and he always comes around to his religious duty. Remember that he was with that other wretched creature for more than thirty years, and left her in the end. And he is turning against you already. I know the signs. As for his money, if that's what you're waiting for, I've seen to that. There's not going to be any settlements this time. That was his mistake with Mrs. Eeles, as I told him. And he quite agreed. After she had nothing more to expect she did just what she liked and treated him abominably. No, he's had his lesson. You will never get your settlement, Mrs. Jimson or Monday, or whatever your real name is." And out she went, quite raging.

But, I thought, what is my influence worth, when Mr. W. drives away Bobby to Canada and lets Tolbrook, with my kitchen and my garden, so that I can't see it again for seven years?

None of that came out at the trial. But how could it? There was no room.

Chapter Seventy

BUT AS for my robberies, that was another thing and I still wonder at myself. For at this very time, when I was helping Mr. W. to economize, and cutting down even his own dinners, I was still cheating him. How I came into this double way of life, I cannot tell, except that I got used to my pickings; and that I was bound to send something to Gulley; and I had made an agreement with myself never to use my savings.

You may wonder how I got any money from Mr. W. when he went through the bills every week and counted the legs and wings of the chickens, but I had a dozen tricks. I must have been a born rogue for I was never at a loss. For I told Mr. W. it was a great economy for me to have money in my pocket to get bargains when I saw them, of fruit and dusters and cleaning stuff and brooms and mats. So I would take a pound a week and spend five shillings or less, and bring up to Mr. W. a bundle of dusters and say: "Isn't this a bargain?" To be honest, the one bundle did for six bargains. For how was the poor gentleman to know how long a duster lasted, or a drying cloth!

Then I would bring him a broom and he would feel the handle, and raise his eyebrows, and look down through the hairs and say: "H'm, that's the weak part, in brooms, but I admit this one *seems* all right," as if he knew all about brooms. But, of course, he had no idea if they cost a pound or a shilling.

So I cheated the poor man. And yet I was always in debt. A pound a week was the least I could send to Gulley, who never asked much from anyone and could fairly have asked for my life, and though I was getting, then, seventy pounds a year wages, I was expensive in clothes. Nothing would fit me from the cheap lines, and the truth was, I could never bear cheap stuff anywhere near my skin. I believe my stockings were often as good as Mrs. Loftus', though, of course, I did not show them. Mr. W. liked his servants in the old long skirts, and I was very willing to wear them, for they gave me height and took off from my hips, but I always loved to have some yards of good silk dashing around my ankles. So I made a bargain with my conscience by telling Mr. W. he could take something off my wages to cut his staff expenses. And he was so pleased and so grateful and so respectful of my goodness that I nearly confessed to him the truth. But I did not, thinking of all the trouble it would make, and he took off five pounds, which gave me some comfort in my conscience for that time.

Chapter Seventy-One

THAT WAS just when Bobby had gone to Canada and Mr. W. was still so upset I thought he would lose his wits. I was upset too, for the boy came to say good-by to me, one afternoon, without warning, and I was out, so when I got his note, I had to take a taxi to Victoria Station and run all the way down the platform, and I was in such a state of heat and worry, I hardly knew how to speak to him. Then, too, with the excitement, I lost hold of myself and began to cry, which I never did before, on a platform. So I forgot all I had to say and only hoped he had said a proper good-by to Mr. W.

But he said no. He had only wanted to see me, who had been as good as his mamma.

I said nonsense, he mustn't quarrel with Mr. W., who was his only friend in trouble, having the capital to set him up; and he must write a very kind letter that day and explain that he had not been able to see him in the rush. He promised me, and so we parted. But I was upset for a week after, fearing I would never see the poor lad again and perhaps didn't look after Mr. W. as well as I should have, especially in his time of trouble. I had noticed, indeed, that he was restless in the house, that he did not come to see me as usual. But I had thought it was because I kept on speaking of Bobby, and how good he was, to make his peace with Mr. W. Perhaps too much. But as I say, I was upset and not myself.

However, it was one afternoon, I think it was the Saturday after Bobby left, for I know I was having a good cleanup of the kitchen copper and the brass, which I usually did on Saturday, to be bright for Sunday, when I looked up through the area grating and saw a policeman turn in at the door with two girls, and one of them making a hullabaloo.

Then my heart fell into my stomach and I thought: It's come at last, the poor unhappy gentleman. But what have I been thinking of? I ran upstairs as fast as I could go, to answer the door myself.

The gentleman asked if there was a gentleman in the house with a white face, a bald head and spectacles, in a gray suit and spats. I said no. But the girls began to scream that they had followed him and saw him come in at this door. The policeman asked who owned the house and if Mr. Wilcher answered to the description given. I said no, but he asked if Mr. Wilcher was in.

I said no again, so he said that he must examine the house. He came in then, and left the girls in the hall to watch the door, and looked through the whole house. But he found nothing, and went away, saying only that when Mr. Wilcher came in he had better report at the police station. I couldn't make out where Mr. Wilcher had gone till I was shutting up the attic and heard a noise on the roof. So I put my head out of the window and there the poor man was, down behind a chimney stack, only his head looking around and terrified to move. It made my heart turn over to think how he must have crawled along the parapet to get to the stack. So I said: "I beg your pardon, sir. Shall I get the cleaners with the ladders? I could say you were looking at the broken slates."

"No, no," said he, "I will come back if you will kindly hold out a stick—I believe there is a curtain pole which would reach me."

228

So I pulled out the curtain pole and jammed the end behind the parapet and he crept along again and I helped him in. You never saw such a state he was in, dirt from head to foot and both knees out of his best suit.

But he was trembling too, and pale as china. I didn't say anything about the policeman for I thought: He knows I wouldn't be here if they were here, and as for going to the station, I'll say I forgot it and so it will be my fault.

"I thought I would have a look for that leak," he said, "but it was not as easy as it looked."

"Good gracious," I said, "no indeed, you might have been killed." I felt so sorry for him then, trembling like a frightened child and so brave, too, in keeping up his dignity, that I could have cried. "I hope you'll never do that again, sir," I let out. But he gave me a sharp look as if to say: "Mind your own business, my girl," and answered dryly enough: "Perhaps you'd better bring me up another suit, I don't want to be seen in this state."

So he changed in the attic and told me not to say he had been on the roof.

But he was summonsed and there was a paragraph in the paper; and though luckily they had the address wrong, the family were all in terror. They went to lawyers and Mrs. Loftus was for putting him in an asylum, if he would not go abroad. Miss Clary was the only sensible one of them all, as usual, and she came to me in the kitchen and said: "What he wants is a wife. It's what he's always needed. Why don't you marry him, Sara, or couldn't you stand it?"

"How could I marry the master?" I asked her.

"You could make him if you liked. He's terrified of scandal."

I was shocked at that. "So am I," I said, "and I have too much respect for Mr. Wilcher to think of such things."

229

"And you used to be a lady," she said, "if you forgive the word—you're quite equal to the part, you know, more than many."

I told her no, that I had never been a lady, and though Mr. Monday had been a gentleman of very good family, he had been a simple good kind of man too, and easily satisfied in everything.

"If you don't marry him," she said, "he'll end in jail. It might even come to murder—the old idiot is so tied up in himself that he's not safe. I can only thank God that it's not children he gets after, or he'd be there already."

So I said that Mr. Wilcher was a good man and a natural man in all ways, given a natural life.

"Well," she said, "I'm not married and I don't feel any necessity to run about the streets and exhibit myself with pocket torches or tickle women in Hyde Park."

"It's different for women," I said, "because of the build."

The poor child said that it was, very different. For a man could always get a wife if he wanted one and a girl never be sure of a husband.

"They tell me it's a time of confusion," she said, "when the young people are so muddled with nonsense they don't know what they want or what to believe; but I don't see any confusion. I know what I want and what I believe but I can't get what I want and it doesn't make any difference what I believe because the papers are making such a silly noise."

She meant about the young. For as she always said to me, she never saw anyone like the young in real life. Miss Clary hated all the papers.

"Well," I said, "the papers must live and they say the

230

competition is terrible. So they have to make a bigger noise now than they used to."

"I wish it wasn't such a silly noise," she said, "because poor old mummies like Uncle Wilcher swallow their papers whole and think we are a terrible lot, and that the country is going to the bitches."

That was to shock me. So I was not shocked. I said only that Mr. W. was no mummy, but a living man and living men could often change their whole minds. Just as Mr. W. had surprised us about poor Bobby's scheme.

"Men can do a lot," the poor child said. "It's a man's world and so it will be until we have polygamy, like the Africans, and we can all live at peace in our own families and just send for a good husband when we need him. Then I could borrow my flower among men for a day or two."

"Perhaps it would be enough," I said.

"Of course it would," she said, "I know I'd be tired of him in the house. But that's no consolation as you ought to know if you've ever been in love."

She was laughing at me; but almost crying too. And so we changed the subject.

I was always heartbroken for Miss Clary and the waste of such goodness and sense, and indeed for all the waste of nice sensible girls going on everywhere. For, of course, there weren't enough men at that time for these girls born to be wives and mothers, and wasted in singleness. Not that I agreed with Miss Clary's plan, which was half a joke. But I remembered the old country ways, where I know if there were not enough men, still the girls managed to find babies, and to bring them up too, and to make a home. As widows must do; and often the best of homes.

Chapter Seventy-Two

THE SUMMONS was put off for a week by Mrs, Loftus, who got a medical certificate that Mr. W. had a heart attack. Mr. W. promised to stay in the house, to save the doctor's face, but he seemed to take no interest in the case. He said it was all nonsense and a mistake. And he did not even obey the certificate, for at night he went out into the gardens or the streets and walked about. But I could see that he was shaken, for he came to me all times of the day and night and we had long interesting talks. It was then I really got to know the master and his true religious heart. For true religion is in the heart or it is nowhere. Of course, we never spoke of the summons, but sometimes of new savings, which Mr. W. was always thinking of. I encouraged him indeed, for whether he needed to save or not, it was a hobby for his mind, and kept him out of mischief. Or he would talk of books. This was the time he began again to speak of reading. For one evening I went out to the garden to find him, seeing by the lamps that there were some nursemaids still there, and I saw him on a seat, doing nothing. And before I could slip away, he saw me and asked me to admire the sky. "I often see you in the garden," he said. And I said that I always liked these gardens because the elms reminded me of Tolbrook.

"But you won't see such a sky," he said, "except in London, because only the smoke in the air can give that color. It's like old varnish, and makes every London view into an old master."

It was true that the clouds were like old fiddles and the blue between as dark and rich as ammonia bottles, full of light too, because still soaking in the sun. I always liked that time when the gardens were in shade and the shadows of the chimney pots on the odd side fell on the evens; but the tops of the trees were still like African islands, in the warmth.

It was late October, but some leaves were still hanging in the top branches, twiddling in the breath of air as bright as new sovereigns. I said I wished all that gold could pay the taxes, but he was not in that mood. He answered that beauty was a jewel beyond gold just because it had no price. "Any poor outcast could enjoy it, perhaps better than we, having no worldly cares. But you understand that better than I do, Sara."

It was always one of his ideas since Tolbrook, that I was a very religious woman, and I think he always had the idea that the poor were nearer Heaven than the rich. In prayers he would always read those bits about the rich man and the camel and the needle's eye, or the young man with great possessions, who turned away sorrowfully, with a very strong voice. He would even pause after them, as if to let them sink in. And would say to us: "How could the rich, with all their comforts safe, feel God's mercies; and without feeling, how could they remember Providence?"

So, too, he would pick up some country word of mine and improve it, like:

> Grace and disgrace
> Are twins in every place.

or:

> The first breath
> Is the beginning of death.

Then he would say to me that it did him good to talk about religion with me because of my good, old-fashioned training. "You believe that we have souls to be saved or ruined and so do I. But you have kept your soul alive and I have nearly smothered mine under law papers and estate business and the cares of the world. Under talk too, for I talk too much about religion and forget that it is not a matter of words, but faith and works and vision."

I thought that he did not know my soul. But I did not say so, for it would have done no good. Mr. W. was a truly religious man, but he was also obstinate in his own way.

Chapter Seventy-Three

SO TONIGHT I saw he was in a religious mood and not ready to talk about the bills. And sure enough:

"How is your reading going?" he asked. "I was looking into one of your favorites only today, the *Pillars of the House*, where poor Underwood dies leaving a sick wife and thirteen children."

Then he said that no modern writer would dare to write such a book; people would laugh at it. "They laugh at everything good or noble or unselfish. They don't seem to understand what life can be like, and that people really did feel and do fine things and lead noble lives or try to lead them, when that book was written."

So then I was delighted and said that was what I had always told my girls, and believed. That it was not Miss Yonge's fault if the men in her books seemed too good or the women too gentle, but the world's. Because I knew from my mother that in her time, before the old queen lost her prince, there were many good clergymen, who tried to be saints, and that many girls were brought up just as soft and forbearing as Violet Martindale or Amy Marville. It was the fashion then for good men to be saintly and girls sweet and dutiful, and so they had been, many of them.

Mr. Wilcher was so eager to agree with me that he would not let me finish. "Yes," he said, "exactly. Just what I tell Clarissa," and "People are what you make them. They may laugh at Underwood, but he wasn't a drifter, at any rate."

Now I have always thought that in real life I mightn't have been so patient with Mr. Underwood, having a child every year; but still I'm sure it was better for a clergyman to be a saint, even if difficult in life, and to obey God's law as he thought it, of multiplying, than stay just an ordinary man and make nothing of himself or of life either.

So I said. And Mr. Wilcher answered me that it was the big clergyman's families made the Empire when it was a great thing, with a Christian purpose. "My own father," he said, "when he went to India as colonel of his regiment, would have no subaltern that did not go regularly to Communion, and he had prayer meetings for the men too, and taught them how to fight the good fight. For it is a fight," he said.

So he was so interested that when I went in to begin the cooking, he followed me to the very kitchen, to go on about the fight. We had only one maid and a daily woman then, in our saving time, and luckily both were out. So while I was stirring up the fire, for we had no gas stove yet, except a ring, he walked around the kitchen table like an admiral on the deck and said that life was truly a battle, a terrible

235

battle, "and the trouble is the enemy goes on changing his uniform and his plans. Now, in my father's day," he said, "a country gentleman knew what he had to do and felt his responsibility—so did a lawyer like my Uncle John, who was my father's eldest brother. They always worked together and fought cheap corn and tried to keep up the country life and the country ways and parsons."

For Mr. W. loved the old ways, as I did. When the parlormaid came in, he pretended to have come about the dinner, and went off and had his dinner like a gentleman, dressed and bathed, with candles. But at night he was up with me from ten o'clock almost till morning, talking, till, indeed, my head went around. For though I could sleep while he talked, especially since all our lights were fused, on the top story, for the last six months, and he would not waste candles by keeping them alight—yet if he heard me breathe a little loud or snore, it naturally put a damper on his spirits, poor gentleman. For he was too polite to wake me, except by fidgets or coughing, as if he did not mean it, even to himself.

Chapter Seventy-Four

ALL THIS time, the family were having the greatest trouble with him to get him to defend himself in court, or even to put off the case. For there was a hope that if the case was put off, a little longer, the girl would cool down and perhaps come to a settlement privately. But Miss Clary told me it was regular diplomacy to do it, for if she should get an offer and change her mind again, then she would have a fine tale to tell and the case would be lost. So the thing was to go through a friend of hers, and first by hints.

But Mr. W. would do nothing and even I could not get him to see the lawyer or the doctor. Yet the summons was put off, and the next thing we heard, the girl would say she had made a mistake; and the police had caught somebody else who had a title, and the case would make a bigger noise than Mr. W.'s and so do the government good, in Wales.

We were all delighted and Mrs. Loftus, I'll own, had won a great triumph. For it was her go and her contrivance that had done it all. I always admired Mrs. Loftus for her great backbone and her never letting go. You couldn't beat her down.

But Mr. W. went really very queer, at least for a while. I must confess it for the truth's sake and to cover myself. I have said that he had been strange all that week and more talkative than ever before. It was Mrs. Loftus telephoned in the evening that "it would be squashed or not come on at all," meaning the summons, for Mrs. Loftus had given orders we must never write or telephone the word summons in case it got to the police; and I took the message, being alone in the house. Then I ran out to the garden to tell Mr. W., but he was talking to the estate gardener, a great friend of his, about the new bulbs to be planted. And when I said: "Oh, sir, Mrs. Loftus has rung up to say that it's all off and you needn't trouble," he only looked at me and said, after a minute: "Thank you, Mrs. Jimson," in a flat kind of voice.

I thought him queer then. And what was queerest still he ate no dinner to speak of and did not come to see me till two in the morning. It gave me a fearful shock to see him

237

then, in his long nightshirt, like a ghost; and without his spectacles, which made him screw up his eyes in an unnatural way.

"Mrs. Jimson, Sara," he whispered, "are you awake?"

Then I waked quite up and said: "For gracious' sake, sir, don't stand there in the draft, with your bare legs." For, as I said, my room was as cold as an icehouse, all winter, with only matting on the floor, and no fire able to be lighted, because there was a brick fallen across the chimney. The ceiling was in holes, too, where the plaster was down and the draft, not to speak of the rain, coming through the slates on the roof.

I was always in terror that Mr. W. would catch pneumonia in those bitter winter nights and, indeed, he had noticed the cold himself, and had said more than once the room was a disgrace, and he must get an electric-fire and a plug. But he had always forgotten or perhaps found that they would cost too much and now the wiring was found so rotten that the electric company wanted us to renew it. I was glad only that, at the time of his many troubles, he took to staying the whole night and keeping warm. I'll own it at once, I liked the feel of a husband again, though it was only to talk about bills.

Now I begged him to jump in quick, and opened the clothes for his poor shaking legs. But he did not seem to listen. He came over to the bed and put down the candle in the middle of the floor, and sat down on the chair with his head in his hands against the bed. I thought he was going to say his prayers, as he did sometimes in my room, though only when he came at his usual bedtime; and I wondered if I had better get out and say mine too, for company. For if he was early, and before I had said my prayers, we would have to say them at the same time. Indeed we

238

had often said our prayers at the same time, though, of course, I would keep a little distance. Our prayers were still our own business, not being man and wife.

But then I heard him talking aloud and I could not believe my ears; he was asking me to save him. And he said all he had said before, in little pieces, over years, about my influence, and my being his help and stay and a messenger from Providence, to save his soul alive. The upshot was, he was going to give himself up to the police, and go to prison, and afterward, if I would have him, he would marry me and live in a poor way, in some quiet place.

I saw now the poor man had gone mad with his nerves, and I knew it was dangerous to contradict him, so I said: "Yes" and "Yes," and of course I would and could do anything if only he would get into the warm out of the draft. For I knew for a certainty that if he did not he would get his lumbago, or perhaps sciatica, and be laid up; and Mr. W., for all his goodness, was a misery to himself and to everyone else, ill in bed, especially on the third story, with only two servants to bring up his meals and his letters.

But he would not get in. He said he was not fit. And he confessed that he had done all the girl had said, and worse to others, for years, out of pure wickedness. He had given way to the Devil all his life, and the worst was he had known all his life his real duty, which was to put off worldly things and follow God's commands.

I saw that he was well started, and nothing would turn him, so I put the eider down over him and tucked it over his shoulders and around his thighs as well as I could.

Then he asked me again if I would take him, after the prison, and I said of course I would. But he would not get into bed until he had told me a lot more about his crimes, and how he saw nothing would save him but a public confession, to break his evil pride and put him right with God.

I thought that there were as many traps in humility as pride, and that the Devil's best hook was baited with confession. For I had found out even as a child that a quick confession could save me a slapping and a bad conscience too, and so, back to the jam. But, of course, I did not say so to Mr. W. in his wild state. I agreed with everything he said and so got him at last into bed and he was as frozen as if he had been out of a refrigerator. I fairly got to work and rubbed some life into him. Not that he paid any more attention than a hospital patient, but went on talking about the badness of his life and the need for a new start, from the bottom.

But I was too late, for he did get his sciatica, and a nice job it was to get him back to his own room before the housemaid found him in mine. Luckily he was a lightweight and so in the end, I took him up, master or no master, and wrapped him in the eider down, and carried him downstairs like a baby. Then I rang up Miss Clary, early as it was, to give her a hint that the poor gentleman was shaking in his mind, and might yet do something foolish.

Chapter Seventy-Five

MR. W., when ill, as I say, was troublesome. And now he would not let me out of his sight. I got the hot-water bottles for his leg and slipped away to get breakfast; but he would have me back, to confess, and to talk. They say mad people must either eat or talk, and if so, I thought, the master was certainly mad.

For now he had got onto religion again and a new wobble. He changed right around from what he had said only yesterday, that the old ways were the best. Now he said that old ways were done and just as a rose will go bad and stink out a whole room, so the old religion, beautiful as it had been, was a poison to the world. We must go back again to the beginning and be as little children learning from our father without book; or like the early Christians, who lived together and had everything in common.

Of course I agreed with all and, indeed, I often thought that you couldn't go back on a fashion. For say what you will, fashions never do go backward, and now if we had saints again, and good family women delighting in children, they would be a different brand from the old, just as are figures since the slump; and now woman need not try to make herself look like a bicycle pump, only for fashion, yet the figures are new, with big waists; a good thing, I daresay, for those that like their food.

So I said to Mr. W. that it was the wine and the leather bottles, and he said: Yes, and the wine was still good; it was only the bottles were rotten.

Chapter Seventy-Six

THE NEXT thing was that when I came in from shopping all the family were there, Miss Clary, the captain, and Mrs. Loftus, who was with Mr. W., and Miss Clary came to warn me Mrs. L. had heard about his offer to me and was getting him around.

"Don't stand any nonsense," she said. "Make him marry you. It's the only way to save him."

"How could I make him?"

"Bring an action. Breach, or something. He's terrified of scandals. They all are. You'd have thought that summons was the end of the world. You've got to fight, Sara, or she'll turn you out. That's what she's driving at."

I said I hated scandals too, and I had to think of my family. Besides, I did not really believe that Mrs. Loftus could get me turned off, till I went up to change his bottles while the Loftuses were at luncheon, and he began to say that I mustn't mind Mrs. Loftus if she seemed a little impatient at times.

"She's young," he said, "and she's had a great deal on her shoulders. She's done wonderful work around Tolbrook, with the Sunday school and the institute and the flower show and the market stall, and now she's going to have a harvest home, quite in the old style. The place is really alive again. She and the captain have given it quite a fresh start of usefulness. All it needed was a little fresh capital and faith."

Mr. W. was always saying that what he admired about Mrs. Loftus was her faith. She really believed in the good old ways and that was why she made them work again.

So the poor man excused himself for his weakness and for not being able to make up his mind quick enough for Mrs. Loftus, who, though perhaps I oughtn't to say it, never had one to make up.

He had talked so before, as when he had let the manor and thrown poor Bobby over, but now I thought he looked more queerly. And when I said something about the case, he answered that it seemed he could not do anything more without bringing the girl into it and spoiling her character.

Well, I thought, as I went downstairs, Mrs. L. is a wonder to turn that poor manny around her finger.

But what a wonder I did not know till after luncheon when she came down into the kitchen and gave me a day's notice, with a month's wages. "I'm taking over the house-keeping," she said, "from tomorrow, and I shall make my home here and a home for Mr. Wilcher. And you will kindly not attempt to communicate with him. He does not wish it and I will take care it does not occur."

So out I went next morning, after thirteen years, with my box and my clothes, thankful only that she did not have me searched, like Mrs. Frewen. For be sure she would have made out that I had taken something; and I was always in terror of the police. I know they had my name in their books for the old trouble about the bad checks.

Chapter Seventy-Seven

THIS WAS on Monday, and on the Wednesday I was going to see my daughter Nancy at Bradnall, who was ill. So I spent one night in a servant's room at Miss Clary's hotel, where she lived then, and went on to Brad-nall on the Wednesday morning.

Poor Nancy was now my only daughter at home, for Belle was always traveling the world seeing sights, and Edith was in China, and Phyllis married in America, or so I hoped. For when she had gone away suddenly from Bradnall, at only seventeen, as traveling nurse to some American children, she had stayed over there and written to me that I was to address her as Mrs. Monday. Not a word of husband. But I thought: Why shouldn't she have mar-

243

ried a man of her own name? However it was with her, I knew she was happy and well, for she sent me presents every Christmas and always a note: "To my darling, with all my love," or "Dearest Mum, from her best lover." And the best note paper. Only a new address every time and she never answered a letter.

For many years, indeed, I had missed my girls. Even Nancy, though not far away, had never found it easy to see me, because her husband and his family had been so upset by my going off with Jimson, and being had up for writing bad checks. I do not mean she did not have a proper feeling for her mother, but only that my visits would have been a nuisance to her. So we wrote and sometimes met in London, for shopping and news.

But now Nancy was getting well into her thirties, and her children were all at school and away from home and she began to feel her affection and to want to see me. She wrote every week, letters which surprised me with their love, and often begged me to come and see her.

So I would go sometimes on a Wednesday when her husband was away from home and see her and let her have a good talk about the children, who, she said, were very unloving and ungrateful, and she was tired of them, and then I would catch the milk train and be back at Number 15 in time to see the master's breakfast on the tray. He never had but a tray to his bedroom, and only rolls and coffee, but yet if everything were not just so, the butter properly rolled, with a shaving of ice, and the coffee just the right strength, and the clean napkin folded around the rolls, he could not touch a morsel.

I had to be back to make sure of his breakfast, or he would go to work famished, and ready to faint.

So on this Wednesday morning, when I came out of the

tube, I forgot that I had been sacked and turned into Craven Gardens. It was habit. And I could not make out what had happened. It was not yet half-past seven and the streets were empty and strange, as streets seem on such a morning when the sky is already light, but no one moving; but Craven Gardens full, and two policemen at the corner.

Then I saw fire engines and I asked where the fire was, and they said: "At fifteen."

I almost fell down. "Oh," I said, "that's my own house and I must get through at once. I must know about the master."

An inspector came along then, with Miss Clary, who was in trousers like a man. She told me that Mr. W. was safe and lying down in one of the neighbor's. The fire had started at the top and he had got out by the stairs. But it had been such a quick and bad fire that almost nothing was saved. An old trunk and hatboxes from the boxroom, thrown out by the housemaid, no one knows why, for they were empty, and some of the collections from the glass cases, which the firemen and Loftuses had saved. The Loftuses had taken all the snuffboxes and gone off to their flat. As for Mr. W., he had brought off only some miniatures and stamps, which he kept under his bed.

Miss Clary said that he was in such a state that the doctor had put him to bed, and no one was to go near him. I could do nothing. So I went back with Miss Clary and had breakfast and afterward we went to see the ruins. But the salvage men would not let us near.

We did not see the master for three days. But he did not see the Loftuses either. Indeed, he had broken off with them, but Miss Clary said it was really because Mrs. Loftus had gone at him till he couldn't bear it any longer.

Instead of going to Mrs. Loftus he came to Miss Clary,

245

but so shaky and worn down, I scarcely knew him. He would jump at a sound, and when he saw me for the first time, he said only: "A clean sweep, Mrs. Jimson—I can't believe it yet."

Then the insurance people came and nearly drove him and all of us mad with their questions. About the wiring of the house, and why it had been neglected, and when the fire was first noticed, and even why I had been away that night from my room, which was next the attic, where, it was said, the fire started. You would have thought they were accusing the master of setting fire to his own house.

Yet I had a fright too, for when I met the housemaid, a girl called Halley, who was in a new place, she told me that the master had been in the attic that evening of the fire only a little while before he knocked on her door and asked her if she smelled smoke. "He went up three or four times before dinner, and it's my belief that he started the fire by tinkering at those wires—and not just all by accident, either."

I thought perhaps Mr. W. might have had an accident with the wires, trying to put in a fuse, and that was why the insurance company made him so angry, fearing it would not pay him. So I told Halley, the master was the last man to burn his own house, where he was born. "No," I said, "you've been reading about the fire-raisers in the paper."

"So has the master," she said, "and if it was his home, perhaps he didn't want Mrs. Loftus to take it from him. He wanted to keep on in his own way."

She meant to keep on with me, so I answered her pretty sharply:

What nonsense, a gentleman like Mr. W. didn't go in for fire-raising and she'd better keep such scandalous talk to herself. "The fire was a fire," I said, "like any other and we had been due for a fire anyhow, with the bad state of the wiring, and that old house full of treasures, and no other fire or even a robbery since it was built, eighty years."

"Of course, I wouldn't say a word," she said, "except to you. Didn't you see how I answered the insurance man? As if I was going to save money for the insurance, with their millions, when they take sixpence off my wages every week."

What a providence, I thought, to send us a girl that was a very good maid and clever enough to see so far into her master; and yet so foolish that she mixed up all the insurance together, and thought a gentleman's company, like Mr. W.'s, was all one with the government robbers.

Chapter Seventy-Eight

THE MASTER was so ill that we thought he would die. But on the Saturday he took a better turn and on the Sunday he got up and carried me off to early service. Not a word about my notice nor the Loftuses. Though I knew he had quarreled with them about my notice, of course he could not well say anything against Mrs. L. to me. But when I was going to a separate pew, he took me by the arm and turned me into the same one with himself. Afterward he seemed very cheerful and spoke of the great consolation of the church; how it gives the same comfort to all, good or bad, if only they will receive it. I saw he had taken a good turn and I told Miss Clary to see that he had the best dinner the hotel could give, and some wine, even if she paid for it. The good girl did give him wine, though she had to pay for it, and though he had given her only a ten-shilling note for her birthday; and it did him so much good that he came to me afterward up the back stairs, among the servants' rooms. Luckily I heard his step and slipped out and warned him that the hotel was very strict with servants and that the walls were very thin, and he might be reported, if he came in to me.

So he went down again. But the next day, when I was coming up the back stairs from our breakfast room, which was in the basement, he popped out from the dining-room floor, where he must have been lying in wait for me, and said: "Put on your hat, Mrs. Jimson, we're going out."

He looked so excited that I knew he had some new scheme and, sure enough, he took me straight to a registry, and before I knew whether I wanted to marry him or not, he gave in our notices. And from there he went straight, by the same taxi, to a place called Ranns Park, all new built, rows of little houses, red and green with pink roofs, like pastries in a shop window. We went to the office and out came a young man who took us to see one of these houses, to be finished next week, and for sale now.

Mr. W. went jumping on the floors and trying the windows and sniffing at the drains and he said to me: "You'd better look at the kitchen, Mrs. Jimson—that's your province."

"But are you taking it?" I asked.

"Why not?" he said, "I must have somewhere to live and this is clean and new, and I'm told the firm is moderately honest, as builders go. But, of course, if you don't like the kitchen, we'll try somewhere else."

Since he had given the registry notice Mr. W. was like a boy, full of briskness and mischief too. But he was not so polite to me. He said: "Do this," and "Do that," as if we had been married for years.

248

The kitchen was good enough, though no proper larder and a cellar like a boot box. But I hardly looked at it, I was wondering so much at Mr. W. coming to live in such a place, like any clerk. Yet he took it there and then and went and bought a houseful of furniture the next day and sent me for new pots and pans. I was settled in before the electric light was joined up or the plaster dry. But Mr. W. was mad to get the carpets down and the garden dug.

He himself was not going to live there until we were married. For he said he was not going to start his new life, in a new place, with a scandal. So he went back to his hotel every day and only came out to Bellavista, as the box was called, in the afternoon. But then he worked like six men, laying carpets and arranging the furniture, and hammering nails in the new plaster.

If Mr. W. still talked about his ruin, he was quite a new man from what he had been latterly at Number 15. I don't think that I ever saw such a change in a man. It was something that Miss Clary and I never stopped wondering at. I thought it was because Mrs. Loftus never came to see us and so never troubled him, for she had been so furious about his engaging to marry me at last that she said she would never speak to him again or come to the house while I was there. Only the captain came, as was his duty, but he never wondered at anything, he was too sleepy. He followed his uncle about while he was shown the garden and the kitchen and the bathroom and drawing room with its new furniture, and said only: "A bit poky."

Mr. W. was angry with him, and then he laughed and said that he had forgotten already how the rich felt. What most surprised me was how Mr. W. could like the furniture. I thought it was an ugly cheap lot, but he kept on saying that it was wonderful what they could do at the price. Then he bought tools and began to dig in the garden and set me to dig too. He would say in the evening before he went: "Sara, don't forget to try that new polish on the drawing room floor," or "Don't forget to dig the front bed —it will need double trenching."

It was a great pleasure to see him lively and interested. Miss Clary would laugh when she came out and found us both cutting or digging or staking, and say: "I wonder what Higgins would say of your efforts."

Higgins was the head gardener at Tolbrook. But Mr. W. never bothered to answer Miss Clary. They were very good friends, but I don't think he ever thought of her as more than a little girl whose talk was no more to him than a window rattling, or less. "Here," he would say, pushing a hoe into her hands, "can you hoe?—Don't cut down my new roses. If you hoe the whole bed, I'll give you a glass of sherry."

But he did not say when, and indeed he had no sherry in the house. For if we had lived carefully before and saved, we counted every penny now. The insurance people were still fighting Mr. W. They even sent a man out one morning early to ask me about the electric wires on the top story and why they had not been put in order, and if I had ever touched them or seen Mr. W. touch them. I said, of course, that both of us had put in new fuses several times, until we found that it was no good, because they always blew out the first night.

Mr. W. was so angry when he heard of this peeping work that he wanted to bring an action for defamation of character, but the other partners in his office would not let him.

So, as Mr. W. said he had no money, I had to live on kippers and margarine, and scrag end. I don't know how I would have managed for some extra expenses with Gulley if I had not had two lucky strokes in the same week. First, the salvage came in, and Mr. W. told me to throw away some old rubbish saved in a cardboard box. But I found some old brass chains in it which were a curiosity and which I sold for three pounds to an antique shop. The second was that Mr. Hickson, when I wrote to him for a loan, gave me fifty pounds for the drawings which were stored in his house all these years.

Chapter Seventy-Nine

NOW I must explain how I came to be having more expenses with Gulley. About two years before the fire, I met him in a strange way.

I hadn't seen much of Rozzie for the last years after Jimson and I took up together. She would never come to see us at Ancombe and we went only twice to see her at Brighton, where Jimson and she kept digging at each other all the time, and meaning to hurt. But just after the slump was at its worst, I had a letter from Rozzie saying she was ill in hospital, and would like to see me. I got leave that very day and went straight to her, for I was frightened. I wondered then at myself for not keeping up with her better. The truth was, I was never a great letter writer and she was worse, and so, though she was often in my thoughts, she had become a stranger. For the one in your thoughts is not the real one; and no loving thoughts will ever keep up a friend in the flesh as duty commands, and your own good.

I could not believe my eyes when I saw my poor Rozzie in the hospital, gone to skin and bone. She was not sixty, and she might have been eighty, with a folded face like an old worn-out shoe.

She had been knocked down by a lorry and lost her leg at the thigh. "And the same day," she said, "I heard that all my money was gone in the Mortimer Hotel's crash. I heard at breakfast and the lorry got me at half-past ten, going over to the Three Crowns for my morning drop, and when I woke up in hospital, I had my best laugh for years."

"Nothing to laugh at," I said, for I was almost crying. But Rozzie gave a heave and a kind of laugh and said: "You wouldn't, Sall—it wasn't your money and your best leg. I've still got the bad one."

The end of Rozzie was very sad. For when they got her well enough to go on crutches, she was still not fit to be about; and she had no money left. There was no place for her but the workhouse infirmary. Her only relation was her brother-in-law and he was in India and had his own wife and family. Besides, Rozzie would never be a burden on anyone. So there she was and there I went to see her three more times, before the leg broke out again and she died of blood poisoning.

"A good thing, too," she said, when they told her she was going. "I've been a fat lot of good, haven't I? I wonder why I was ever born—but I expect I was an accident— one at the start and one at the finish."

I told her how I respected her for the fight she had made, but all she said was: "I was bound to be tough and so you, too, had better be tough—the world being what it is."

But I thought that I could never go by Rozzie's way, for with all her fighting, what good did it do her? She was fighting for nothing.

I was shocked by the waste of her and I wanted to say a prayer for her or read something from St. John, espe-

252

cially the Revelation, which the old squire had been used to read at deathbeds. But she would not have it. "No consolations," she said, "I may be a good-for-nothing, but I've got my pride. And if I can't die happy, I won't go out howling. Don't break me down with your Bible stuff, Sall, or you'll make me sorry for myself. And I've no right to it."

So she still kept joking in her old style, saying: "If only they'd let me have my stays. They were always my best support in time of trouble and I wish I had them now to meet what's coming."

I asked her did they treat her kindly and she said: "Yes, but no allowances. Human nature can't be happy without that, as you know, Sall, and I tell you this place has more human nature to the pound of bones than you'd get in a stone of steaks, anywhere else, cut where you like and duchesses not barred."

Poor Rozzie, she wouldn't let me read to her or say a word of kindness, and she held herself up like a soldier, only to the last breath, when her face gave way, as if she was going to cry. But thanks to God, she had no time for it, her jaw fell, and she began to settle in. It was only then that a little water came out in the eyes.

Chapter Eighty

I WENT to the funeral, and indeed I paid for it. There was no one else and I couldn't bear to leave Rozzie in a pauper's grave behind me. I could never have slept in peace. But who should come to the funeral, the only other mourner, but Gulley. I didn't know him at first when I saw him in the chapel, among all the chairs turned wrong way up. The light was bad, and I thought him only one of the paupers. For he had a regular pauper's face, with his nose come right down to his lip, and his chin sticking out under it, and his eyes gone back into his head. I was crying too and could not notice anything except the miserable place, like a cellar, and the bearers yawning in their hats, while they pretended to be serious; and the clergyman gabbling, a mortuary clergyman paid by the piece, I suppose. It seemed so miserable an end for any human, let alone Rozzie with her great go and jump, with strength for two men and a heart like a lion; I was torn in two and fairly sobbed.

I must have looked quite drunk at the graveside with my hat crooked and my red eyes and nose and my hair coming down with my hat. I knew it, but I did not care, when I thought how I'd neglected Rozzie, all for a quarrel about a man like Gulley, who was not worth a day of her life.

It was only when I threw some Parma violets, Rozzie's favorites, into the grave, that I saw another bunch go down and I looked up, and there was Gulley, full face, looking up at me across the grave. He grinned at me and I got such a jump that I said, right at the grave's edge: "It's not you!"

"Oh, yes it is," he said, grinning still and looking at me as if he would bore me through. He came around the grave and said: "And how are you, Sall?"

But my heart was full of Rozzie, and I could not think of myself, or him. So he took my arm and we went toward the gates.

"Poor old Rozzie," he said. "Poor old horse."

"How did you know?" I said.

"Oh, I used to write. We sent cards every Christmas,

254

and I heard about her accident. I meant to see her, in the beginning, but I never had time."

"I'm glad you made it up," I said.

"Yes, we made it up," Gulley said, still looking at me and grinning. For his idea was that I had been jealous of Rozzie. And perhaps I had been. For God knows I never knew myself.

Then at the gates he said: "What about a half?"

"Oh," I said, holding back. I had not been into a bar for ten years.

"They're just open," he said. And then I thought there couldn't be a better place to see Gulley, for none of Mr. W.'s people or he himself went into bars. So we crossed the road to a public house and had a pint of bitter. It was a regular town bar with little tables and red plush seats and we sat in a corner and had a good talk. It seemed that he was full of an idea for a picture of God, like a glass man, with the people running about in His veins and nerves and some of them fighting and giving Him a pain in His stomach.

It was to be done on canvas ten feet high and fifteen feet wide, and Gulley had his eye on a kind of shed at Hammersmith, which would be the right place for painting it.

"Is that where you live now?" I asked him, for I had always sent his money to a box address, at a sweet shop.

"Why?" he said, grinning at me and thinking I was curious.

"Because if you were alone, I'd like to see it," I said, "and see if you're comfortable."

"Oh, yes," he said, "quite comfortable, thank you." But I knew he had some woman with him, for the top button of his coat was a safety pin. And by that pin I knew she must be a slummock; and I pitied him, poor manny.

255

But he would not tell me his address. He only went on about the picture and, at last, just as I had feared, he asked me for money to buy a canvas. Ten pounds to buy an old Academy picture, which would be half the price of new cloth.

I said I couldn't afford a big sum like that. And Gulley did not say another word about it or pester me. He simply grinned and called for another drink and said: "Well, Sall, I've got to thank you for keeping up the installments— the best patron I ever had. I've often lived on nothing else, for weeks together."

This was Gulley's good side; he never pestered or groaned or pitied himself. And his coat green as cheese mold, and that pin winking at me as if to say: "We live in pigsties." So when the time came for us to part, suddenly I said that perhaps I could find a pound or two toward that canvas.

I never saw anyone more delighted. For Gulley had two smiles, his smile of keeping up, and his smile of joy, which was like any street child's with a sugar bun. It went through your very soul. So the next thing was, I sent him his ten pounds.

I thought myself foolish at the time and I said: "This will bring him down on you every time he has a new dream." And so it did. But not for some new mad picture, only to mend up his clothes and get him settled.

Chapter Eighty-One

HE WAS living with a girl called Lizzie, and just as I had thought, she could neither sew nor cook nor clean nor contrive. He was in a nest of such. For I found him in a slum and his flat in the dirtiest of the row, with a dozen bells and a string of blowsy trollops laboring in and out like sick bees in a rotten skep.

And the pity of it was that he had got his start at last, if only he had known how to use it.

For as Lizzie told me at our first meeting, he had a picture in a public gallery, at last. She told me, in the National Gallery, which I could not believe. And sure enough, when I took a day off to go to Trafalgar Square only to see it, it was not there at all, but down on the Thames side, in a place called the Tate; Mrs. Bond's portrait.

But even though it wasn't in the National Gallery, it was something for an artist to be proud of. So I told Gulley, but he laughed and said: "The portraits are the winners, you told me so."

I was angry. For I had not told him so; I was not so stupid. What is the good of saying so to any man?—For it does you no good with him, and him no good at all. But he kept on laughing and the end of it was, he gave me a little squeeze as if scorning my brains, but I easily held him off, and told him that I would not come to see him if he did not behave himself.

And so he did. Never once had he struck Lizzie, so she told me, and was surprised to know that he had ever struck anyone. And as for me, he would only take me by the nose, now and then, and pinch it a little and say: "Don't you stick it in too far into my affairs, Sally, or I'll have to push it back again," which made us both laugh. This, of course, at the very time when he was calling out for me to do this or that, to pay the bills for Lizzie, or to get his boots mended. More than once, in spite of my warnings, he telephoned to me at Craven Gardens, only to come and clean him, because Lizzie was too ill, or bring him some colors.

So the first thing was to move him to a better address, where, if portraits came his way, he might do them. And we found a very nice flat down west, near Hammersmith Bridge, and quite near his shed, which was in a builder's yard. The poor man's idea had been to go across London, morning and night, only because Lizzie could not think how to get a better room or to move their few sticks from east to west.

She was a queer girl, a lady by her rights and as pretty as a supplement, though gypsy in her color, but as helpless as a sheep on its back, turning up its eyes at the sky and bleating for the moon to drop grass into its mouth. She could sit all the morning in her pajamas, smoking cigarettes and reading an old magazine. When Gulley came in for a meal, he would open a tin for both of them. As often as not, Gulley made the tea and even the beds and emptied the slops, which was only when the pail was running over.

When first I knew Lizzie I thought she was a drugger or a drinker or worse, to be idle all day, and though not too dirty in herself, yet living in dirt. But no, she was only a dreamer, the worst I ever knew. She would walk about for half an hour smoking and dropping her ash over my clean floor, for the first thing I did, every time I went to see

258

the Gulleys, was a general clean and wash for everything; and then she would say in her soft voice: "Do you see, Sara, there's a million people drowned in China? Did you see, Sara, that skirts are going to be longer again, to use more stuff?" And though her voice was soft, it was never sleepy. You could tell she was full of her news, however useless.

She had been an artist herself, and thought Gulley the genius of the world. Also she was musical and she used to go off a lot to concerts, and come back in such a state of dreams and excitement that if you had put soap into her mouth, for dinner, she would have eaten it and said: "Thank you, Sara—you're too good."

I grew so fond of Lizzie she was like a daughter to me; and I believed she liked me better than my own daughters, except for poor little Nancy. She always had something for me to do, either to wash her stockings or let out her dress. For she was in the family way, and no more fit to be a mother than Gulley a father. Yet there was a child with them too, a boy called Tom. Now I knew when I first went with Gulley that he had one child by his wife, which she had kept. But I'm sure he had others and this was one of them. He would never tell me the mother except that she had been his model. Tommy was nine, he said, though he might have been younger, by his looks, and older by his knowingness, a regular slum boy, and a demon for noise, dirt, and wickedness. Nothing he did not know or wouldn't do.

Lizzie, of course, could do nothing with him and did not try. Gulley would sometimes take him down to the shed, which he called the studio, to keep him out of mischief, but Tommy was away into the streets as soon as he chose. And

259

Gulley would never correct him. He said it was bad for children to be checked, or even taught.

Chapter Eighty-Two

NOW TOMMY was thrown upon me too. For though Lizzie would say that the child was spoiled from never going to school, and that he was very gifted, and Gulley too would say that he was a clever spark, they never did anything for him or to get him brought out. Not that I believed it then, for he seemed to me only wild and bad, and I knew that for Lizzie, all geese were swans or ostriches, and for Gulley, all children were marvels. He was one of those who believe that any child's scrawl is art, and that it is nothing but schools which make fools.

So all I did for Tommy was to take him off their hands, when Lizzie, poor thing, was green with sickness, and Gulley wanted to get on with his work. I would take him to a cinema, or to tea in a shop, which was what he loved and we would walk along by Strand-on-the-Green and look at the river, and the barges going up with the tide, or sometimes an eight-boat, rowing like a toy. Tommy, I say, was a devil, and so Gulley and Lizzie would wonder that he always came out with me and stayed with me. They invented the tale that I had great influence over him, which was to excuse them making me take him off their hands.

Now it is true that on my Wednesdays, young Tommy would run down the street to meet me and hug me and dance on my toes. But that was because I always had a chocolate bar, or a paper of bull's-eyes in my pocket. And if he was good with me when we were out, it was because I let him chatter, and he knew, too, that if he stayed by me and was good, it meant a cream bun, or an ice, or a sixpence. It was all cupboard love in that young monkey, though whether children have anything else before they are twelve and thirteen, I might doubt, and for all I know, one love may be as good as another, to lay hold of a limb.

"Aunt Sara," he would say, while we were walking, and I was longing only to cool my feet or to run into the Black Lion for a draught: "Are there any pirates now?"

"Indeed," I would say, "I don't know, but if not, it's not for want of people ready for any villainy."

"Yes," he would say, "there are privateers in China. Did you ever hear . . ." of some bay or other?

"No, Tommy, I never did."

So then he was well away telling me about the Chinese pirates and Chinese tortures. It was a wonder what horrors that child carried in his head and he loved to talk of them. But my rule has always been, let a child talk and tell all, and though they say I spoiled my children, I think them not so poor, with one doing God's work among the heathen, like a hero; and two wives, and the fourth, though she has not seemed to do anything, yet, when you know her, an upright and honest woman, afraid of nobody.

So Tommy talked about how the Chinese pirates would cut a man into mincemeat or drop water on him in little drops till he went mad, and I would go along under the trees and look at the water, as bright as a new knife, and at the pretty houses which looked all as if they were made for runaway couples, or wicked baronets or good people who have renounced the world and come to their senses, in their old age. I liked the Brighton houses for the same thing and my favorite hotel there was one with mahogany

261

doors, that had been built for George IV, in his gayest time. But Strand-on-the-Green was dearer to my age, for it was more quiet and unfashionable. You could walk there in your old easy shoes and let yourself wag; and if you spoke to someone in the street, to ask the way or the time, it was odds they would stop and chat. You might have been in the country. So I liked my walks with Tommy in spite of his chatter, and thought what I pleased; Mr. W., poor little Lizzie, or often, I'll confess, my tea. For at fifty-seven I was growing to think a great deal of a sit-down, and a good tea.

But I'll say this for Tommy, pest as he could be with his dirty finger marks all over my best silks, and trampling my skirts and shouting in my ear to make me jump, which I hated most of all, he had a sweet heart at bottom, and never bore malice. He would give my hand a great jerk and shout: "You're not listening, Aunty!"

"Yes, indeed I am, my sweety," I would say.

"Then what did I say?"

"Something about torturing pirates."

"No, it was about wireless. I knew you weren't listening. I was telling you how wireless worked."

"Yes, of course you were, my dear—that's what I meant, and it was very interesting. That's just what I want to know, about valves and waves."

And then he was off again. For he wanted to tell me. He was ready to teach the world, at that age. Just like my dearest Bobby, in his. But Tommy bullied me more, because I was older and he younger.

Chapter Eighty-Three

I SAY I didn't think so much of Tommy's brains, that they were beyond ordinary. Until one day there was a summons from the school officer. The Jimsons were always being harried by school officers and mistresses and even masters about Tommy, for he was a devil to play truant, and I think Gulley encouraged him.

So this day Gulley said he wouldn't go to court if they jailed him, and Lizzie said she couldn't because she was too big. She had no suitable clothes for the wife of Gulley Jimson. She was worried to death, poor lamb, when I got to the flat at nine, and Gulley was nowhere to be found. So the end of it was I went and answered the questions. At first they were going to arrest Gulley, but I said he was very ill. So one thing led to another, till I was Lizzie's sister, and she was an invalid like her husband, and I was the only responsible person to look after the boy.

Then the magistrates gave me a good talking-to about the way I'd neglected the child and warned me to be very careful in the future.

I got off easily enough. But just as I was coming out of court, a tall thin man with a big nose like the fiddle of a spoon came up to me and said: "Mrs. Jimson, I believe." So I said: "Yes," for I didn't want to bother him with names, and he answered: "I'm afraid I was too late for the court or I would have seen you before. I'm the headmaster at—" I didn't take the name, "where your son will be coming on Monday."

"I'm afraid he is a great nuisance," I said.

"He is a very great disappointment to Miss Stoker," he said. "I don't know if you realize that he is exceptionally gifted—quite exceptional, Mrs. Jimson, Miss Stoker put him down long ago as a certain scholar. You understand what a scholarship would mean to your boy, Mrs. Jimson?"

So he went on telling me that a scholarship would take Tommy to a secondary school, and to Oxford or Cambridge. He might be a doctor, or a scientist, or even prime minister and sit down with the king at Buckingham Palace.

I saw that he threw in the prime minister and the king to catch my fancy. For he took me for the kind of slummock that would let her son go to waste and dress up in her best only for the court, and I thought to myself: It's a great pity a man can't know that you're in clean linen and could strip against queens, except by the nose. Half of them can't smell anything except their own nasty tobacco.

But he was a very nice man and what I liked about him he was so keen about Tommy.

"You will excuse me, Mrs. Jimson," he said, "if I am making an unfortunate mistake, but I did hear that Mr. Jimson is somewhat opposed to education, as a general principle."

"He may have said so," I said, "but I don't think he means it. He is an artist, you know, and talks a good deal for his own pleasure."

"Perhaps I might speak to him."

It wouldn't be any good, I told him, for I thought that it would be awkward if he told Gulley he had been with Mrs. Jimson, meaning me. But he insisted. So I took him to the shed, to keep Lizzie out of it and when he began to say "Your wife," I said: "Excuse me, I'm not Mrs. *Gulley*

264

Jimson—I thought you meant Mrs. Gulley Jimson. Mrs. Gulley Jimson is Tommy's mother. I'm only his aunt." So he thought it was his mistake and apologized nicely and went on about Tommy's great chances. Gulley, of course, was in a fury. He hated government and he used to say that he could be useful to burglars because all his hairs stood up if a policeman came within fifty yards, even in a tail coat.

"No," said he, "you're wasting my time and I'm wasting yours. You can't expect me to co-operate in the destruction of my own son."

The headmaster apologized politely and said that, of course, he greatly disliked compulsion, and so on. He couldn't have been more tactful. I liked him very much. But when he came out with me, he said: "Is the mother in the same way of thinking?"

"Oh, no," I said, "but I'm afraid she hasn't much influence over the boy—he's too wild."

"In fact," he said, and he looked at me, "what we want to do is to get him away from his parents."

Why "we," I thought, but I had been thinking what a pity it was if Tommy was so clever to leave him at home. Lizzie was no mother to him, and Gulley a worse father, with his cranks.

And if they were bad for Tommy, Tommy was a plague to them, and would be worse when the baby came.

"We want to get him into a special school," the master said.

But it seemed to me a terrible thing that any child with gifts like Tommy's should go away among a lot of savages to learn devilry. Of course Gulley and Lizzie said the same. Gulley wanted to shoot the attendance officer, till he forgot about the whole thing, in five minutes; and Lizzie wanted to send the boy to a school where the fees were two hundred pounds a year. The end of it was, I was to see the headmaster and he recommended a school he knew of, not a special school, but a pay school where they might take a clever boy like Tommy at half fees. He said that most of these cheap small schools were bad, but this one had a very good master.

It was not three miles away, on the trams, so I went to it and made inquiries.

The school seemed a nice enough place for a town school. It had a garden and a playground. I liked the master better; he was very kind and said he would examine Tommy, and if he did well, he would take him to board, for twenty-two guineas a term, which was a third off the fees.

Gulley and Lizzie said at once that this was cheap and they would pay. So they did pay, more than I expected; for Lizzie had a little money of her own. Between us we managed very well for the first year, even the clothes. For I had some old castaways at Bellavista, which had been Bobby's, which fitted Tommy like tailor's work. It was only in the second year, when Lizzie had another baby and the first was ill, and Gulley's shed had to be refelted, to save the poor manny from pneumonia, that we fell a little behind. And then, as I say, I had a lucky stroke, as I thought, with the antique man.

Chapter Eighty-Four

NOW I'LL admit that I never told Mr. W. about my half days at the Gulleys', and when I got away to them as I sometimes did, of an afternoon, I would invent some excuse in case Mr. W. found me out. For I knew Mr. W. had no opinion of Gulley and would not want me to see him again. All the worse if he knew how I enjoyed those days. For I don't know how it was, I looked forward all the week to my Wednesdays, and in the second weeks, when I went to Nancy, I would always manage an afternoon or evening on some other day, if it was only because they could not do without me, poor things, and Lizzie would keep all her washing and hold her mending till I came. But I loved to go down to the shed and even to hear Gulley say, as in the old days: "Give me your hand, Sally," or "Show me a leg."

I had always loved, since Woodview days, to sit in the same room when Gulley was working; even to hear the poor manny whistle and hum, and to see him skip up and down his ladder, gave me pleasure. For though Gulley looked old, because he would never wear teeth, yet he was spry as a boy still, and whether it was his liveliness or the perfect content of him, or only the memory of old days or the sudden way he would cut a joke at me, I liked nothing better than to take the mending there while he worked.

And I had never known him more content. He was stuck only twice in the two years, to my knowledge, and then he only went out and got drunk. Lizzie, to be sure, was upset

267

about that, for she feared for his health, but I thought she had got off lightly, and I thought too, God forgive me, that it might be no harm if Gulley did die in his drink, suddenly, before he finished his picture and came to himself, and saw that he had been wasting some more of his time, that his whole life was wasted. For if the Garden of Eden had been a mad kind of picture, it was nature to the Living God. As for portraits, of course, he would never do one. He refused a dozen good commissions, saying he had no time to waste on them.

Now it was made out at the trial that I was only playing with Mr. W. and that my real mind was with Gulley at his shed. But this was not so. For fond as I was of Gulley, in his old peaceful age and busy gaiety, and pretty Lizzie who hung upon me like a daughter, and Tommy writing to me every week, by his father, for sweets and sixpences; yet I knew Mr. W. was worth three Gulleys, a better and a deeper man, and a more tried. I knew myself honored by him and I meant to make him a good wife. And though I loved my river dawdlings and my chitchat in the shed, I had grown fond of Ranns Park too, as any young bride-to-be. Bare as it was, with not a tree over man size and even the pillar boxes as fresh as toys out of Christmas parcels, it was so new and fresh, and full of young couples.

When you went out in the evening to the little park they had, with a little new pond, and a bandstand like a cruet, and when they played twice a week, on closing days and Sundays, and you saw a couple going along with the man's arm round the girl's waist, and head on his shoulder, or lying on a seat by the bus stop, you had not to be worried or to wonder if that was another poor young girl getting into trouble or poor young man got caught by a minx; for

268

you knew that they were married and had their lines. Their courting was a double pleasure to you, because it was love and religion too, as they had vowed.

Even the babies were nearly all new and you should have seen the new prams. Though I don't like these new box prams as deep as graves with the babies buried so far you can't see the poor little mites and they can't see the world either as babies love to do, yet I had to allow that they were bright and gay, and brought back the lovely old carriage work in the horse days.

The shops were all new too, with new paint and tiles, and the shopkeepers so keen and polite, to get your custom. You would hope they would get on and watch them getting on. But the shopkeepers had to be keen for so were the shoppers. There were no blowsy old things with sore feet dawdling along the arcade at Ranns Park, and no notion in their heads for dinner or anything else, and no method, drifting to a tin of salmon or a box of sardines, enough to break a shopman's heart and a husband's spirit. There was nothing but young mothers marked with the first baby wrinkle between the brows, and eyes like gimlets for the cream on the milk or the lean on a chop; or brides going out with shopping baskets and notebooks and silver pencils, fresh from the wedding presents, and a look as if to say that they must fight this fight and feed their men, or die. But though they were fierce and even the sound of their heels was fierce like soldiers rattling to war, yet they were gay too. You couldn't walk out at night without hearing young girls laughing and often they would romp too, mothers as they were. There was a couple on our other side, with two babies already, but they would chase each other about the garden like children, and laugh till they could not stand, yes, and give each other such smacks, I wondered they were not black and blue.

On a summer night with all the windows open and the chatter coming out like birds going to bed, and the new lights showing on the new little trees with leaves so bright as newborn buds, you would feel the sweet joys of being alive and having your comforts, even though you were too old for romps and babies, and used to managing a man and a house.

As my mother would say: "The young donkey complained of his long ears, but the old horse thanked God for grass." It was a sweet thought to lie in bed at Bellavista and think there was more happiness there, to the acre, than in whole towns; more worries too, I'll be bound, but a young worry is like a baby's cry, half for the joy of it.

Chapter Eighty-Five

AND WHAT a pleasure to see Mr. W. so lively and joyful, as any young clerk, just married, with his new furniture and his garden. He was laying down a path now and I was mixing cement and wetting bricks all the afternoon till my hands were like nutmeg graters. But I could not be sorry seeing that Mr. W. had a new hobby, for it kept him amused and out in the open air, and gave him an appetite, which was just what he needed. As I'd found out long ago, Mr. W. was a very natural kind of man, who only needed something to occupy his mind, and plenty of exercise, and good regular meals, to be as happy as a boy and as sweet and easy as an angel. It was not only that he treated me kindly and never forgot his politeness and respect, as a gentleman, but he would go out of his way to show his kind thoughts of me. He never came from town without some sweet biscuits, dear as they were, or sometimes peppermints, which he knew I liked, or even flowers, and he would give them to me like any prince making his offers to royal blood.

So it was till the very day before the one fixed for our wedding. I ran down that afternoon, while Mr. W. was at his lawyer's about making a settlement, and just looked in at the Gulleys' to tell him that he need not worry about his colorman's bill, which was a pest to us all, and to see if there was a note from young Tommy and to get raw fruit for supper, as Miss Clary was coming to stay the night in proper style on the last night before the wedding, as bride's friend. And when I came back, there was Mrs. Loftus and a policeman going through my box.

Now I might have turned them out, as Miss Clary always said, and had Mrs. Loftus up for breaking locks, for there was nothing in that box to shame me, except some of those old rubbishy trinkets which Mr. W. had given me long ago and which I had not yet sold to my antique man. Miss Clary never ceased to wonder, that same night, that I did not do so, but only went back to my kitchen to put the supper in.

Then when Mrs. Loftus followed me down and accused me of robbing the master, I said only that so she said, but the truth might be different, when the master came home.

But they had found my letters from the antique dealer, and a check from him and my post office book, and some little bills too, from dress shops and sweet shops, and what

271

was worse, a grocer where I got whisky and brandy for my visits to the Gulleys', and presents to them.

So they sent for a cab to take me off to the station. I'll never forget Miss Clary's face when she came in and found a policeman in the kitchen and me mixing a salad, and Mrs. Loftus in the hall waiting for the cab. She could not believe her eyes or her ears.

"What are you thinking of, Sara? You're not going to let them take you before Uncle comes home." But I only showed her the pie in the oven, not to leave it too long, and the cream for the custard. For I did not want to see Mr. W. then. I knew I was a guilty woman. I felt like the ghost of myself, just floating along in the draft from the stove to the sink and back again. I was not even afraid or unhappy. I was only surprised at myself and my devastations.

For the truth was that I had been picking and stealing for years past, and especially since the Gulleys had come upon me. It was not only the old trinkets I had taken to the antique man, but a gold watch, and silver fruit knives, and an ivory statue with his head knocked off, and two stamp albums, leaf by leaf, which I had found tied up with string under a lot of old clothes.

It all came out soon enough when the policeman began his inquiries.

But what was most shocking, I was told, to Mr. W., as it shocked the judge, was that I had 237 pounds in the post office and 23 gold sovereigns put away. It seemed as if I had robbed Mr. W. when I had money saved, and I could not explain that I had promised myself never to call the post office money savings, until I had neither place nor home. That was why I had never used that money for bills.

272

You would think that I was a mad woman to go on so, for years, and to take such risks of being found out. So it seemed to me then and I could not believe how I had done such things. But now I know, and the chaplain agrees with me, that it was a case of little by little, and that the seed of sin was in me from the time when I ran about wild in a pigtail and flirted with three boys at the same time, because I could not refuse any pleasure. I was all in the moment, like a dog or a cat, and indeed, I suppose it is nature to be so, and as the good chaplain says, there is no way for man or woman to remember his duty, from one day to another, and keep upon a steady line, but by stringing his loose days upon a course of religious observance, not just Sundays, I mean, but every day and as often as he is tempted.

Chapter Eighty-Six

FROM THE time that the detective took me to the station, I never saw Mr. W. again. He went back to his hotel and he sent Miss Clary to me with the name of a lawyer to take care of my case, and a hundred pounds to pay him. He said, too, that if they gave me bail I could stay in the house till the trial.

I wrote to tell him how badly I felt and to ask his forgiveness, but all I had back was a note from Mrs. L. to tell me that if he died, I could consider myself responsible. It seemed that Mrs. L. had carried him off to the rectory and even Miss Clary could not get to see him or hear from him, after the first day.

Miss Clary was in despair with him. She said that he ought to stop the case and that he ought to marry me in spite of all. "The old fool," she said, "his heart's broken. I never saw any man so changed. But when I tell him that it's his own fault for not marrying you long ago, he says this shows it was a mercy he didn't because you have been sending money to Jimson all the time. I believe he's just jealous."

Miss Clary even wanted me to bring out how Mr. W. had lived with me, and so it did come out in the end, but not by my fault. It was the Loftuses trying to show how I had got hold of the old man, and to frighten Mr. W. too, out of ever coming back to me. It was because of the Loftuses the case made such a noise in the papers. And so too, I ought to tell the truth, for his sake as much as my own family, that he was never to blame and I was no grabber.

As for the case, it seemed that it had to go on, for the curiosity man was to be charged with receiving and the police had wanted to catch him. Besides, Mr. W. had always a great opinion of the law and he did not like to interfere with it just because it didn't suit him. So the case went to the assizes. Then, of course, it came out as well about my paying bad checks in 1924, and I got eighteen months in the second division.

I deserved no less, as the chaplain said, for no one had better chances and more warnings. Neither had my luck left me, for just when I was fretting for our quarter day at Gulley's and Tommy's bills on top of that, this kind gentleman came from the news agency and offered me a hundred pounds in advance for my story in the newspapers, when I come out. Paid as I like. So that will pay the school bills, at least, till I'm free, and I've no fear then. A good cook

274

will always find work, even without a character, and can get a new character in twelve months, and better herself, which, God helping me, I shall do, and keep a more watchful eye, next time, on my flesh, now I know it better.